Dark Solus
An Assassin's Tale

by
David Andrew Crawford

ISBN: 978-0-9876773-1-0

Design: Dedicated Book Services, Inc. (www.netdbs.com)

Dedication

To my Mom who believed and for Baron, a friend I lost along the way.

I

Let me tell you a story—but not your typical story, where the prince saves the princess, or even the one about the knight who slays the dragon and becomes king. No . . . this is not even a story at all, but rather a tale. This is an assassin's tale.

The sun had set and nighttime had fallen upon the City of Duergar, so named for the Dwarven King who had built the city and ruled here many years ago. The moon was full and the stars were shining brightly, lighted by Nyx, the goddess of the night sky. Usually a time of mischief and thievery, eventide in the City of Duergar was a time when the creatures from the dark would venture forth, performing ungodly acts of evil. Duergar had a reputation for being the greatest city in the world, full of wonder, magic, and mystery, as well as being the wickedest, filled with villainous and powerful entities.

With the onset of darkness, the once bustling and hectic streets became silent. Shops closed as most of the citizens retired to the safety of their homes. The coming of the night tide opened the taverns, brothels, and gambling dens, with numerous merchants and innkeepers willing to relieve a traveler of his cumbersome load of treasure.

City constables were common during the hours of daylight, but to keep the peace during the witching hour, the Night Watch, an elite group of guards, was required. Maintenance of law and order fell to this group, which incarcerated any individuals who committed any offenses against the Code of Justice in Duergar. Silence reigned in the city this night, as people tended to desert the streets, seeing only those with dishonest intent venturing out into the capital after nightfall. The members of the night watchmen were thus a common sight on the boulevards of the city after dark. But on this night, there were no patrols, no citizens—no one.

The city was indeed quiet, uncommonly quiet. But a creature did stir this night—two, in fact. Scurrying along the rooftops were two dark-cloaked figures clinging to the shadows so as not to be seen. Bounding from one building to another, hastily making their retreat, they passed the high market in the garden quarters, a residence for the rich and wealthy. They made their way to the Grand Bazaar, both stopping atop the Great Library of Duergar and quickly ducking behind two sizeable gargoyles for cover.

The Grand Bazaar, located in the center of the city, was a huge open area with numerous stalls, tents, and a plethora of little booths. Large, two-story shops surrounded the grandiose market, and located at the core was the Ring of Champions. The Grand Bazaar was known for its many different shops, galleries, and specialty shops that you couldn't find anywhere else. Its cobblestone streets teemed with skilled craftspeople selling their unique wares, numerous elegant taverns, and a monument to the city's greatest heroes.

The monument was comprised of five, forty-foot-tall statues resembling the brave martyrs who sacrificed their lives to save the city from almost certain destruction. Among the stone goliaths was the female priestess from the Holy Cross Order, mace in hand. Next was Dwaric the dwarf fighter clad in chain mail, his oversized axe held high above his head, ready to cleave a man in two. The third and fourth were the thief Baal, named after the demon lord, and Haffaer the wild mage with his famed crimson crystal staff. Finally, there was the most widely known and celebrated champion of Duergar, Sir Tristram Aeronenbras, the Knight of the Red Branch, his great shield and sword in hand, ready for battle.

The silence was finally broken when the larger of the two cloaked figures turned to his smaller companion and began to speak.

"Leynorr . . ." His voice trailed off as the second cloaked figure held her hand up, cutting his sentence short, her eyes darting left and right, searching the night sky. Drawing back the cowl exposed small, pointed ears and an elven heritage. Removing the veil revealed the slender, beautiful face of a half-elven woman with a slim nose and chin and thick, red lips that quivered slightly as she looked back at her confrere.

"The Arch Mage has found us," she spoke fearfully, her face showing grave concern.

No longer crouching, the bigger of the two companions threw off his black cloak, hurling it onto the cobblestone streets below the library. What stood there now was the figure of a demon with a wiry physique. Armor made of tiny, dark scales covered his body from head to toe, and he had claws for hands. He wore a helmet that held the image of the face of a demon with two short horns and glowing, red eyes. At his waist was a plain, black bag.

The once clear night began to darken as black, ominous clouds started to form and swirl about overhead. Tiny droplets of fire began raining down, striking the demon character and making a hissing sound as they quietly extinguished upon contact.

"Is this supposed to stop me?" the dark man said defiantly, turning to look at Leynorr.

"No . . . it's the beginning of a spell," she said, looking extremely annoyed at her brash partner.

"What spell?" Leynorr's dark consort asked curiously with little or no concern in his voice.

"A spell of animation," Leynorr stated worriedly, gazing in the direction of the five huge statues.

"What could he possibly . . ." The scaly armored man's voice trailed off as he, too, looked at the stone giants standing before him. "Shit!" he swore. "You need to get out of here . . . now! The docks are just past the cargo gate. Get to the *Albatross*, and get to Mephisto's and tell him what we know." His tone was now angry as he faced the Grand Bazaar, his eyes glowing red.

"I am not leaving you, Demon!" Leynorr shot back with stubborn conviction in her voice.

Demon turned back to Leynorr as drops of fire fell all around them. Leaning over, he held the slender half-elf in his scaled arms and placed a claw-like gauntlet on her abdomen. "You carry our son," he said, gently rubbing in a circular motion on her stomach. "Your safety and his are all that matters."

"Or her safety," she sang back with a smile.

"Leynorr, you need to go," the dark demon spoke gently, but with conviction in his voice.

His focus turned toward the ring of heroes as he pulled a white, rolled up parchment from deep within his black bag and unfurled it. Leynorr's lips began to move, but her words were cut short as the fire from the sky stopped falling and the two gargoyles perched in front of them began to stir. Both heads turned simultaneously and stared with grey stone eyes at Leynorr and her dark protector Demon. Little shards of rock fell around their feet as the two stone sentinels turned slowly to face them. The two gargoyles had the bodies of lions with extremely large claws, gnarled teeth, and oversized horns atop their demonic heads. Free from their bonds, they extended their stupendous stone wings and crept forward on all fours, looking ready to pounce, but instead sat down on their hindquarters.

"Have no fear, Leynorr," the animated gargoyle on the left said in a deep tone.

"We will not harm you or your companion," the other stone twin said in turn.

"How do you know my name, guardian?" Leynorr snapped back, demanding an answer.

"Her Majesty instructed us to watch over you," the beast on the left spoke up quickly.

"Mother sent you?" Leynorr shouted in response, visibly upset at what she had just heard.

"We don't have time!" Demon flared up. "We have bigger problems at the moment," he said, pointing to the ring of heroes as he spoke. "Ugly twins," he began again, staring directly at the now-animated gargoyles. "You have a new job now," his tone became cold as ice. "Make clear the way from here to the *Albatross*. Then guard the way to Mephisto's," Demon's determined voice whispered.

They did not move or budge an inch, nor did they pay heed to the demands of this man called Demon.

"Do as he says," Leynorr spoke out quickly, staring directly at the stone twins.

The two gargoyles turned without hesitation, leapt down onto the floor of the Grand Bazaar, and loped away down a dimly lit alley toward the wharf. As the stone sentinels vanished into the darkness, booming sounds like rolling thunder were heard as stone began to crack and break and the five huge statues started to animate. Large shards of rock fell, smashing onto the cobblestone streets of the great city as each one of the sculptures lurched forward from its marble pedestal.

The first to break free and turn toward the two fugitives was the thief Baal, his curved short sword of stone being raised up to strike as he lumbered forward. Leynorr walked toward the edge of the library rooftop, arms outstretched, hands held high in the air. She began chanting an ancient passage known only to the druids of the elven clans. The dark clouds in the sky began to whirl around faster and faster, like a rapid, vorticose current of liquid. The air around her seemed to snap and crackle with intense heat and electrical energy. Bolts of lightning began flashing down in vertical streaks, with caps of thunder instantly following. Bolt after bolt burst down, striking both the thief and the priestess and shattering limb after limb. The most spectacular was the explosion that slashed through the head of the giant thief and down through his torso, launching large, stone fragments like catapulted missiles everywhere. Both statues soon lay shattered in heaps of crushed rock, billows of white wispy smoke rising skyward. Demon had moved quickly, snatching Leynorr by the waist and rolling both of them to the hard surface of the library's marble rooftop. He used his own body as a human shield as a rather dangerous and large piece of stone debris came hurtling by where Leynorr had been standing.

"Sorry I destroyed your statue," she said with a smooth smile, kissing his steel-clad cheek.

"I never carried a short sword," Demon declared. "It doesn't even look like me. I'm clearly more handsome," he mused mockingly.

They both sprang to their feet as the rumbling beneath them meant the remaining massive giants had finally broken free of their bonds and were heading straight for them. Demon removed his clawed gauntlet from his right hand, flexing it gingerly, indicating he had not been quick enough to escape the flying projectiles.

"I wonder if it still works," the dark, horned figure said, looking at the cracked, plain silver ring on his index finger.

Demon had no time to check. The three surviving statues were his first priority, and the Arch Mage would soon be upon them, if he weren't already. Picking up the parchment he had dropped, Demon now turned to face the last of the stone behemoths. With one longing last glance at Leynorr, he ran to the edge of the greatest library in the free world and jumped.

"Get to the *Albatross*!" roared Demon in mid-flight.

As the cry from Demon rang in her ears, her beautiful green eyes began to well up, and a single teardrop ran down her cheek. She wiped the tear from the side of her face as the drop of clear liquid magically transformed into a small, blue gem. Leynorr pushed her lips together and blew on the precious stone, causing it to glow in a brilliant blue hue. The gem quietly shot from the back of her hand like an arrow shot from a longbow. The blue jewel plunged in between the last of the stone abominations, making a faint ping, like a small bell being rung.

A circle of runes and strange symbols in radiant light flashed out brightly, encircling the three larger-than-life heroes. As the circle of symbols faded away, a thick sheet of ice now held fast the giant's feet to the cobblestone floor. Demon landed on the icy rink, pressing his clawed gauntlet into the now frozen battlefield, leaving large scratch marks behind him. The three animated stone heroes struggled to break free from their icy incarceration as Demon came to rest between them.

Leynorr took from under her cloak a wooden baton the color of obsidian with strange hieroglyphs carved deep into the wood. Holding the baton out in front of her, the hieroglyphs began to glow faintly as the baton extended to the size of a long pole. Running toward the edge of the library rooftop, she planted the black pole and launched herself skyward toward the other side of the Grand Bazaar. The staff extended to a great length toward the ground and retracted to secure a safe descent to the cobblestone below. Two more times she extended and contracted her magical pole to dizzying heights, until finally touching down on the roof of Reginald's Arcane Emporium. Hopefully not for the last time, Leynorr turned to cast a glance at her dark demon prince. Making an about face, she once again started her journey along the rooftops toward the cargo gate. Searching for the night watchmen that were usually on guard, she found none.

"Strange, not one guard," she muttered to herself.

Near the Peasants' Playhouse, a seedy sailors' tavern next to the docks in Duergar, she found her longship tied to the end of a pier. The longship called *Albatross* looked more like . . . well . . . an albatross. It had a stout, heavy body with a shallow-draft hull designed for speed. Unlike longships that were double-ended, it had one bow with the head of an albatross, a long, hooked bill, and long, narrow wings that wrapped around its hull to the stern. There was no mast or sail, no visible rudder, and the cockpit had only seating enough for two—maybe three, but it would be a tight fit. The leeway told her the current was strong and heading out toward the Solstice Sea. Leynorr boarded the vessel, and almost immediately the boat came alive and spread out its gigantic wings in preparation for flight.

"Not quite yet, my friend," she said, talking to the *Albatross* in an ancient elvish tongue. "Let's start heading out. Just over there will be sufficient," she said, pointing to an area just ahead of them.

The *Albatross* started to move, making its way past a set of piles on the port side. The ship was planing just above the water, leaving no wake in its trail. The *Albatross* stopped just far enough from shore as to keep away from the lighted lamps at the end of the many piers that lined the docks. Leynorr's keen elven eyes darted back and forth, searching the shoreline frantically for her dark champion.

"Hurry up, Demon," she said in a slightly worried tone.

She caressed her belly with her slender hand and found herself wondering if she would have to leave without her husband and raise their child alone.

"Stop that!" the half-elf exclaimed suddenly. Scolding herself silently for thinking such thoughts, her mind now focused back on the task at hand. After all, this was Demon, one of the world's greatest assassins, and if anyone could take care of himself, it was he.

"No one could stop him from returning to me." She paused, as if reflecting on her own words, and resumed watching vigilantly for the return of her dark hero.

Coming quickly to his feet after his surprising first-time skating lesson, Demon held the ancient scroll at either end and began reciting the ancient incantation. A nearly invisible ripple of magical energy waved down through his body, and a small circle of smoke and flame in the center of the scroll began growing in size. From the core of the flaming parchment, a ball of red-hot fire sheathed in arcane energy was launched toward Demon's gigantic stony opponent. Upon impact, Dwaric the battle dwarf exploded into millions of tiny shards, with sparks raining down like pyrotechnics on the eve of Summer Solstice. Haffaer, the great battle mage with crystal staff in hand, now had one foot loose and was trying to free the other entrapped limb. He too had suffered the same fate as the dwarf after a second ball of orange, red, and gold flames with a fiery tail of sparks collided with the big mage. The violent release of energy from the flaming globe detonated with a low roar, sending more debris shooting out in all directions. The smoking parchment disintegrated into flaming ash as Demon turned toward the huge stone knight and let loose the last ball of fiery doom.

The glowing orb streaked toward the last of the stone giants, but was deflected by the knight's great shield. The diverted blow crashed into a group of assorted shops and apothecaries, leveling the area and spraying more deadly debris skyward. With a mighty blow, the great knight brought down his enormous sword, smashing the thick ice that held fast his feet. The colossal Red Branch Knight began striking at Demon, hitting only the cobblestone street, leaving vast craters in its aftermath. Each powerful blow that Demon skilfully evaded violently broke the surface of the ground, creating wavelike crests and troughs through the earth. The hulking stone statue raised its shield high and slashed down toward Demon, shattering its shield and left arm as it struck the solid bazaar floor.

Demon, now on the offensive, pulled a small, translucent vial from his ebony bag and smashed it on the ground. The solution, upon mixing with the air, created a misty vapor that arose all around him, obscuring the stone monument's vision. With great dexterous ability, Demon leaped onto the stone pillar in front of the library and, like a graceful cat, bounced easily on the knight's back. Demon held on with one of his clawed gauntlets, digging deep into the leviathan's stone shell. On his scaly forearm suddenly appeared a small-hand crossbow crafted from solid black wood, inset with red rubies, and with the bowstring dyed black.

"Block this, you giant, stone bastard!" he hissed, firing flaming bolts in rapid succession into the back of the statue's neck.

The stone-visored head snapped free from its giant torso, crashing loudly to the ground like a huge redwood to the forest floor. Now headless and missing its shield and arm, the still-animated Goliath swung its mighty sword wildly in the air. Demon scarcely held onto the back of his mountainous enemy as the headless knight jerked left, then right in sudden and abrupt motions.

Reaching into his black bag, Demon yanked out a small grappling hook with a red silk rope attached. With great force, the dark assassin rammed the barbed hook into a voluminous fracture in the statue's neck. Grasping the silk rope firmly, Demon descended the tall statue, wrapping around its massive frame like a barber's pole. With tremendous agility, Demon dashed in between and then around the stone sculpture's legs. Quickly, he darted behind one of the wide marble pillars of the library, wrapping the silk rope around like a giant pulley. Bracing his feet, Demon with superhuman strength strained backward, forcing his gigantic adversary off balance. The stone monument to Sir Tristram Aeronenbras, greatest hero and knight to the people of Duergar, fell onto the steps of the Great Library with a resounding crash.

From the large dust cloud, amongst the piles of ice, wood, and stone debris, Demon emerged, running toward the route taken by Leynorr. He quickly bounded up onto the rooftop of Reginald's Arcane Emporium, not glancing back from whence he came, but forward to where he needed to be. After passing the strangely unguarded cargo gate, Demon saw the Witch Raider's mark atop a warehouse right on the docks, his stopping point.

In this part of the city was a mixture of boarding houses, taverns, and warehouses, holding much of the cargo brought down the river to be stored on the quay. Duergar Harbor at night was usually a symphony of noises with flickering torches and blazing lamps, but tonight it was empty and quiet. Peering over the edge of the warehouse rooftop, he saw the calm waters of the Solstice Sea below, with many ships of different shapes and sizes lining the piers.

"This is all wrong," Demon mumbled quietly to himself.

Warily, he set his feet down upon a pile of boards below, no doubt used to repair this highly used port. Looking down the long, torchlit pier in front of him, he saw two large galleons docked on either side. These were large, heavy ships, broad in the beam and characterized by high multiple decks on the fore and aft. Climbing off the stacked planks, Demon bent to one knee, placing his clawed gauntlet on the wooden floor, his eyes glowing. A mystical light in the form of a shadowy illumination stretched out, coating the lamps and torches around him and down the pier, extinguishing each flame in turn. Making his way in between the two castle-like galleons, he paused, turned back around, and came to a standstill.

From the docks of the boats sprang forth dozens upon dozens of leather-clad little halflings holding short bows with arrows drawn back, aimed directly at him. From around the bow of one of the galleons strode a tall man with pale, white, weathered flesh, making his bones horribly visible, with shaggy eyebrows that knotted fiercely over a long, flat nose. The hideous man was cloaked in long, flowing, deep-red robes and had large, jeweled rings adorning every finger on both hands. He had greying hair, balding at the crown, and a thick, fresh scar running from just below his right earlobe halfway around his throat.

Following behind the pale figure was a weasel of a man with greased-back black hair, wearing dark leather armor, and with a broadsword at his side. He stood half as high as a human, with large, hairy feet, olive skin, and balding, brown hair, and his robust belly showed a lust for food. The halfling butterball wore a fur jacket two sizes too big that dragged on the ground behind him, and a large cross was draped around his swollen neck. Bringing up the rear was another halfling with an athletic build, ruddy skin, the same hairy, jumbo feet, curly, black hair, and dark, brooding eyes.

"Kalifen, how nice of you to see me off. And I see you brought the circus with you," the horned assassin said, with obvious disdain in his voice.

"Hold your tongue Demon . . . or better yet, let me cut it out!" the weasely man said with a raspy voice while sneaking his broadsword from its sheath.

"I didn't know puppets could speak on their own," was the quiet retort, Demon's eyes glowing a bright red.

"Enough!" the pale wizard screamed, clutching his scarred throat with his bony hand in obvious agony.

"I may not have taken your head, Kalifen, but the poison will finish the job I started." Demon's speech softened a bit, his mask hiding his icy stare.

The pale wizard's face turned hard. "Where's the Witch Raider? I sure hope the Grey Elf hasn't found her . . . yet."

The wizard's speech was almost inaudible, showing obvious signs of discomfort.

"I don't know how you're still alive, Kalifen. Maybe I should just finish you off . . . here and now!" Demon bellowed, his hands moving to rest on the bag about his waist. The Arch Mage paused suddenly, his grim features lined with anger.

"The Wallet of Perseus won't save you now . . ." The skeleton figure began again, but his words stopped short as he once again clutched his throat in obvious pain.

The fat, furry halfling waved his hands in a secret gesture only known to the Halfling's Guild, sending ten more halflings dropping from the ships behind Demon, bows drawn and ready to let death loose.

"Kill him!" the rotund halfling shouted, his eyes wide with bloodlust.

"Wait!" The cry came from Kalifen as he noticed Demon wearing a silver pendant in the likeness of a broken arrow.

His outcry went unheeded as the arrows were let loose, speeding steadfast toward their intended target. Seconds before certain impact from a myriad of arrows, the silver pendant glowed slightly, dispatching the missiles in reverse, each returning from whence they came. Halfling after halfling fell, each bearing a look of shock and surprise upon receiving the rebounded projectiles.

Kalifen flicked his wrist as if brushing away a fly, sending two arrows hurtling into the large halfling who sprang in front of his fur-clad boss, his eyes no longer brooding. The repellent, greasy-haired man had picked up a halfling archer, using the diminutive creature as a living shield.

Kalifen returned his stare back at Demon, but his eyes met only dark shadows as the assassin had vanished into the night.

"No . . . NO!" Kalifen's screams trailed off as both of his hands now clasped tightly around his scarred throat.

"Find them," he said, picking up the fat halfling by his neck making his face turn blue from lack of air. Dropping the little humanoid on the ground gasping for oxygen, he turned with the weasely-faced man, walked toward the cargo gate, and disappeared into the darkness.

Leynorr, who was watching and waiting anxiously, turned her head to see Demon pulling himself slowly into the *Albatross*. Splashing water into the boat as he brought his legs over the side, he laid his head back and breathed a deep sigh of relief.

"You took too long," Leynorr said, wrapping her arms around his neck with tears streaming down her rosy cheeks.

"I had to see the circus one last time," he said, laughing.

"Can we go now?" Leynorr asked with a smile forming on her lips.

"We're all leaving," Demon said, gently touching Leynorr's pregnant stomach. "*Albatross*, take us to Mephisto's . . . and hurry," Demon said, facing Leynorr.

The *Albatross* cocked her long, hooked bill skyward, stretched out her slender long wings, and lifted them into the night, flying out toward the sea.

II

He passed into the darkness and the forests of tall maple trees, periodically riding beneath a canopy of pine trees that overlapped one another, blotting out the sun. His deep blue eyes followed a trail unfamiliar to him as he disappeared into the thick forests of the highlands, reappearing only for brief glimpses in the thinly spaced clearings of the woodlands. In the silence of shadows, he moved slowly and cautiously, keeping his keen ears alert, but the chirping birds and a lone wolf howling in the distance were all he could detect. He crawled down behind a wall of foliage and began pushing through the leafy branches as an adumbral image passed sharply before him. Pulling down a densely covered branch of bright green leaves, he could see a modest, timber-framed house with a small porch and a ground floor supporting a slightly sloping roof. From around the back of the house, a dark figure appeared, a man with a wiry frame, sooty, black hair, and a slimness to his nose and jaw, with the most noticeable feature being deep, penetrating black eyes.

Dropping his hand to the sword sheathed at his waist, he noiselessly pulled it free and waited for the dark figure to cooperate and turn his back so he could strike swiftly at the unaware intended target. Like a huge, black shadow, he detached himself from the brush and enveloped his victim. The blows were silent as he struck again and again, his great sword flashing dully in long, wide slashes. The wirily built man fell forward heavily onto the hard ground, making an audible groan. Then, straining his muscles, he managed to roll onto one side and, with great effort, glanced up at his would-be assassin.

For a brief moment, no one moved. Smiling guilefully, he looked fleetingly at the quiescent form that now lay silent at his feet.

"Now you die," he declared pointedly, breathing heavily with his sword raised high, ready to strike down the final deathblow and complete his assignment.

Then, suddenly, the heavy wooden door to the longhouse opened, swinging ponderously outward. Its iron hinges creaked slightly, causing him to hesitate and break off his assault. Silhouetted against the faint light, a black shape like a dark wraith hung motionless, awaiting his attention. In its hand was a strange, slender object. Slowly, the dark figure moved toward him and, stepping from the shadows into the sunlight, a woman appeared.

He turned to face the strange newcomer, a woman with small, pointed ears, a thin, beautiful face with thick, red lips, and a tiny, slender frame with long, straight black hair. She wore a long, dusty black dress with a white, frilly apron tied about her waist, and in her hand she held a large wooden spoon.

"Dark . . . Elim, dinnertime," she said with a gentle smile.

"Ah Mom," muttered Dark under his breath.

"Do as your mother says," Elim broke in.

"Can't we play just a little longer?" Dark asked hesitantly, trying not to look directly at his mother.

"No," was her quick and short reply.

She paused for a brief moment and looked again at the two dirty combatants, both of whom were staring sheepishly at the grassy floor, neither one willing to make eye contact with her.

"Your grandfather will be here any minute, so go and wash up . . . NOW!" commanded the queen of the castle while waving her scepter, making her decree official.

"Yes ma'am," both chimed in unison.

Surrounding the house lay heavy-laden orchards and fields of high grain. Above was a rosy sky where faint, glittering stars could be seen. In the distance, on picturesque mountains that loomed behind the fields and orchards, a strange light glimmered and streamed out in golden shafts.

"Go wash up, Dark. Your grandfather will be here any second," Elim barked at Dark before turning and hurrying into the house.

Dark quickly ran to the front porch, where a wooden bucket lay at the foot of the steps. Taking hold the handle, he walked to the back of the house to the well and filled his vessel with water. With both hands gripping tightly, he walked awkwardly back, splashing water over his feet with almost every step he took. Without warning, from the west, at the far edge of the field, a rider appeared, moving fast. The horse was a white one, crowned, bridled, and shod with silver. The rider had short, black hair and a black beard streaked with silver. He had sharp, hazel eyes and a prominent, aquiline nose. He was dressed in voluminous, rich robes of black with silver decorative threading, and a silver cloak made of fine silk was draped around his shoulders.

"Hello Grandfather," Dark said, his eyes resting on the old man as he struggled to keep the jostling liquid in his bucket.

"Dark, my boy," he announced loudly as a familiar smile crossed his face. "Have you been keeping up with your studies?" the tall man asked, looking at Dark sharply.

"Yes, Grandfather," Dark replied quickly, nodding and smiling as he struggled with the bucket of water that seemed to somehow have gotten heavier.

"That's good, because it's very important you keep up with your studies," the tall man began again, his face softening as he climbed down from his white horse.

With two snaps of the old man's fingers, the white horse began to shrink, smaller and smaller, until finally appearing to be a miniature statuette only a couple of inches high. The man bent down, picked up the tiny figurine, and placed it in his pocket on the inside of his robe. The tall traveler stroked his dark, silver streaked beard with a lean hand and smiled, cocking one dark eyebrow in wonder.

"Have you gotten bigger?" he asked after a moment of studying his grandson.

Dark thought to himself for a moment, and then a little more, then shrugged. "I don't know, maybe?" Dark said, looking back at his grandfather.

"I think you have," the tall, bearded man said, smiling warmly. "Now let's go see what your mother is up to."

Dark stood less than half the size of his grandfather, with short, sandy blonde hair and large, deep blue eyes. He was a little skinny, but small muscles were forming, and he had solid legs for running quickly in the tall fields or climbing the apple trees in the surrounding orchards. From behind them, Dark's mother appeared, standing in the doorway stirring a rather large wooden bowl of whipped potatoes. "Mephistopheles . . . you're late," Leynorr said with a mocking smile.

"I know. But to be fair, I am an old man, Leynorr," Mephisto interjected quickly, slouching forward slightly and placing his hand on the small of his back.

"That is a distinct possibility . . . OLD MAN," Leynorr conceded. Making a wry face and shaking her head, she turned and went back to continue the preparations for the night's meal.

His grandfather's lean hand reached over to grip Dark's shoulder firmly, and both began making their way toward the steps of the house.

"Could you help me with this heavy bucket of water?" Dark asked, glancing up at his grandfather and displaying a large set of puppy-dog eyes.

His tall grandfather smiled briefly at the question. "Of course, Dark," he nodded thoughtfully as he sauntered over to the door and flung it wide open, then motioned for the boy to proceed.

"Thanks," Dark replied, frowning deeply as he sourly passed by his grandfather through the front door.

"Don't mention it," Mephisto said, sporting a huge smile as he closed the heavy, wooden door behind him.

The sky was growing lighter as the night came to a melancholy close, and the stars disappeared altogether as a new day was about to begin. Dark's mother thrust open the curtains to his bedroom window, revealing the rising morning sun in its first glow.

"Dark, time to get up," she demanded.

"Ah Mom," cried Dark gloomily.

"It's time to get up," repeated his mother, this time with a more austere tone.

Dark mulled the situation over in his mind, wondering what could be done to prevent the inevitability of leaving the comfort and warmth of his bed, or to even just get a few more minutes of needed sleep.

"Nothing," she replied softly, leaning over and kissing the little boy's forehead.

Dark thought a moment, then finally nodded hopelessly and reluctantly obeyed, pulling himself up and into a sitting position, his eyes still closed tight.

"Can Dad make his famous scrambled eggs?" he asked hopefully.

"He sure can," his mother smiled, running her fingers through his curly hair before moving out into the hallway and starting for the kitchen.

"Let's go, Dark," his father's voice echoed suddenly from the hall in a mild but stern voice. "Your grandfather wants to start out early."

Dark could recognize that unmistakable voice and demeanor anywhere. And it meant, "Get a move on . . . RIGHT NOW!" Dark finally sprang out of bed and began rifling through his personal belongings and clothes, noting what he needed and setting aside items that he didn't need or would not use. He pushed clothing, his favorite pillow, and a picture his grandmother had given him of his parents and himself as a baby into a leather pack and quickly made his way down the hall to the kitchen.

There he found his family sitting around the marble kitchen table, made a brilliant white in color by mineral deposits of the purest calcite. What was unique about this heavy, stone table was that it had nothing supporting it—no legs of any kind—but it hung there in a quiescent state.

It was no secret that, in actuality, Dark's mother prepared all the meals, even the famous ones. Elim's contribution consisted only of a single ingredient, his secret ingredient—parsley. Elim's famous scrambled eggs were eaten hastily, and no sooner than Dark had finished, he leaped for his belongings and bolted for the door.

"Freeze!" was his father's shouting command.

The little boy guardedly spun around to face his not-so-smiling-faced father. All he did was look down at Dark's plate, with utensils lying on top, and shot glaring glances back at him. He looked to the plate, then back at Dark, to the plate, back at Dark . . . the plate . . . Dark. This seemed to go on for hours until the silence was cracked like an egg.

"Aren't you forgetting something?" Elim sat there with an expressionless face focusing on his son's.

Dark hastened back to what he thought was a pretty darn clean plate. All that was left was an infinitesimal piece of parsley, which he promptly shoved into his mouth, chewing theatrically.

"Mmmm . . . I almost forgot the best part," he said, smiling mockingly at his father.

"Are you ready?" Mephisto asked softly, massaging his full belly.

Elim was looking over the plate that his son had cleaned, inspecting it closely, searching for any little speck or morsel of leftover food. Finally, he nodded his seal of approval, then carefully handed the now clean dish over to his wife, who only stared back in disbelief, shaking her head slowly in a quizzical fashion.

"I have a surprise for you," Mephisto said, standing up from the floating table. "It is just outside."

He smiled at the delight he got from his grandson, then moved silently across the room and disappeared through the front door.

"Now you make sure you do as your grandfather says and be good," his mother insisted stubbornly.

Dark once again reached for his pack, slung it over his shoulder, and quickly followed his grandfather out the front door.

There, as he stood on the porch, was his surprise. His grandfather sat tall on the same white charger he rode in on the day before, only next to him was a large, powerful dray horse, tall in stature with an extremely muscular build and a coat as black as a tinker's pot. Flames wrapped around its steel-like hooves like a wreath as it spouted fire from large, flared nostrils. Its mane and tail were like pyres. With glaring eyes as black as ink, the hellish beast stared hauntingly back at its new master.

"His name is Nightmare . . . and he's yours," Mephisto said, smiling broadly at his little grandson, who was grinning with glee.

"What is he?" asked Dark, curiously watching the great horse, which was now moving slowly toward him.

"Nightmare is a Hell horse," Mephisto spoke again. "His home was in the very stables of Hades himself."

"A Hell horse?" Dark repeated wonderingly.

"Watch your hands," his mother warned sharply as she silently came to stand on the porch with her arms folded.

"He will not harm his master," Mephisto declared, boldly staring directly at his overly protective daughter.

"It better not, old man," Leynorr warned sharply, giving a look only a mother could give when the welfare of her child was at stake.

"I'm pretty sure your father knows what he's doing," Elim laughed shortly.

"I promise you he will never harm Dark," Mephisto spoke, quietly looking at his daughter with reassuring eyes.

"Is he really mine to keep?" Dark asked after a moment, breaking the awkward silence.

"He sure is," was his grandfather's quick answer.

Mephisto paused, looking over at Leynorr and trying to judge her reaction. Leynorr hesitated slightly and glanced sharply at her father, then a broad smile slowly spread over her beautiful features.

"Okay . . . but you be careful!" The smile was gone from Leynorr's face, and her features hardened as she stared at Mephisto. "I normally wouldn't allow my little ten-year-old boy a spawn from Hell as a gift, let alone allow him to ride such a beast. But since your grandfather gives me his WORD no harm shall befall my boy, then I am perfectly fine with it . . . right Elim . . . ELIM," she said coolly, her eyes never leaving her father's.

Elim closed his eyes tight and breathed a deep sigh.

"Whatever happens to Dark happens to you . . . sorry," he said, shaking his head with his eyes still shut. Leynorr stood there, her hands on her hips with a smug smile and feeling quite pleased with herself. Mephisto's smile grew wide as he reined his horse around to meet his daughter's steady gaze. Then, with a simple wave of his hand, Nightmare was adorned in Hell-forged, plate mail barding of the darkest metal. Crowning his head was a gilded chamfron, having a short spike projecting from the front with decorative etched detail and a silver saddle with a low cantle and high pommel to protect the rider.

"Do you two realize the trouble I went through to procure this incredible beast?"

"I appreciate it, Grandfather," Dark burst in suddenly, his huge smile showing his appreciation for the thoughtful gift.

"Thank you, my boy. Your sentiment is much appreciated. Do you both realize the backdoor deals that took place?" His voice trailed off as both his daughter and son-in-law burst out laughing.

Elim almost fell from the porch, but quickly caught hold of the railing, stopping his fall.

"Father, you are the most powerful wizard in the world, and Dark is in no safer hands than yours," Leynorr said, trying to control her laughter. "We were just having a little fun at your expense. I love you, and your gift is absolutely fine with us."

The anger that had set hard on Mephisto's face quickly faded, as he, too, softly began to chuckle.

"So does this mean I can have the horse or not?" Dark sputtered with a look of confusion, unable to see what was so humorous.

"Yes Dark, you can have the horse," exclaimed his mother, still chuckling in delight. "Now thank your grandfather for his fantastic, but unusual, gift."

"Thank you, Grandfather," Dark said smiling, then quickly stared with starstruck eyes at his new gift.

"Well then, what are you waiting for?" Mephisto declared in an eager tone.

"Hang on, Dark," Elim interrupted, still chuckling from his thin attempt at humor. "Come give your mother a hug before you go."

Dark managed to pry his attention from the Hell horse long enough to quickly ascend the porch stairs and hug his mother and father goodbye.

"Mephistopheles, you very well had better have Dark back here on time," stated Leynorr flatly. "You know how angry Mother gets when you don't . . . and she knows you do it on purpose. She also made me promise to tell you that, the next time, she will come straight to your house for HER grandson."

Mephisto was about to respond angrily, but instead held his tongue and seemed to smolder in fury for a moment, fighting hard to control his quick temper. Then, calmly, he looked at his daughter and nodded stubbornly in agreement.

"Father . . . when will you ever just forgive and forget?" the hushed voice of Leynorr gently pleaded with her stubborn father in earnest.

"Never!" Mephisto exclaimed harshly, his face stony and impassive.

"All right, mount up," Mephisto's impatient voice cut through the air like an arrow.

Dark leapt down from the top step of the porch and ran hurriedly back in response. He stared a final time at the huge, dark, flaming beast, then cautiously climbed onto his waiting mount, gathering the reins hesitantly in his small hands. They turned to leave with Mephisto motioning Dark to follow at his side, and seconds later the two horsemen were moving down the tinker's trail at a slow trot. After taking several strides with his new mount, Dark glanced back over his shoulder and waved a last farewell to his parents, then bade his eager mount for a faster trot.

They traveled for some hours along a worn path of tall oak trees in fading light and passed through the deep grass of a low hill into a place of mist that curled around the bottom of thick tree trunks like a shawl. Mephisto slowly reined in his horse and produced in his hand a small, black pouch with the symbol of the sun embroidered on both sides. Opening the pouch, he poured silvery dust that shone like a thousand tiny stars in the middle of his palm. In the fading light, he whispered ancient incantations from a language long since forgotten, tracing mystic symbols in the air that illuminated in a prism of colors then quickly faded. Instantly, the mist that surrounded the trees steadily grew skyward like a wall from the tallest castle.

"Are you ready?" Mephisto announced softly, sitting back in his saddle.

Dark only smiled and nodded as the two riders urged their steeds forward and both vanished through the misty veil.

In the next moment, the mist parted, revealing a land of meadows and green valleys laced with sparkling streams. In the distance, a forest-shrouded mountain rose sheer from the plain, the peak surrounded with a ring of white, circling clouds. Beside the mountain lay Dragon's Mouth Lake, a blue sheet of still water that mirrored sailing clouds and was framed by tall, green reeds.

"Ah Sommerset . . . my home sweet home." The grin on his face showed the fondness he had for this mystical land of the faëries. Life here seemed to be lighted by a different sun, for Sommerset was a green and magical land, rich in wildlife and a reminder that powers from the elder days still existed.

"Shall we see what these two can do," he said, raising one eyebrow.

"Finally . . . I've been waiting all afternoon to let Nightmare fly," Dark spoke excitedly.

"First one to the mountain wins!" Mephisto hollered.

"You're on," Dark cried, gripping his reins tightly and kicking his horse to a full gallop.

They flew down a well-worn path edged with multi-colored flowers and hedges with birds singing amid the blossoms and fruit trees. Nightmare sprang over any obstacle that got in his way, his head heaving forward as flames trickled from his flared nostrils. Mephisto rode a little distance behind Dark with his ivory horse flickering among the trees, trying desperately to catch his young grandson. In long, sure-footed leaps, the powerful dray horse from Hell easily cleared low shrubs, hedges, and a large, mysterious pond that suddenly appeared in front of them.

"No fair." Dark cast a quick, angry stare back at his cheating grandfather who was closing ground.

The two riders weaved in between large oak and birch trees, quickly climbing the gentle, sloping embankment toward the ivy-covered entrance to Mephisto's cave.

Dark brought his mount to a jolting halt. Almost immediately he saw it, the shadowy figure of a horse and rider was cast against the large, smooth boulder that lay beside the entrance to Mephisto's home. The problem wasn't the shadow, for the great wizard received many visitors who rode horses. The quandary lay in who emitted this dark shadow, for there was no rider and no horse, but only the cast of their shadows was visible.

"What is it, Dark?" Mephisto pulled back tightly on the reins, his hard-ridden steed coming to an abrupt stop, its flanks heavy with sweat.

Quickly, the old wizard pulled in front of Dark to shield his grandson from any possible harm, his eyes coming to rest on this shadow creature of sentient darkness. This foreboding mass of shadows stood motionless, but only for a mere second. Then, slowly, from the surface of the flat rock the shadow of a man and his mount peeled away from the stone canvas like a painting coming to life. There, from the depths of darkness, stood a huge, horse-shaped beast with curved horns, deep-socketed eyes, wide, flat nostrils, and a long, slender serpentine tail. It had no mane, but instead long, curved spikes peaked behind the head and down its long neck with tiny scales of the dullest ebony covering its entire body. Its master was of medium build. His face was covered by a black, expressionless mask that was as dark as a moonless night. His breastplate seemed to have been scorched black from the fires of Hell. His body was draped in a long cape and a cowl that kept most of his masked face hidden in shadows. A strange, silent sensation of death clung about him.

"It's good to see you, my old friend. You always did know how to make an entrance," the elderly wizard greeted him calmly, managing a slight smile.

Dark sat astride his horse, watching in a mixed state of shock and confusion. His mind raced wildly as he looked at this dark figure who, somehow, not only knew his grandfather, but apparently was his friend.

"I take it you were successful," the lanky wizard queried.

Mephisto's dark friend did not speak, but nodded his head slightly in acknowledgement of the task he had completed. From his saddlebag he produced a long, slender wooden box with the image of a dragon carved into the top.

Dark's blue eyes went wide when this being from the depths of Hell handed over the package, as the figure's silk sleeve fell back to reveal no arm attached to his hand.

"*Moinnaich, dè fon ghrèin*!" Dark caught himself abruptly, covering his mouth with both hands.

Mephisto and his motley friend both paused simultaneously, cocking their heads to glance sharply at Dark.

"Did your father teach you that?" Mephisto's face was flushed with anger, his eyes fierce and narrowed. "Maybe you'd like to repeat that in front of your mother?"

"No sir," Dark stammered fearfully.

"Then get over here and meet an old, dear friend of mine," the old wizard spoke quickly in a tone of indignation and pointed just to the left of him.

The little boy edged his mount slowly next to his grandfather, then dismounted Nightmare, still holding his reins in his hand.

"Dark, this is the Warden of the Stygian Depths," Mephisto declared, his voice softening.

"Hello sir," he mumbled hesitantly, his eyes peering into the darkness, trying to discover some semblance of humanity. "It's nice to meet you," he spoke in a slightly braver tone of voice, relaxing his guard a bit.

The black figure sat silent and only nodded slightly, though Dark could feel his eyes running quickly over his slim countenance, as if studying the boy.

"Before you go inside, I am going to teach you two magic phrases," Mephisto began speaking to his grandson. "First, place your palm on Nightmare's shoulder and speak these words, *Cer at annwfn."*

Dark did as he was told, placing his palm on his new mount's shoulder and reciting the words. The instant the last of the words left his lips, a burst of white-hot fire sprang into existence around Dark's horse, swirling and twisting dangerously. A brightly glowing sigil appeared only briefly, branding harmlessly into the surface of the Hell horse's ebony coat. The swirling, shimmering field of flame twisted and spiraled into a cone of fire, sinking all it engulfed into the palm of his hand in an unsettling fashion. The light glowed brightly only for a moment before fading to invisibility. There on his palm was a sigil in the shape of a flaming wreath of white fire.

"That's how you send Nightmare home," Mephisto broke in once again. "That mark is a Hell's Eye rune. It is used for summoning and grants the magician a measure of control over the beast. To summon him once more, the invocation is *Adfer chan'r ffagla*."

"Now give me a moment with my friend, please," he smiled gently and turned again to face the dark ward.

Dark nodded dumbly, quickly turned, hastily made his way down the stone steps of his grandfather's limestone cave, and faded into the darkness.

III

Dark, now thirteen, found himself for the first time traveling alone to study the mystical arts in the land of the faëries and at his grandfather's home. Traveling on the Eve of Beltane, which marked the beginning of summer, he crossed over from his island home of Faëroes into the land of Sommerset by mid-afternoon, and slowly made his way toward the entrance to Mephisto's cave. As Dark pulled back the reins, his great steed came to a stop amongst several rows of redolent flowers that were lilac blue in color with greenish grey, narrow leaves. Dark dismounted, gently rubbed his hand on the side of the wild horse's neck, then invoked the spell that transported Nightmare back to the stables of Hades. He smiled as the glow from the sigil on his hand faded, remembering the day he received his gift and the strange, shadowy figure he had encountered. It had been three summers since Dark's first meeting with the Warden of the Stygian Depths, the black guardian to Hell. That macabre image, along with that four-legged creature he rode, haunted him for quite some time.

"Such fearful thoughts are for children," he said to himself aloud, because at thirteen Dark no longer considered himself a child.

Straightening himself to stand tall, the boy made his way down to the mouth of the cavern and descended the familiar stone steps into the inky blackness below. There, deep in the rock, the familiar glow of the well-stoked fire sent smoke twisting toward the cathedral-like ceiling. His grandfather's home was a massive natural cavern where stalactites and stalagmites abounded, but over time, most were faded and blackened by what must have been an extremely hot flame. The air was not dusty, but moved and flowed freely throughout the large cavern and its many chambers, and there always seemed to be the sweet, aromatic fragrance of lavender throughout his grandfather's underground home.

As you entered the great room, books of all types were scattered everywhere, spread about on large chests of oak, packed in solid ranks on tall, dusty shelves and piled like pillars on the floor, along with crisp parchments of magical theories and scrolls that dealt in the secrets of the black arts. Mephisto's own works, in various stages of completion, were scattered about and accompanied by the materials he used in writing them.

Other paraphernalia included candles, exotic oils and oil lamps, many, many hourglasses, as well as various lenses and prisms in the assorted colors of the rainbow. White skeletons of a wide selection of animals and otherworldly creatures both known and unknown, vials, jars, and mechanical devices littered a long and elaborately detailed wooden table. Silhouetted against the blaze from the fire was the tall, statuesque figure of his grandfather, his arms clasped behind his back. Mephisto was standing in front of a large, golden gaming board on which silver and black men did battle, moving effortlessly. The horses cantered over the gold surface on a cushion of air without the aid of human hands.

"Hello, Dark," his grandfather greeted him cheerfully, but his gaze on the game remained steadfast.

The contest came to a quick and surprising end for Mephistopheles, the wise silver mage, as the opposing force surrounded the last of his silver men. The old enchanter's remaining piece, a heavily armored dwarf knight in a defensive position with his shield raised high, sat in a corner, unable to move.

"That's my best knight, Taliesin—you haven't won anything yet," said Mephisto calmly.

A black game piece resembling a beautiful female dark elf with a large crown adorning her head moved forward to meet the defensive knight. In the figurine's hand, a slender, dark staff glowed brightly, causing a misty cloud of dark green energy to twist around the silver knight in a whirlwind of deadly decay. Mephisto's last piece turned black and disintegrated, leaving behind only a trace of fine dust and grey, smoldering ashes.

"You lose again, Old Wizard!" The voice came from a magic looking glass made from the rare beryl stone that was being held in the fingers of a giant, wooden hand that sat in front of the game board.

"The boy distracted me, Taliesin," Mephisto's voice became icy cold with displeasure.

"Of course he did. How else could I beat you . . . AGAIN?" Taliesin's voice laughed mockingly from the large scrying device.

"Alright, Taliesin! We have played our little game, and still you need help to beat me. Next time we play, I will put forth a little effort—but for now, revel in your tainted victory." Mephisto's voice trailed off and the icy tone of displeasure melted as a hint of mockery emerged with a short laugh. "My grandson is here for his tutoring, so I must bid you goodnight, until next time."

As Mephisto snapped his fingers, the clear surface of the looking glass gradually turned blue and misty as Taliesin's voice became silent.

"Why did you let him win?" Dark suddenly broke in with a perplexed look on his face.

"I didn't," was the old wizard's quiet retort.

His grandfather then turned to look at his little grandson, smiling gently, his voice softening a bit before he began to speak again.

"You must learn that everyone can be defeated, no matter who or how strong they are. This is a lesson you must always remember. Now then, shall we get on with your studies?" His grandfather clasped his hands together, eager to see if his grandson had kept up on his assigned studies.

"I just got here!" exclaimed Dark sourly.

"Yes, you have," his grandfather agreed cheerfully. "Now, shall we begin?"

Mephisto breathed deeply, locked his hands behind his back, and ascended the heavily worn limestone steps, humming softly to himself, not once looking back to see if his grandson was even following behind him.

Dark shook his head and looked up in silent despair at the old conjurer, dropped his leather backpack, breathed a deep meaningful sigh, and quickly scrambled up after him. They both exited the cave and made their way down beside Dragon's Mouth Lake, coming to a stop on a wide, smooth plain that was cloaked in green and white flowering clover.

"Though you have become quite well-versed in the ancient arts, especially at such a young age, it is important to learn the limitations of magic, its mystery, and unpredictability," the old wizard began, his voice spoke in a very serious tone. "Knowledge of magic and the technique in learning how to control it propagate in very different ways."

"Does this mean I finally get to blow things up?" Dark cut him short.

"Yes, Dark, we are going to BLOW THINGS UP!" Mephisto shouted. "Just like your mother," he murmured under his breath.

"You do remember I have the sharpened senses of an elf . . . right . . . so I can hear you," Dark stated flatly.

Mephisto hesitated for one brief second, remembering that Dark was still just a child, so he bit his tongue and motioned for his grandson to stand before him.

"Well, then, you tell me which we should start on first, offensive or defensive spells," Mephisto asked quite plainly.

"Offense, Offense!" Dark exclaimed loudly, his arms in the air, fists clenched and his eyes wide with excitement.

"Defense it is," Mephisto grinned mockingly at the youth.

"Defense, what about offense?" he sputtered desperately, his arms dropping suddenly to his side.

"Defense must come first, my boy . . . always first." The old mage shot a quick, teasing glance at his grandson, gently tapping Dark's small, un-smiling face several times.

"Offensive skill in battle is not enough—you must also guard against the attacks of your enemies," the Archmage began again, speaking directly to Dark in a bold, stern voice.

"A well-forged defensive spell can mean the difference between life and death." Mephisto stood there stroking his finely combed beard, when suddenly his eyes opened wide.

"Missile defense!" the old man bellowed.

With an intricate wave of his left hand, he began to sing in the language of the dark elves, calling upon the plane of negative energy. Bolts of dark, pale energy sprang forth from his fingertips and, in an instant, missiles of magical energy flew unerringly to strike sharply at his young grandson. Dark reacted quickly and instinctively, remembering without thinking all that he had learned since he was four years of age. With a word and a thought, a winding ribbon of glowing white translucent force, like a wall of glass, sprang forth from his outstretched hands, shielding his entire body. The barrier became visible when struck by the barrage of bolts, flashing a brilliant electric blue, with silvery sparks falling softly around his feet. When the last of the magic missiles struck the wall of force and the dark elven energy had dissipated, the wise wizard spoke.

"That was an excellent use of shield magic. Job well done, Dark . . . job well done."

"Thank you, Grandfather," Dark replied slowly, his face showing visible signs of fatigue.

"Now you know the greatest lesson a wizard must learn," Mephisto's voice rolled out as the silver mage came up to his exhausted grandson. "That power and magic has its price. That feeling you have is your connection to the arcane energies of this world around you slowly slipping away."

"Yeah, I feel weak," Dark replied slowly.

"When you summon a spell, you feel a forceful confidence manifest within you. When you cast that spell, you release a focused blast of deific energy that flows throughout your body. That feeling of weakness and exhaustion is the end result and cost of performing any of the arcane arts," he concluded.

"Is there any way around this?" Dark cut in.

"Yes, Dark. The more knowledge you gain increases your powers and lessens the effect, but it is your sheer will that is the greatest determining factor. He who has the greater will, not the greater power, is usually the victor," was the tall wizard's reply. He paused to straighten his robe and to see if his grandson was able to continue.

"I think you are ready for a more advanced defense," he began again. "This spell is known as the Mantle of Magic. Now, in your mind's eye, concentrate on the energies of light and dark, invoking the powers of good and evil. Now speak these elven words . . . *Lioght 'n gethin nghyfuno*."

The magic words once spoken caused a shimmering, white field to come into being, with arcing dark energy that surrounded Mephisto like a glowing cloak.

"Attack me!" his grandfather's cry was muffled by the magical field of energy that enveloped him.

"With what?" queried Dark, unable to think of a single spell.

"Oh, I don't know . . . maybe you could try . . . MAGIC!" the ancient enchanter growled irritably, shaking his head in disgust.

"Like what?" Dark snapped back.

"By all the gods, I don't know . . ." the old man paused, placing one finger to his bottom lip. "Try lightning!"

Dark took several steps backward and began calling on his reserve of personal power, causing his eyes to glow with an unearthly radiance. Sparks flitted among his fingers as electrical energy formed from the surrounding air. "*Llucheden*!" the little apprentice spoke the true name of lightning.

The energy that welled within him suddenly surged outward in a furious blast. Flashes of crackling electricity struck his shielded grandfather, but quickly faded as the magical barrier seemed to grow brighter with each pounding blow. Then, making a grand circular gesture, the shimmering field that draped around Mephisto burst skyward in a blinding, dazzling flash of white light. The arcing energy stopped, and the glowing cloak disappeared. Dark's grandfather then walked over to him and firmly patted the little boy's lean back.

"Well done, Dark. I am so proud of you," Mephisto commended, heartily clapping the young magician on his slender shoulder. "You know you're better than your mother was at the same age."

"Really?" was his excited response.

"Absolutely. She couldn't focus sometimes—probably too busy thinking about boys," the wizard said, laughing.

Still chuckling at his thin attempt at humor, he paused, then as suddenly as the laughing had started, it stopped, and the old teacher began speaking in a quieter tone of voice.

"Now this is important. The Mantle of Magic will only absorb a certain amount of magical energy, then it will dissipate, leaving you vulnerable once again."

"Then all that arcane energy is lost?" Dark asked flatly.

"Not necessarily. A truly powerful wizard can take that absorbed mystic energy, channel it, and expel it toward your target," the deep voice of Mephisto replied. Watching the reaction of his grandson told the old teacher he was about to lose his student to boredom, because he knew thirteen-year-olds they needed to be entertained, not talked to death.

"What do you say we blow something up," he ventured suddenly, looking at his small pupil.

"Finally!" exclaimed Dark impatiently. "It's about time!"

They practiced the magical arts of sorcery and witchcraft until twilight crept in and both the moons of Sommerset shone like silver sickles against the backdrop of the darkening sky. They returned to the warm glow of his grandfather's cave, ate a late supper, and retired to the comfort of their beds for the evening.

On the ancient Celtic calendar, Samain Eve marked the end of the summer season and the beginning of a new year. It also marked the end of Dark's summer holiday with his grandfather and time to say goodbye to the ancient land of Sommerset. But this time, they left one day earlier, as Mephisto wished to avoid another confrontation with Vanora, Dark's grandmother. Dark once again passed through the misty vale between the faërie world and into his homeland of Faëroes. The night sky was dotted with tiny pinholes of light by thousands of friendly stars that seemed to wink at him as he rode. His grandfather rode silently by his side, smoking a long, silver pipe and forming intricate shapes with the blown smoke.

"Can you make a dragon?" Dark asked with a quick smile.

"Of course I can," the old wizard replied easily.

Mephisto took a long draw from his pipe, inhaling the fumes from the burning leaves, and released a large billow of smoke. Instantly, the white cloud transformed into a dragon with long horns, giant, bat-like wings, and a long, spiked tail. This idyllic shape circled around the pair and shot straight for Dark, opened its mouth, and blew a cone of wispy smoke straight into his face. Dark began to cough as the dragon's breath entered his lungs, but with one powerful sneeze, he defeated his smoky adversary. Several large puffs later, they passed out of the deep forest and followed the old tinker's trail east toward his family home.

The smell of smoke permeated the air as the two riders made their way around a large patch of crowded bushes, with Dark thinking of his own warm, comfy bed just ahead. As they drew closer, the familiar yellow glow from the flickering porch lights became visible through the dark, cold night. The two weary travelers slowly slid from their mounts as Dark eagerly led the way up the wooden steps to the top of the porch. The old mage stopped suddenly, grabbing his grandson by the shoulder, and pulled the lean child back to stand behind him. He stood perfectly still and began sniffing the air, listening quietly for something or maybe someone.

The wizard's eyes went wide as he smelled the nauseating stench of a decaying grave that now filled the air around them. Without warning, from the cast of his own shadow, a mass of clawing darkness, crackling with a tenebrous energy, formed around him. A multitude of ribbon-like shadows instantaneously exploded upward, enveloping the old enchanter in a veil of adumbration. By some magical force, a wraithlike grasping hand appeared and reached inside the magician's chest, seized his heart, and began slowly crushing it. Mephisto was wracked with pain. His face and hands began to stiffen as a black, oozing fluid quickly coursed through his veins. His head was bowed and his steely grey eyes began to cloud over with blood, rendering him momentarily blind.

"Grandfather! . . ." Dark shouted, his voice trailing off suddenly.

From somewhere in the darkness beyond the tree line, he heard movement. The young boy twisted about sharply, his keen elven eyes moving anxiously about. Then a huge, black shadow detached itself from the dense brush and from the cover of night emerged Taliesin, one of his grandfather's oldest and dearest friends. Taliesin had thinning blond hair, shifty green eyes, and atop his head was a golden crown with the head of a dragon, a single red gemstone set in the center of its forehead. A cloak of blue-black fur wrapped around his shoulders and hung to his ankles, and in his hand he held a long staff of twisted, fire-blackened wood with a glass eye floating on the scorched tip.

Suddenly, behind him, small, black-cloaked forms violently forced Dark to the ground with a jarring impact. A hawk-like grip from one of the lean, dark figures yanked him like a rag doll to his feet, while another dark, leather-gloved hand came around in front of his face and covered his mouth firmly.

"Not a word," Taliesin's leather-edged voice sounded in his ears. "Don't move; don't think—just stay there and shut up!"

Dark stood helpless, his gaze fixed solidly on Taliesin, hoping desperately that all this might be just a horrific dream and that he would awaken in his bed and all would be well again.

"Taliesin, I should have known," Mephisto sputtered, wincing in obvious agony.

"Yes, you should have, old man. But you didn't . . . DID YOU?" the voice rolled out as the blond enchanter came up to the bound wizard, smiling vaingloriously.

Taliesin was an arrogant man who had a brazen confidence in himself—he was a braggadocio if you would. But his command of the dark arts was undeniable, for no one studied or trained harder than he . . . at least in his own mind, anyway.

"The great tutor, the omniscient Mephistopheles," he mocked, laughing in childlike amusement. "The all wise . . . the all-seeing . . . the all-knowing . . . fooled by his youngest student—and so easily, I might add!"

The beguiling enchanter stood proudly before his shackled ex-master, smiling arrogantly and waiting for the wizard's antiphon, even so much as to place his hand next to his own ear in mocking gesture.

"No response . . . nothing to say . . . hmmmmm. Shall I tell you what's going on then?" Taliesin grinned wolfishly at his old mentor.

With a loud snap from Taliesin's fingers and a quick word, a shimmering ball of light came into being high above them and illuminated their small circle. As the light grew brighter, so did the circle, until it uncovered a host of a hundred creatures amassed about them. This motley crew consisted of several massive warriors, all fully armed with weapons at the ready, and in front, short childlike creatures wrapped in dark robes with short bows drawn. Feral masks with the likenesses of otherworldly animals in intricate detail concealed their faces.

"First, let me show you how I trapped your daughter, your son-in-law . . . and now you," Taliesin said, once again smiling slyly, his voice trailing off into a sinister whisper.

From directly behind him, the horde parted, and from the darkness emerged four females, each one carrying a lighted lantern. The four women were identical in description. They had small, light frames with smooth, ebony skin, and their angular, ageless faces made them quite a rare beauty to behold. Their long, braided hair was a pale blue in color and hung down past the smalls of their backs. Their eyes had a deep purple sheen to them. They wore jet-black breastplates, each with an elven-headed spider embossed in a macabre, blood-red design. In their hands they carried hooded lanterns constructed of black iron in the shape of a demonic face, its mouth wide and bearing sharp, jagged teeth. Each had a single semi-translucent panel tinted a bright ruby red. From the lit lanterns radiated a mystic light that cascaded a shadowy illumination onto the ground that flowed toward Mephisto.

"I take it you remember these lovely ladies," Taliesin whispered harshly into the entrapped wizard's ear. "The Daughters of Lolth used to be six, until their encounter with you. Needless to say, they were more than happy to aid me in seeing to your demise. It was their idea to use the Lanterns of Lolth against you."

The fur-clad enchanter spoke a few words in the dark elven language, and the four priestesses moved one by one to take up positions at the north, west, south, and east points around Mephisto.

"Are you familiar with this spell, Dark?" Taliesin now turned his attention to the young, struggling captive, looking at the little boy humorously as his voice sharply pierced the night air.

"I'm familiar with the spell, you gordderch," Mephisto mocked scornfully.

"Then you know no human, once bound, can break the spell's dark binding!" the enchanter stormed menacingly, his angered face contorted savagely. "The boy's father found this out . . . as did his mother!"

"What did you do with my parents?" Dark managed to free his mouth as he cried out, his voice edged in a harsh tone of desperation.

"SILENCE!" Taliesin demanded angrily as his voice thundered out in the chilly air, magnified by the aid of magic.

The evil enchanter turned toward Dark, his face red with rage and his twisted staff pointing menacingly at the boy.

With a single word, the floating glass eye began to glow as a surge of burning energy blasted outward in a shower of hissing sparks. A burst of white-hot flame struck in an explosion of brimstone and fire, the scorching blaze engulfing every inch of Dark's body, launching him deep into the dense, black forest.

"Noooo!" Mephisto's voice resounded about them with unbridled fury. He then directed his eyes to focus his vindictive anger upon the blond enchanter. "I shall set Hell on you!"

Taliesin turned to his captive and brought his staff in contact with Mephisto's forehead. "You are not in any position to make idle threats, old man," his chilling voice exclaimed angrily. "Do you see, Mephisto, what Kalifen has given me . . . POWER!"

Taliesin's shifty green eyes stared steadily back at the shackled wizard, the strange hatred flaming anew, then turned away suddenly as a slow smile crept over the evil enchanter's lips, relaxing his anguished face for a instant.

"You fool . . . you know not what you have done!" exclaimed Mephisto.

"I have bargained you and your family for true power—power I would have never obtained under your pathetic tutelage."

"You made a deal with the devil," the old wizard cut in shortly, his words coming slowly out in a strangled effort.

"For too long I have stood under your ancient shadow, but no longer," he shouted venomously, his shifty eyes widening. "I now possess the knowledge of dragon magic, and I have mastered the great Wyrm's ancient secrets."

"Power, Taliesin . . . this is what you desire?" the old mage's rough voice sounded almost in his ears. "You were not ready . . . nor were you worthy!"

There was just a trace of fear in the fur-clad braggart's hard gaze, and then a broad, devilish grin spread slowly across his crooked mouth.

"I was ready . . . and I was more worthy than that little brat you call a grandson. Or should I say . . . used to."

"Kalifen should have told you there are powers of which a human can never have true knowledge . . . powers you cannot possibly obtain, and powers you will never, ever understand!"

"And you have knowledge of this power, old man?" Taliesin's strong voice trailed off as Mephisto, still trapped in his shadowy shell, turned a steely gaze to face him.

"Not knowledge of . . . I AM POWER! NOW FEEL ITS WRATH!" As Mephisto roared, his words echoed out like a sudden crash of thunder, causing each of the dark lanterns to shatter simultaneously, sending tiny fragments of metal shrapnel hurtling in all directions and striking down several of the masked intruders.

Taliesin's attention quickly focused back on his old master. Taliesin stared at him incredulously as a shimmering surge of bright, silver light seemed to radiate from every fiber of the binded mystic's being. Before his very eyes, Mephistopheles began to transform. Taliesin quickly remembered there was an old tale, which was thought to be only a myth, of a polymorphous silver dragon that befriended the humanoid races. The myth went further still, as this ancient beast not only involved himself in the life of mortals, but also married a queen who bore him a child.

The mighty force of elemental energy flooded Mephistopheles' body, forming powerful muscles as he expanded rapidly in size. A brilliant sheen of silver scales, resembling little miniature plates of armor, replaced his normal skin, and his fingers grew into sharp, razor-like claws. From the base of his spine, an unwinding tail sprouted, along with two leathery wings that burst from his muscular back. Now looming over the host of evil figures was a mountainous, ancient silver dragon covered in silver-white scales that sparkled and gleamed under the moonlit sky.

He now possessed large, cat-like eyes that were the cold color of a frozen northern ice field. He had wings the size of sails from a galleon and two smooth, shiny horns with black tips extending out from his enormous head. Mephistopheles stood now in his true form as a silver dragon, a shining vessel of wrath. Anger flashed in his eyes like lightning as he stared down at the now-cowering blond betrayer. The great beast swiftly thrust his head forward, letting forth a blast of vengeance and fury. A blinding light of pure, white energy washed out over the cowardly enchanter. Taliesin, in a futile effort, raised his twisted staff to shield himself from the fatal blow, but to no avail as the master of dragon magic slowly vaporized, leaving behind only painful screams of agony that echoed hauntingly throughout the cool night air.

A ripple of fear swept over the horror-struck brood like a tidal wave as the mass of shadows and men tried in vain to escape winged death. Mephisto's strikes were terrible and swift, spewing spurts of white beams that silenced three of the remaining dark witches. His huge, silvery tail coiled around the last of the dark-skinned priestesses, then raised her high overhead before driving the screaming witch downward, smashing her headfirst into the cold, hard ground. The last of Taliesin's company swiftly fell prey to the dragon's voracity for bloodshed, leaving them writhing in agony until their final screams of loathing were forever silenced by the brutal, unforgiving beast. When the carnage was over, only Mephisto emerged from the grisly scene of battle, blood dripping from his sharp teeth and strips of flesh clinging to his claws. When he had finished, the ground was littered with the mangled, cold, lifeless bodies torn and bloodied, their sightless eyes staring blankly up at a canopy of twinkling stars.

IV

When Dark's eyes finally opened, he found himself immersed in a pool of crystal clear water that slightly glowed with a bluish tinge. In the center, a geyser spouted upward, but it did not cascade into an umbrella of falling water. Instead, it flowed outward in all directions, forming thick branches like a tree, complete with a dense, shimmering liquid of blue foliole. His head was aching and his sore ribs reminded him that trees are very, very solid. Lost in deep thought, he wondered how he was still alive and how he still had any skin left after being engulfed in fire? He should be dead like his parents. That thought he replayed over and over again in his troubled mind.

The memory of the previous night lingered painfully in his mind as he wearily looked around. He assumed he was at Sommerset in his grandfather's cave, but he had never seen this section before. Dark noted the ancient austerity of this massive chamber as his blue eyes curiously darted about. Tall stone columns surrounded the structure, and chiseled on their surface were strange, unfamiliar hieroglyphics in long, vertical lines. The floor was covered in a mosaic of colored tiles that resembled the roots of a large tree. Placed evenly about the room were several statues elegantly carved from a deep, rich redwood. Each statue was beautifully detailed, and each one depicted a different type of dragon, with its name engraved on a silver nameplate that was attached to its base. The chamber was lighted by crystals set into the ceiling that glowed with an incandescent radiance.

"Unbelievable!" The familiar voice that echoed loudly against the smooth walls was that of his grandfather.

Dark leisurely turned with a slight wince and glanced back over his shoulder. There he saw Mephisto standing in front of a huge fireplace built into the rock wall. He was applying a thick, blue aqueous material to an open wound on his side from a bubbling black caldron that hung over a well-stoked fire. Within seconds of applying this strange, syrupy substance, it slowly disappeared, leaving no trace of the injury, not even a scar.

"What are you doing?" Dark asked quietly.

"Just trying to heal these old bones of mine," he replied with a quick smile. "So how are you doing?"

"My head hurts, my entire left side aches, and, oh yeah . . . my parents are dead," the soaking teenage boy said bitterly.

Mephisto let out a great sigh and turned to face his understandably angry grandson. "I know, Dark, I am angry too."

"What happened? . . . And WHY?" Dark asked a question that Mephisto knew would only lead his grandson down a most certainly dangerous and perilous path. He took a moment and thought to himself before responding.

"Taliesin used the Lanterns of Lolth to bind both your parents' souls . . . and both bound to serve Hades for all eternity," the old wizard began again with a pained expression showing on his face. "What you saw happening to me is exactly what happened to them. The spell was the Mantle of Malice—it binds your soul in darkness, and it is then separated from the mortal flesh and sent to the plains of Hell."

Dark never moved from the soothing, cool water, but instead listened intently, soaking up every word like a dry sponge. "They're gone then . . . for good?"

The words seemed to hang in the air for an eternity as a slideshow of memories flashed wildly in his mind.

"Where are their bodies?" His words came out slowly and sadly.

"I buried them in your mother's favorite place," Mephisto replied slowly.

"There must be something you can do," Dark pleaded emphatically. "Why can't you just bring them back?"

The tired old magician stared at his grandson uncomprehendingly for a moment, and then slowly shook his head negatively. "Not even I can help them now," his grandfather responded in an almost inaudible whisper.

"Can't you just try?"

His plea was cut short as Mephisto broke in.

"Don't you think if I could I would have done it?" the wizard's anger broke free. "She was my only daughter, and my heart mourns for her as well as your father!"

The anger faded from his grandfather's wild, wide eyes, and a slow smile crept over his ancient lips, his face relaxing the anguish it previously displayed.

"I'm sorry, Grandfather," Dark said soberly, but his eyes remained vacant and detached as he tried to fight the inner rage that now consumed him.

"I'll let you rest for now, and later I'll bring you something to eat," Mephisto spoke hastily, but still trying to sound of good cheer. "Let the pool work its magic, and if you need me, just call my name."

With that said, he pulled his cloak close about his body, and with one final glance at his grandson, the old enchanter spoke a single word. In the blink of an eye, he vanished. With his grandfather gone, Dark was left alone in silence. In the dark corner of his heart, a strange, restless anger began to emerge.

Resting for a few minutes longer, Dark decided to leave his peaceful pool and dry off by the warm fire. The bruised and battered boy rose sluggishly, picked up a blanket and wrapped it around his waist, then slowly made his way to stand in front of the cooling hearth. The flame had extinguished itself, leaving only the faint rosy, glowing embers behind. His curiosity about what exactly was in the blackened pot was cut short as his elven eyes spied a new prize. There, sitting atop the stone mantle, was a familiar looking wooden box with the carving of a dragon on its surface—the same wooden container that the strange Styg had delivered to his grandfather just a few years back.

Dark opened the case anxiously and peeked curiously at the contents of the strange package. Inside, he saw a slender wand that was about a foot or so in length. It had a long, sinuous dragonhead of silver embedded with sparkling diamonds in the shape of a dragon eye. A silver band encircled the neck, with the words "Dragon's Breath" inscribed in the language of the grey elves. The body wrapped around a smooth cylinder of dark metal that was covered in faintly glowing runes. The intricate detail of hundreds of interlocking dragon scales showed that a master artisan had constructed this artifact.

Dark balanced the wand gently in his right hand, moving it back and forth and then finally in short, tight circles, testing its weight. He suddenly wheeled around and drew the wand from beneath his blanket, pointing it forward.

"Dragon's Breath," he spoke the words, half expecting the wand would immediately do something wondrous. Nothing happened. Dark quickly repeated the words in the tongue of the ancient elven clans, but again, nothing happened. Again and again he tried, using every known language with which he was familiar. First he tried pixie, then spoke in faërie, and so on and so on, trying one obscure language after another. But again and again as before, nothing happened. Now bored and disappointed with his new toy, his attention turned back to his previous curiosity—the contents of the pot.

The caldron hung high inside the fireplace, supported by a thick, iron-hinged arm that allowed for slow stewing. Peering inside, he saw what he thought to be just a puddle of dark blue water. So, using the horns of the dragon's head like a fireplace poker, he pulled the fire-blackened vessel toward him for further inspection. He tilted the now cool caldron and inhaled deeply, but to his surprise there was no smell or aroma of any kind.

"What is this stuff?" Dark mumbled to himself.

The next step to further his scientific study into this foreign blue liquid matter was evidently clear to him—he must poke it. The wand in his hand became the perfect instrument for this task, as the intricately sculpted dragonhead was slowly submerged into the magical solution. He quickly noticed that the substance was quite similar to thick molasses rather than water, as his stirring became increasingly difficult. The wand now seemed stuck, caught by some unseen force that snatched free the artifact from Dark's grasp, burying it deep beneath its slimy skin.

"Uh-Oh," was all he could say shaking his head in disbelief and frowning deeply. He couldn't hesitate now, because if his grandfather came back, all hell would break loose and come screaming to Sommerset. The frightened boy desperately plunged his arm into the alien compound and began frantically searching the contents of the caldron for the dragon wand.

"What are you doing?" a voice exploded with anger from behind the startled boy.

Dark stood up slowly with fear gripping tight at his heart. "Hi, Grandfather," Dark grinned happily at the familiar voice, quickly hiding his blue arm behind his back.

"What have you done?" gasped the angry wizard. "Have you lost your tiny, wee mind?"

"No," Dark stammered fearfully. "I just dropped the wand in the caldron."

"Dragon's Breath!" his voice rasped menacingly. "My wand!"

"By accident," declared Dark abruptly with a scared look on his young face.

Mephisto paused and looked directly at Dark, his ancient eyes hard as they burned into his young and impetuous grandson. "That is an ancient recipe used to replace skin and to even restore lost limbs!" exclaimed the magician. "So, whatever you place inside that iron caldron gets dissolved and becomes one with the liquid!"

Mephisto moved hurriedly forward and caught his grandson's arm roughly, holding it up for inspection before he began again. "Then, once applied to the desired area, the object is restored as it merges with your body . . . you little nitwit."

Dark was aghast at what his grandfather had just said and, for a moment, stood there speechless, fearful of what would happen next. The thick potion began to sink into his flesh, bringing into existence a trace of glowing blue energy that promptly faded. In seconds, the silver dragon's body and tail sprouted painfully from the back of his wrist and coiled around his arm like a serpent. Dark fell to his knees, screaming in horrific pain, his eyes wide in terror as an opening in his palm began to form, slowly widening to the size of a gold coin. From the depths of the dark orifice, the animated silver head of the dragon emerged and opened its mouth full to bare long, sharp teeth. Suddenly, from its gaping jaws, an icy sphere of blue energy rapidly formed then blasted outward, spraying the cavern wall in a sheet of ice. Amid the new frigid and icy environment, the air within the cavern began to freeze and, as a result, snow began to fall on the tile floor.

"I didn't do anything," Dark insisted stubbornly as the pain subsided almost immediately.

"You didn't do anything?" Mephisto growled, breathing heavily, his finger pointing to the falling snow above.

"I didn't do anything . . . on purpose," he alibied shortly. "YOU left the wand and the pot here. . . . Besides, I'm just a kid. What did you expect me to do . . . just leave it alone?"

"Yes, that is exactly what I expected you to do," the enraged wizard began after a moment. "Now what do you suppose we do?"

Dark thought for a second, tapping his lips with his finger, and finally shrugged uncertainly.

His grandfather's angry face stared at the young boy incredulously, and then a broad smile slowly spread over his handsome features, as all he could do was shake his head. "Well . . . you now are the most powerful thirteen-year-old on the planet," he murmured gently. "What's done is done, and now you need to learn how to properly wield this great power you now possess."

"So you're not mad at me?" Dark asked hesitantly.

"With you Dark," he replied quietly. "How could I possibly stay mad at you . . . you are all I have left."

His grandfather choked slightly on his lugubrious words and glanced with tearful eyes at his grandson.

Dark reached up and quickly brushed the tears away from his own cheek, then smiled at Mephisto as he raised himself to his feet. “You’ll always have me,” he answered him somberly.

The weary old enchanter smiled back at his grandson, gripping Dark’s shoulder tightly. “I think it is time we go and pay our respects to your mother and father,” he spoke softly. “And say our last goodbyes.”

They remained a few minutes longer as Dark dressed himself. Then, glancing up at his grandfather, Dark spoke. “I’m ready.”

Mephisto placed one hand on the boy’s slim shoulder and, in a flash, they stood in front of two freshly covered graves with two stone statues of his parents serving as both grave markers and as dedications to the deceased. The sullen pair stood in humble silence until the day approached its close and the goddess of the night drew her black veil across the sky. Mephisto, tired and weary from the day’s events, left his grandson and retreated inside to find the temporary peacefulness of sleep.

Deep within Dark a vast empty space opened, and inside was a feeling of despair as dead as dreams. Sinking to the forest floor, he called out to his parents until his throat was raw and sore, but the only reply was the faint, hollow cries of the wind.

V

That night, Dark's sleep was restless, tormented and haunted by nightmarish images of his parents trapped inside a shadowy coffin. From out of the misty darkness, his mother's distorted and muffled screams for help sounded out like howls in the wind. Taliesin appeared suddenly out of the darkness, then faded silently into the forest and had disappeared before Dark could strike even a single blow. Dark heard the chanting of the dark witches that rolled out deeply into the night, the sound still ringing hauntingly in his head. In menacing defiance, his father's cries for Dark to avenge them echoed deafeningly in his elven ears.

When Dark awoke the following day, it was almost noon. Still half asleep, he slowly rose, forcing himself into a sitting position, and looked about sleepily only to discover that he was indeed still at his grandfather's home. Everything was hazy in his mind, and at first he could remember nothing about the dream that tormented him during his restless sleep. Then, all at once, his nightmare came flooding back like a surge of rushing water. He remembered the misery and destruction caused by not only Taliesin, but also someone or something that was clearly commanding the evil enchanter. He also remembered the pain his mother and father suffered and the final words from his Dad repeating over and over again. "Avenge us . . . AVENGE US!"

So many questions were now racing wildly inside his mind, but he had no answers to these riddles. Why did Taliesin kill his parents? Who really were his parents? Who or what was ultimately responsible for their deaths? And how was he still alive? Then, like a clear, bright light illuminating in his mind, Dark had an epiphany. He didn't need to know the answers because he knew who did . . . his grandfather. He quickly bent down and rummaged wildly through his leather pack. He quickly dressed himself in a white cotton shirt and a pair of brown leather pants that his grandmother made for his last birthday. Like a startled rabbit, Dark bolted for the great room, hoping to gain the answers to the riddles that eluded him.

As Dark entered the vast cavern, the tall figure of his grandfather was seated in his favorite leather reading chair next to a crackling fire with his fingers drumming against the arm holds. He was wearing heavy, dark, somber-looking robes. On his upper left arm, he wore a large black armband, which was usually worn during periods of mourning. Mephisto smiled slightly as his grandson, then walked over and seated himself on a small stone bench that was conveniently placed in front of him.

"I guess you need some questions answered," he stated simply, turning to his grandson. His dark countenance was worn and grim, but still he managed to smile warmly. "I'll try and answer them as best I can."

"Just like that?" Dark spoke abruptly, thinking to himself this was way too easy.

"Yes, Dark, this much is owed to you," retorted the smiling wizard.

"I have many questions that need answered," Dark cut him short. "And I need those answers . . . now."

"I don't doubt that you do," was his grandfather's reply. "What do you want to know first?"

"I guess the first thing I need to know is who sent Taliesin to kill my parents?"

"Let's start with an easier question first . . . alright?" Mephisto asked shortly. The pained expression he displayed clearly showed that he was not quite ready, nor willing, to talk about his daughter.

"Alright, then why am I not dead?" Dark asked without hesitation.

"That's easy . . . you are part dragon," Mephisto stated simply, as if the answer should have been obvious.

"What?" was the only response Dark could think of as he glanced back at his grandfather. A look of confusion and shocked disbelief was noticeably evident on his lean face.

"I am an ancient silver dragon, Dark," admitted Mephisto plainly. "Therefore, my offspring would be of dragon descent . . . ergo . . . making both you and your mother part dragon."

Dark paused for a moment, wondering if the old magician, his own grandfather, could actually be a silver dragon. The astonished little grandson of Mephistopheles, the silver mage, stared in stunned silence back at the speaker for a moment, in awe of what he had just been told. Dark thought about the centuries of history behind the old man and how much power he must truly possess.

"Did Mom and Dad know about this?" he asked shortly.

"Like you, I eventually told them, but very few know my true form," Mephisto finally spoke after a long pause, the words slow and reluctant as a single tear ran down his cheek. "And I'd like to keep it that way."

"Does Grandmother know?" asked Dark slowly.

"Yes. Actually, that is what first attracted her to me," responded his grandfather fondly. "But that was a very long time ago."

Mephisto stood up and sauntered sluggishly over to a padlocked plain, wooden cabinet, produced a small brass key, and quickly unlocked it. From within the little cabinet he took an exquisite-looking crystal decanter that was filled with a dark amber liquid, poured out the contents into a globular glass with a small top, and drank heavily.

"One day, Dark, you too will find a woman that drives you to drink," his words were garbled as he drank four more fingers' worth.

"So the flame strike from Taliesin didn't turn me into ashes because I'm immune to fire?" interjected Dark.

"Yes, and you are also immune to other elemental energies such as cold, electricity, acid, and, as you now know . . . fire," came the wizard's firm retort as he drained his brandy snifter.

"So exactly how old are you?" Dark asked finally.

Mephisto arched his eyebrows and produced a furtive smile on his face, amused by the question that had been asked so often throughout his long lifetime. Refilling his glass and quickly taking another large gulp, he paused momentarily to reflect on his years, as his young grandson eagerly awaited his answer.

"I have lived well over ten centuries," he admitted coolly, looking back at Dark with the same sly smile. He refilled his glass vessel and returned to take his seat in front of his grandson.

The son of Elim and Leynorr Solus shook his head slowly, trying to believe that what he was hearing was possible. "Are you really a thousand years old?" Dark muttered dryly, still shaking his head.

"Yes," was his grandfather's short reply.

"Really?" Dark asked in quick response.

"Yes, Dark, I really and truly am over a thousand years old," Mephisto replied even more quickly, but in a slightly annoyed tone.

"Really?"

"Yes, for the last time . . . next question!" a now-irate Mephisto demanded as he put away another stiff belt of brandy.

"That's insane . . ." Dark muttered softly, shaking his head. "Then the blue mixture is for dragons?"

"Yes. It is the only way to replace scales that I have lost," replied Mephisto. "Whatever object comes in contact with that liquid immediately dissolves, breaking down to its most basic element. You then apply the substance to the desired area, and the liquid then acts as scaffolding and stimulates skin regeneration and biodegrades . . ."

"Huh," Dark's eloquent retort cut short his grandfather's explanation, a look of total confusion visibly displayed on his young face.

The old historian paused and smiled to himself, cocking his head in the direction of his now-confused grandson, then began again. "Basically, Dark, when you dumbly put your left appendage into the blue goo, the dissolved wand reformed and grafted to your living tissue. . . . So, in other words, it became one with your arm."

"Yeah, it's pretty *aingidh,*" Dark said, tracing his finger along the silver body that wrapped around his arm. "I bet I can cause a lot of damage with this."

"That is a very powerful weapon in your possession, and you must be schooled in its proper use!" his grandfather declared vehemently, his fine brandy sloshing along the sides of the crystal snifter glass and threatening to escape.

"I bet if I had this a few days ago, my parents would still be alive!" Dark paused after he spoke and sat silent, staring blankly, his mind deep in sorrowful thought. "Why did this happen to them, Grandfather?"

The tall historian paused for a moment, uncertain as to how much he should really divulge to his still young and only grandson. "Where do I start, Dark? . . . Where do I start?"

"Dad used to say all good stories start at the beginning," Dark replied quickly. His voice gave way, exposing his true sadness over the loss of his mother and father.

Mephisto slowly rose from his soft leather chair and walked away from his grandson, thinking to himself, not sure how these questions should be answered. He then turned around abruptly, walked back, and slumped down heavily into his desk chair with a loud, grievous sigh.

"Alright . . ." his grandfather replied slowly, his eyes looking up from the floor to meet Dark's. "I guess we will start at the very beginning."

"Don't leave anything out," Dark cut in sharply.

"A very long time ago," he began again, still considering his answer as he spoke. "Before boundaries formed between the mortal world and the faërie world, the High King of the Tuatha Dé Danann reigned over the entire Eorth. He was the father of all, known as the Lord of Knowledge, a kind and just sovereign, and he was named Dagda, which meant the 'Good God.' Dagda created four separate kingdoms and gave each to a different race he felt was worthy of such a great gift. The first kingdom he kept for his own faërie race, the second to the elves, the third to the dwarves, and the last to the humans, but still he remained ruler over all. It was not long before mortal man and his lustful greed saw fit to break the treaty set by Dagda, the Faërie King, and thus the Race War began. The war raged on for a hundred years. Despite their magic talismans and enchanted weapons, and even with the great powers they possessed, the faëries were eventually conquered. The Tuatha Dé Danann took refuge in invisibility and left the surface of the Eorth forever, never to be seen by mortal man again, hiding their kingdoms beneath lakes and islands far across the sea."

"What does that have to do with who killed my parents?" the abrupt interruption came from Dark, who smiled coldly at the old historian.

Mephisto's face grew dark as he stared back at his grandson with deathly silence. Dark knew instantly that he was asking for trouble, and his flushed face had gone pale at the thought of a confrontation with the weary wizard.

"Shall I continue, or would you like to interrupt me again?" demanded Mephisto blankly.

All Dark could do was nod dumbly, for he knew the old mage would reveal the story in MT, or Mephisto time, and only when he saw fit.

"I don't know if I should even tell you this, but I am . . . so shut it!" Mephisto stared at Dark, seeing if his lips would dare move, then slowly continued. "Many years after the Race War, the Dwarf King founded the City of Duergar, and it became a beacon of culture, as well as the center of learning in the ancient world. Duergar had become the largest city on Eorth with an extraordinary mix of races and cultures, but was always careful to maintain the distinction of its population's largest ethnicity, the dwarves. The ever-expanding population of the human race grew and began to encroach upon the Dwarf King's territory. Being a good king, he allowed them to settle around his kingdom and even take up residence inside the city."

Dark's grandfather rose once again and walked slowly to his cabinet of spirits, this time taking the bottle with him as he returned and sat back down in front of Dark.

"This was the downfall of the dwarves and their city," began Mephisto again, taking massive swigs straight from the decorative decanter as he spoke. "Out of the greed of man and their lust for power rose up the Bandit Kingdoms from the North and the Warlords from the East. It was about this time a strange sickness began to infest the entire population. The great Dwarf King commanded his messengers to send for the wisest wizard in the world, wise above even some gods—Mephistopheles, the silver mage."

"So the king asked for your help?" Dark quickly interrupted as he shifted slightly to sit more comfortably, eager to hear more of the engaging story.

"Yes, Dark, but no more interruptions," was the silver sorcerer's quick response. "With arduous research and investigation, I identified the source of the strange illness. A rare and obscure poison had contaminated the city's water supply. This fatal substance was known as Monk's Head, said to have been created from the saliva of the three-headed Cerebus, mythical guardian of the Underworld. The only known cure was from a rare plant called Lady's Mantle, as the morning dew collected from the funnel-shaped leaves had magical properties. On a remote island far to the south, near the end of the world, lay the Shrouded Isle, the only place where the exotic plant existed. However, on this island, guarded by a great antagonist, was Typhon, the hundred-headed hydra. Having to stay and attempt to slow the lethal poison's effect on the denizens of Duergar, the king then assembled a brave party to wrest the much-needed herb from the clutches of the island's guardian. This hardy band consisted of my prize pupil, Haffaer the wild mage, and Lozelle, a female priestess from the Holy Cross Order. Her longtime companion and infamous champion of the people, Sir Tristram Aeronenbras, Stoic Knight of the Red Branch, joined as well. I sent word to the Styg to send forth his best student—your father presented himself in the guise of Baal the Thief. Finally, with great reluctance, the king sent his only son and heir to the throne, Dwaric Duergar, to lead the party."

Dark was openly captivated and quite enthralled by the epic events depicted by his grandfather, and tried to restrain himself from committing any further interruptions.

"The party made the perilous journey in their quest for the magical healing herb, and as many more lives faded, the battered group returned victorious and surprisingly intact. With the magic antidote found, the weary band was hailed as heroes, and colossal statues bearing their likeness were erected in their honor. The king, however, became mysteriously ill while the entire city was still celebrating the triumphant return of the new heroes of Duergar."

"Was it the poison again?" Dark asked meekly.

"No, this time it was something quite different," the ancient historian acknowledged. "The king's limbs became atrophied and his skin began to turn to stone, transforming even his garments. I was dumbfounded and unable, even with my skills, to save the Dwarf King from certain death. A master of ancient medicines and botany, Blackthorn, an old and highly esteemed elder of the Druid Council and Ambassador to the King, was summoned immediately. Shortly after his arrival, from Duergar's own Guild of Thieves and from their network of spies, they informed Blackthorn that the Shadow Lord, leader of the Bandit Kingdom, was responsible for the king's illness and the attempted genocide of his people."

"Wait a minute," Dark interjected boldly, "I don't trust that Blackthorn. Why would the Thieves' Guild help out the city and its king? And why would they report this information to Blackthorn and not to Dwaric, the king's son and heir to the throne?"

"I don't know," Mephisto conceded. "I too asked the same questions, but let me continue with the story. He then received news that the Shadow Lord and a small contingent of soldiers were camped at the foot of White Mountain that lay to the North. Dwaric, now full of rage, once again gathered the still-recovering heroes to seek out this Shadow Lord and end his reign of terror once and for all. The only heir to the throne proclaimed to the citizens of Duergar that, in his absence, Blackthorn would temporarily assume rulership of the city until his return or their king recovered."

"Why didn't he leave you in charge?" Dark asked, now sitting on the edge of his seat in anticipation as to what would come next.

"Because this time I decided to accompany the small party for fear that something foul was afoot," was Mephisto's response. "As I expected, a trap was sprung and we were ambushed, surrounded by well over a thousand Bandit warriors. I also found out too late the party had indeed been betrayed from within, for leading this strong force that encircled us was the Druid Blackthorn. Blackthorn must be the Shadow Lord, or so we all thought. Then, from behind the circle of ready and armed men, a huge red specter seemed to rise up slowly and traipsed forward to reveal a tall and exceptionally lean man. His long frame was wrapped in a flowing crimson cloak with a loose cowl pulled close about his head. The darkened face was long and his eyes were kept in the shadow, completely hidden from view."

"The Shadow Lord!" Dark interrupted again.

"With a single gesture his army set upon us," Mephisto began again, paying no attention to his grandson's interruption. "During the battle, our magic collided, with both of us seeking dominance over the other. In the end, the day was lost and we luckily made our escape. But the cost was high as the fates were not kind to three of our comrades. Sir Tristram, along with the Priestess Lozelle and Haffaer, my best student, all succumbed to the bloody assault. With the remaining survivors, we made our escape and fled back to the safety of Sommerset. There to greet us was the Styg with the sad news that the great Dwarf King was dead and Lord Blackthorn now assumed control of his city. He also informed us that Dwaric, the son of the king, was said to be responsible for his own father's death, and I, his cohort, was indeed the Shadow Lord."

"How could anyone believe that nonsense?" Dark interjected excitedly. "And no one thought to question any of this, especially with the king's murder and only Blackthorn constantly by his side? With Dwaric the only heir to the throne and you both now conveniently put in the role of the villains, there's no one to stop him from gaining control of Duergar!"

"Exactly my boy," his grandfather acknowledged. "Which means they must have had help from some of the more seedy guilds, most presumably, the Assassins, Thieves, and Halflings' guilds. Now, about this time, your father formed a plan to go back to Duergar and assassinate both the Shadow Lord and Blackthorn, but that approach would never work. They were too well-guarded and would surely expect such a quick retaliation. And, as skilled as your father was, he was no match for the Shadow Lord's magic. So a new plan was devised where Elim would enter the Assassin's Guild, rise in the ranks of the guild hierarchy, enabling him to gain enough trust to get close enough to destroy them both. The feeling was he needed some support from inside the city and, since no one there could be trusted, your mother was the only logical choice to accompany him."

"It was also around this time they fell in love and were secretly married . . . is that right?" was Dark's question to his somber-looking grandfather. "Or at least that's what they used to tell me."

"Yes, they were . . . and so happy," Mephisto paused for a moment, lost in thought and still showing the visible signs of a grieving father.

"The Styg escorted Dwaric to Agnarock, an ancient stronghold of the dwarves and a safe house from the ever-searching emissaries of the Shadow Lord." Wiping a tear from his eye, Mephisto once more began telling the all-too-painful tale. "Your father arrived at Duergar as Demon the Assassin, and your mother now the Witch Raider. Lord Blackthorn then appointed a new court magician, an archmage named Kalifen. Evil in nature, this conjurer of black magic also became his personal consultant and advisor."

"Do you know who this Kalifen is, Grandfather?" was Dark's curious question.

"No, and that is the strange thing," his grandfather stroked his beard as he answered his grandson. "In all my years, I have never heard of an archmage named Kalifen, nor have I ever heard that name spoken in any of the schools of magic. Anyway, two long years passed, and your father sent word that he finally received an audience with Kalifen—and inside his very chambers . . . finally alone. That night, Demon struck the unsuspecting wizard, slicing open his throat, but his venomous shadow sword failed in its attempt to sever Kalifen's head from his body. With his subterfuge now known and Kalifen somehow still alive, Elim and Leynorr swiftly retreated, running along the close-knit rooftops, and by some miracle managed to escape unharmed. Now you know the whole story," his grandfather's voice died away in a weary murmur as he slowly sank back into his soft leather chair.

"Now I know who I need to kill," Dark said in an ice-cold tone.

"Dark, I did not tell you the story so you would go off and get yourself killed!" exclaimed Mephisto, a look of consternation clouding his ancient features.

"You told me yourself that I'm the world's most powerful thirteen-year-old boy," cut in Dark sharply.

"Yes, Dark, you are quite powerful, but you are still just a boy," protested his grandfather.

"I may not be as powerful as Kalifen, but this is!" Dark exclaimed loudly, holding up the arm that now housed the wand called Dragon's Breath. "And I will sneak into the city of Duergar and find their murderers and kill them all!"

"So you are going to do what your father and countless others could not?" rasped the angry wizard in barely controlled fury. "That's absurd, ridiculous, and unbelievably stupid! You could not possibly win, Dark. . . . You would just be throwing your life away."

"Even with your help?" asked Dark quietly.

"Even with my help," Mephisto smiled gently and quite unexpectedly. "You're not going up against a thirteen-year-old bully from school. He is as powerful a wizard as I am, and with help from the other guilds . . . almost unstoppable."

"Can't you train me more?" asked Dark quickly. "I promise I will try harder and I will study every day."

"You will need more than just my training—you need training I cannot give you," his grandfather said slowly.

"Can't give me or won't give me?"

"Both!" was the magician's straightforward and quick reply. "Do you honestly think a mere child can match skills with an archmage, let alone all those who serve him?"

"You can ask the dwarves for help," protested his grandson further. "Maybe we can ask Grandma. . . ."

"ENOUGH!" cut in Mephistopheles sharply, his tone as cold as ice and muttering a low oath of fury. "This is utter madness. You would be committing suicide . . . so I forbid it!"

"You're not my father. . . . You're not my mother. So you can't tell me what I can or cannot do!" Dark leapt to his feet, knocking his stone seat to the floor with a crash, and moved swiftly across the room, quickly ran up the stairs, and escaped outside.

Mephisto called desperately for his young grandson. Again and again he tried in vain, but nothing came back except the echoes of his own despondent cry. It was too late, for Dark had already made his escape on horseback and was heading at a rapid pace for the misty veil.

VI

Dark passed through the wall of mist and entered back into his homeland of Faëroes, still extremely upset at his old and obviously senile grandfather. He shook his head in disgust, then halted Nightmare in annoyance, grinding his teeth in anger as a fierce flame of indignation spread across his face.

"It's not like I'm a child anymore," he shouted bitterly aloud, somehow hoping his grandfather could hear him.

The young half-elf wanted to get off this island immediately, but with no real plan of travel, where would he flee? He had no supplies, and the trek to Seabrooke, the capital of Faëroes, would take many days. The lands beyond his home were unfamiliar to him, except for a few well-traveled roads and a handful of hamlets that he had visited as a child. Given his present situation, with no money or food, it would be impossible to do much more than just point in any general direction, follow it blindly, and hope that fate would find favor with him.

Dark considered the alternatives as he once again began making his way down this road to nowhere. But as he rode, still pondering his predicament, there seemed only one reasonable alternative. He would first go and spend the night at his old family home, the house that his mother and father had built themselves and the only home he ever knew. From there, he could form a new plan of attack. And from his new hideout he would travel to the only person that would possibly help him . . . his estranged grandmother. Even though he only saw her but once a year, and each visit he felt more than a bit out of place for he never really spent any time getting to know her, Dark was still certain she wouldn't turn away her only grandson.

Feeling better about his not-so-bleak situation, he made his way with great haste amongst the tall oak and pine trees, the sun still hanging high overhead in the clear, cloudless sky. His horse he rode hard, galloping over fallen leaves and acorns that were scattered beneath the wide branches that veined the deep sky overhead. Dark, still angry with his grandfather, did not pause to look back, but only looked ahead to what he thought would be his new life and new beginning with his grandmother. His large black horse easily flew across the uneven ground, moving nimbly among the tall grass that was still wet with early morning dew. Nightmare seemed to fly with ease over thick clumps of bushes and small boulders that blocked his path. His faithful steed's stout muscles worked tirelessly in an attempt to reach his master's home before nightfall. The terrain beneath them had passed by quickly, as did the hours in the day. The sky was growing darker as the afternoon came to a wistful close, and the first twinkling stars began to awake from their deep slumber.

Dark had set a brisk pace, moving quickly and quietly amongst the heavy clumps of trees and through large stretches of mixed woods that dotted the highlands of Faëroes, until finally coming to the slow, sloping tinker's trail that led to his old home. Suddenly, his sharp elven eyes recorded a blurred image of a horse and rider as he passed through a small cluster of woods near his house. He jerked hard on the reins, causing Nightmare to come to an abrupt stop, and dismounted surreptitiously before returning his faithful steed to Hell. In the midst of the shrouded gloom of the trees, his keen pointed ears picked up the resonance of low speaking voices. Dark fearfully dropped flat amid a crisp carpet of colored leaves and some gnarled, broken branches. Hastily he crawled, trying to keep low and out of sight, praying the vague rider had not seen or heard his arrival. He lay unmoving, his mouth dry as he slowly visualized what would happen to him if he were to be discovered.

"No one's here," a childlike voice sang out strongly. "And it looks like no one ever lived here."

Bravely, pushing his fear aside, or maybe it was just curiosity that overtook him, Dark inched forward cautiously and peered through a break in the thicket of birch and tall oak trees that cloaked his presence. Dark could now see clearly who the intruders were and, more importantly, how many. He immediately concluded the leader of these unwanted interlopers must be the medium-sized man sitting atop a beautiful white mare. The rider had well-groomed, wavy hair and brown eyes with half his face curiously painted gold. He was dressed ostentatiously in long, thick purple and gold robes, and in his hand he held a quarterstaff made from petrified black wood.

"No, this is the place," the painted horseman shot back at the four small humans who stood in front of Dark's old abode.

"Are you sure this is the right house?" a husky voice said as two more unwanted guests strolled out of his front entrance. "Maybe we're on the wrong island . . . there are hundreds of them, you know."

These evil little creatures were halflings that stood about three feet tall, with most of the brood sporting long sideburns, each wearing an identical grey cloak embroidered with a large, gold triangle and set in the middle two curved, black daggers pointing straight down. By their waists, short swords were still sheathed.

"Taliesin must have failed in his attempt against the rodent's family," the horseback rider exclaimed angrily. "I fear our master has underestimated the old wizard's power."

"I hope that means I can still show the Witch Raider a little love . . . if you know what I mean, boys!" one of the halflings said, laughing boorishly while using the porch railing to make a rather rude gesture that caused the enraged son of the Witch Raider to stand.

The anger he held inside finally erupted like a volcano, his eyes frightful to look upon as they blazed like fire with new hatred. These halflings looked innocuous enough if you happened upon them, but from the stories his father told, they were hardened killers who had been doing the guild's dirty work for years. He could not and must not underestimate them, for if he did, he would surely find a blade emerging from his belly. The fear that left him pressed against the forest floor had vanished, and in its place was a pernicious malice for these loathsome and revolting creatures. His deep blue eyes turned straight ahead as he walked out into the open, his blond brow furrowed in deep concentration. He marched undaunted toward the small party, with anger in one hand, fury in the other, and with no real plan of action. But one thing did occur to him—don't miss.

The first to catch sight of the visibly angry thirteen-year-old boy was the still laughing halfling comedian, his words still burning in Dark's ears. His laughter stopped as he stood frozen, his eyes opened wide in amazement at what he thought must be an optical illusion. The last thing he ever saw was a streaking silver projectile in the shape of an arrow that burst forth from the pointed finger of the lean, blond-haired boy. The stunned victim's jaw dropped as the rapidly moving magical bolt entered his gaping mouth and exited through the back of his skull.

Dark, still charging forward, began to call on his reserve of personal power, which caused his eyes to glow faintly. Static began to fill the air, surrounding him in a field of electrical energy while sparks danced around his fingertips.

"*Llucheden arc*!" Dark shouted out his call for lightning.

With a sudden surge, a bolt of hissing electricity flashed outward and, with tremendous force, struck the halfling closest to him. The lightning bolt arced between the first, then simultaneously to two more of the little spies, creating a magical current that ended in a frightfully loud, thunderous clap.

A quick survey saw four out of the seven trespassers now lying lifeless on the cold, hard ground, but also causing the remaining three to be made aware of their own little intruder. With the invaders now alerted to his presence, Dark remembered his grandfather's insistence of defense first and promptly spoke aloud the incantation for the Mantle of Magic. The young conjurer then focused his keen elven eyes on the robed rider as the last of his words caused a shimmering white field with arcing energy to flow out, draping over him like a thin diaphanous cloak.

Dark paid no attention to the last two maddened halflings charging wildly toward him as a green ball of arcane energy was about to collide into his thin shield of magic. The attack came from the glowing quarterstaff of the purple-clad horseman who now displayed a look of shock and utter disbelief as his eyes met Dark's, and with it came the realization that this would-be assassin was nothing more than a small child. The glowing orb smashed into the enchanted barrier that sheathed the pupil of Mephistopheles, but quickly faded after only a few pulses. Channeling the absorbed energy with a grand circular wave of his right arm, the shimmering field began to glow brightly. With a wicked smile, Dark gestured toward his mounted foe. A blinding aura of light burst forward from the little mage's outstretched hand, striking the mystic's unprotected body. The aura tore through his gold and purple abdomen, leaving behind a large, gaping blackened hole.

Whether it was foolishness or bravery, Dark was unfazed by the throwing knives that whizzed quickly by his face, with one blade even cutting off a lock of his sandy blond hair. The sudden movement brought his hate-filled eyes to rest on the two remaining hostile attackers, who were rapidly gaining ground on him. Dark acted instinctively and whirled swiftly about with a cry of hatred that caused a brightly glowing sigil to appear briefly in front of him before gently fading to invisibility. As the last of the combatants loomed several yards away, hundreds of slender, razor-sharp blades began to swirl around his lean body. Both halflings felt eagerly for the handles of their own short swords, each one drawing the steel blade from its sheath with grim determination etched on his face. Dark met the rush of angry little men with a word and a gesture sending the circling blades flying only moments before they were upon him. The lethal blades flew invisibly to their targets with blinding speed and fell silently upon the unprepared bandits. The last two who stood against him dropped heavily to their knees, then finally fell in still, unmoving bloody heaps.

In amazing disbelief, Dark stood and gazed slowly about the battlefield, glancing down wearily at his father's enemies who now lay dead at his feet. As the last faint tinges of light began to fade, the surrounding area seemed to grow strangely silent, so quiet the exhausted little wizard could hear his own breathing rasping heavily amongst the calm. Then he heard something and glanced about, his elven eyes traveling quickly as he searched for the cause of the noise and listening intently for something further. Long moments passed as Dark waited and peered cautiously about for a second time, convinced it must be just his imagination, until he heard a scarcely audible sound from somewhere behind him. Dark twisted slowly around and blinked in disbelief at the slim figure standing motionless behind him, brandishing a sharp long sword that pointed only inches from his throat.

"Impressive!" the leather-edged voice sounded suddenly in his ears. "Very impressive, but I would expect nothing less from the Son of Solus."

The man had an arrogant, pugnacious look about him. He had a tanned, worn face, short, sandy brown hair, and a small, pointed nose with a black stripe painted across his deep eyes and a short goatee that he had dyed black. He wore armor consisting of a black leather breastplate with two red, criss-crossed blades inside a golden triangle that was embroidered on the front. Both hands were covered in spiked gauntlets, and a small hand crossbow was mounted on his right forearm. Dark took a moment to study the man's face, and found he couldn't take his eyes off of what was his most noticeable and dominant feature—two deep, criss-crossed scars that had been carved into both of his leathery cheeks.

"You know who I am?" Dark quickly sputtered.

"No, but I guessed you must be Demon's son," the strange thin man began again. "And the magic you used here tonight I assume was taught by your witch of a mother. . . . Also, why else would you be here, and unaccompanied?"

"You must have me mistaken for someone else. You see, my name is Vale and I seem to be . . ."

"Enough of these lies!" the stranger warned sharply, cutting off Dark in mid-sentence. "Lying only leads to more lies."

The hostile thief looked at him for a long moment, an amused smile crossing his lips as he now grinned wolfishly at his captive, obviously feeling quite pleased with his unexpected catch.

"I also failed to mention I knew your father very well," he said, pointing to his two scarred cheeks. "He graciously left me these as a memento of our first encounter."

"I would have made them deeper," Dark mocked bitterly. "And a lot more permanent."

"I see looks are not the only thing you inherited from your father, but his smart mouth as well." As he spoke, anger flashed sharply in his eyes. "You see, I wasn't the only person he did this to . . . I was just the first. There were others . . . many others . . . and all of those who crossed him or got in his way received this parting gift. . . . So you can imagine how many enemies he must have made."

The scarred man paused in remembering thought and stood in silence, staring mesmerized at the ground in front of him for but a moment, dangling the sharp tip of his sword dangerously close to Dark's own cheek.

"A reminder, he would say, to always know who his enemies were. This is why I volunteered to search for the whereabouts of Taliesin and his party . . . and to make certain my master was rid of Demon and that bitch, the Witch Raider."

"Do you want to know what happened to them?" Dark broke in coldly. "Taliesin and all his little friends are dead!"

"I figured out that much, but I also believe he completed his appointed task, or else your parents would be here to defend their child, and a mere boy wouldn't be left alone as you are now. You see . . . BOY, my reason for being here is twofold. One . . . I'm here to confirm the death of your parents, and the sad, pathetic look on your face verifies that for me. Two . . . use this worthless crew as a diversion, keeping Mephistopheles engaged while I sneak around him . . . like I just did to you, then, backstab the old bastard and once and for all end his pathetic life. But to my surprise, what did I see killing my men? Not the old wizard, but a young one."

You're very sure of yourself, whoever you are," came Dark's quick reply.

"Where are my manners? Allow me to introduce myself. My name is Criss-Cross, assassin extraordinaire." The stranger smiled faintly and bowed his head slightly, his sword lowering to his waist. "And you are?"

"I'm the world's most powerful boy!" he roared, raising his left arm upward, palm open as he tried to unleash the power of the wand on his unsuspecting captor . . . but nothing happened.

The assassin easily caught Dark's exposed hand in a grip like iron, twisting it down and sharply forward, bringing the world's most powerful boy to his knees in obvious pain, all the while smiling faintly down at him.

"No, you're the little brat who is lucky to still be alive . . . unlike Mommy and Daddy!" Criss-Cross sneered mockingly at the wincing youth, his smile gone, brandishing his steel sword once again to his young prisoner's throat. "And you're the little brat who's going to help me kill your own grandfather!"

Dark's grimacing face became distorted in sudden hatred and fury. His youthful features turned villainous as a storm now raged in his eyes. The cocky assassin looked on in astonishment. A faint trace of surprise registered on his face as he saw his youthful captive grab the tip of his blade and, with a demonic grin, began to stand.

"That's how little boys lose fingers!" his voice rasped menacingly, but the young magician did not loosen his grip.

A thirst for vengeance now burned like fire deep within Dark's very soul, and giving that metaphor literal truth, his vengeance did indeed turn to flame. Gripping the blade tightly, his hand now slick with blood, he began to concentrate. His eyes seemed strangely more focused, like the calm before the storm.

"Now let me show you the mark I give my enemies!" Dark cried venomously as the energy that had been building up inside him was released, causing his eyes to vanish, looking like the very fabric of space itself.

The assassin shot a quick, startled look at the young apprentice of Mephistopheles as a dull, wispy blue flame began to cover Dark's arm, giving off a shadowy illumination. The unearthly fire crackled down the length of the long sword and covered the assassin's hand in a sheath of magical fire. In a flash, Criss-Cross' body became outlined in the blaze, erupting in a powerful burst of the bright blue flame that bathed the area around them like sunlight. His sword began to soften and flow like running water. Charred tissue melted off his face as he writhed in horrifying agony, shrieking loudly. His flesh turned black as his body crumbled into ashes and sank to the burning ground. The last of his chilling screams erupted upward into ear-shattering sounds until finally disappearing into the night air. The only thing left of the overconfident assassin was the pungent smell of hot metal and burnt flesh emanating from his smoking remains.

VII

Dark's arrival back at his grandfather's home was a triumphant one as he silently congratulated himself on his successful confrontation with Criss-Cross and his little band of spies. He paused momentarily as his foot came in contact with the first of the stone steps that led down to the cave, feeling more than a little afraid of facing his sure-to-be-even-angrier grandfather. Reluctantly, he eventually proceeded downward, knowing he had no other choice than to endure the tongue-lashing that would be inflicted upon him and whatever punishment was sure to follow. The fearful young magician had not taken more than two steps beyond the archway when his elven eyes met the grim, hardened face of his grandfather, his cold, callous eyes staring back in deep disapproval.

"What do you have to say for yourself?" the deep voice of his grandfather boomed out piercingly, his silk cape billowing slightly as he moved toward Dark.

"I won!" was Dark's abrupt declaration.

"You were lucky!" his irate grandfather began again, his face flushed red with anger. "If it were not for Teigue watching over you . . . well . . . you could have been killed!"

"I thought you fought very bravely and your use of the arcane arts was masterful," a familiar tiny voice blurted out from behind the tall, infuriated magus.

From behind the cover of the mystic's voluminous robes emerged Teigue, emissary to the Faërie King, longtime friend to Mephisto, and someone Dark had known all his life. Teigue was comely of feature and resplendent in his garb of blue and white petals and glowing blue circlet that seemed to float slightly above his head.

"You're not helping, Teigue," Mephisto warned harshly as the little faërie darted out of reach of the wizard's grasping hand.

"You weren't there. I was, and what I saw was not a young apprentice, but a skilled magician in total command of his craft and of the situation!" Teigue snapped back, flying even farther away, making sure to keep a safe distance between himself and the quick hands of Mephisto.

"He fought a group of amateurs, probably just a scouting party," Mephisto spoke suddenly in retaliation.

"He fought and killed six members of the halfling pack, as well as a young, pompous apprentice magician," the little faërie said defiantly.

"Six lowly rats and one . . ."

"Criss-Cross was leading the party," interjected Teigue quickly, cutting short the old magician's rebuttal. "And he, as you know, is an experienced and deadly assassin, or should I say . . . was."

Mephisto looked over at his grandson and managed a slight smile, inwardly pleased with his young student.

"Were you not afraid?" he queried shortly, his look one of concern.

"At first I was as I crouched in fear," Dark began slowly. "Then this uncontrollable anger forced me to rise, and that's when I decided I needed to do something."

"And he did something alright," Teigue broke in again, trying hard not to laugh. "I don't even think there is anything left of Criss-Cross to bury."

Mephisto seemed to hesitate for a moment, then looked to Teigue, smiling coldly as a deathly silence settled over the company. The frightened faërie shot a quick look at the foreboding wizard, then desperately raced for cover, but it was too late. Before he could reach the safe shelter of a nearby table leg, a small, well-made silver birdcage appeared instantaneously, imprisoning Teigue inside before falling heavily to the floor.

"I don't care how well he did," Mephisto continued, turning his icy gaze back at his grandson. "What you did was brash, irresponsible, and incredibly dangerous."

Mephisto walked over, stood in front of Dark, and paused for a brief moment to consider his explanation, trying hard to choose his words wisely.

"I know I am not your father or your mother, but I am your grandfather. And I only want what they would want, and that is to keep you safe. I love you very much, and I only want what is best for you, so I need you to trust me. You truly do not understand the nature of the enemy you would be up against and the powerful forces he wields. Is Taliesin's death not enough for you?"

"No . . . that is why I need your help," Dark began slowly. "If you would just help me, I know we can defeat all of those that are responsible for their murders. You just don't get it!" he began again, yelling obstreperously.

"You are thirteen! Do you understand the words that are coming out of my mouth? You are still a boy, going up against full-grown men like Kalifen and Blackthorn, not to mention the thousand or so highly trained and highly skilled henchmen that they have at their disposal! You could not possibly defeat them all. No one can . . . not even I could do it alone!"

There was a moment of ominous silence that hung oppressively in the air as Mephisto's final words echoed back with a resounding sharpness that cut deep into his grandson.

"Then maybe I'll just send for Grandmother to come and take me away from here." Dark spoke softly, his look one of anger and his thoughts sinister.

"How dare you speak that witch's name in my presence. And make sure you remember to whom you are speaking," warned the stern voice from the ancient silver magus. "That woman is no longer welcome in my home, and I am your guardian, not her. So until you are old enough, you will obey my rules."

"You can't keep me here forever!" stormed Dark, stepping forward with absolute disregard for what might happen to him, his small hands balled into clenched fists.

"Watch me!" the furious wizard erupted, his face tightening into a frightening mask of rage.

"Actually," the mocking voice of the almost-forgotten caged faërie volunteered abruptly, which caused Mephisto to roll his eyes and clench his jaws. "Faërie law clearly states, every male on the day of his fifteenth birthday shall be given the status of an adult."

Both Dark and his grandfather looked back at the trapped faërie, who was flashing a huge smile, followed by a slow bow, making his jailer sigh heavily and stare with blazing eyes of hatred.

"I bet you regret incarcerating me now."

"In two years' time, on Samain Eve, I will turn fifteen, and that will be the day I leave from here," Dark spoke defiantly and purposely held up two fingers to his grandfather's bitter face. "And there is nothing you can do to stop me!"

Slowly, Dark walked away toward the stairs to his room and left his grandfather in shocked disbelief with Teigue, the little faërie, clapping his hands in applause.

"You were a great help, Teigue," the weary mystic spoke with thick sarcasm.

"That's what I'm here for," the gentle voice of the faërie cut him short.

"Seriously, what am I going to do with this boy?"

"He has too much of his father in him . . . you know this," Teigue answered quietly. "And there is no way of changing his mind—not now, not ever."

"I fear you may be right," he muttered.

The tired old magician wearily settled his ancient bones down against his favorite leather chair. Worn and haggard, he stared upward toward the cavern's ceiling, lost in thought. For the first time, Mephisto realized the truth about his predicament. His grandson would journey to the city of Duergar, and there his safety would last only until the Shadow Lord found him and destroyed him.

"So what do I do?" the tired magician asked after a moment's silence.

"Well, the first thing you need to do is . . . GET ME OUT OF HERE!"

Over the next two years, time passed quickly, without incident, and with very little communication between grandfather and grandson. Dark, during the day, would continue to practice what he had learned in the magic arts. But without the aid from his teacher, he lacked the natural insight to truly comprehend the secret sciences. His nights were spent immersed in diligent study, usually behind massive pillars of ancient tombs and spell books. He read stacks of manuals and grimoires resembling towers gleaming with gold leaf and bound in satiny leather—and he noted that almost all were annotated in Mephisto's own hand. Dark also discovered that, unlike his grandfather, he could not easily locate any specific volume he wanted, on which line or which page he needed to be, nor even which zone of the study he needed to look to find a specific spell amongst the mass of literature. On many nights, his screams of frustration could be heard echoing throughout the vast cavern, usually followed by a poem of choice curse words.

Mephisto, during this time, could be found rummaging through his vast library searching tediously for some obscure or hidden law that would help his cause. Once a month, he would venture to the king's court seeking an audience with his Majesty, desperately trying in vain to make amendments to the law, citing that Dark was human and saying the law shouldn't apply to a mortal. Each month, Dark always knew the king's answer to Mephisto's plea, especially when one day he found his grandfather standing in the great room amid the dust and debris of fallen rock under a large, brand new skylight.

"I thought the place could use more light," was all he said.

After that, his grandfather resigned himself to walks in the forest and took frequent trips abroad. Where he would be gone for long periods at a time, Dark could only guess. Neither of the two stubborn pair ever relinquished his convictions. Shortly thereafter, communication became only a passing hello or a glancing smile from across the room.

Dark woke that fateful morning of Samain Eve and his long-awaited fifteenth birthday. The birthday boy quickly dressed himself in worn brown pants, soft leather boots, and a white, collarless long-sleeve shirt. Pulling a heavy grey sweater over his head, he paused a moment and thought of all the memories he had made here at his grandfather's, then brought his mind back to the present and what must be done. He gathered up his belongings he had packed the previous night and began his slow descent down the polished stone steps to the great room and, with no doubt, his waiting grandfather. Standing there as predicted was Mephisto, looking rather large and foreboding, which caused Dark to stop abruptly and stare at him wordlessly, slightly afraid.

"I take it you have still not changed your mind," Mephisto stated, sighing deeply.

"No . . . I have not changed my mind," Dark spoke with stubborn conviction in his voice.

"And the fact that you are no match for them still won't deter you?" the silver mage declared, looking warily at his grandson.

Dark clenched his jaws and grit his teeth at the thought of letting those responsible for the death of his parents escape justice. "No . . . I cannot and will not let them get away with this. . . . I just can't!"

"Your father said the exact same thing to me just before he went back after Kalifen," Mephisto interjected quietly. "And he barely escaped with his life, as well as that of your mother's."

"Where my father failed, I will not," Dark interrupted bravely, his eyes locked onto his grandfather's in open anger.

"Bold words from a clueless child!" his grandfather exclaimed heatedly, his words stabbing at Dark like daggers. "And without any of the training your father or mother had . . . not a chance!"

"That's it, I'm leaving!" Dark burst out loudly, turning away and heading for the exit from this cave prison.

"Wait!" Mephisto caught his lean shoulders, jerking him around violently, pausing momentarily while trying to regain his composure before speaking again. "If I cannot stop you . . . then I might as well help you."

"Really?" Dark muttered, his voice still muffled with fury.

"Yes, but on one condition," replied Mephisto coldly.

"Just name it, and I swear it will be done," promised his grandson emphatically, his tone more serious than it had ever been before. "Just name it, and I swear to you it will be done!"

"The condition is that everything is to be done my way," Mephisto's eyes narrowed as he spoke. "Whatever I say to do . . . you do . . . no matter what."

"As long as you actually help me, I'll do whatever you say . . . I give you my word," Dark exclaimed happily.

Dark looked at his grandfather, whose tireless gaze fixed lovingly on his small grandson, remembering the last two years lost on pointless bickering between them. He vowed to himself to never allow that to happen again. He realized his grandfather loved him and only wanted his happiness and safety, and fighting his grandson showed his willingness to do whatever it took to see to his safety at all costs . . . even losing Dark, if need be.

"There is one thing I would like to ask you," Dark asked hesitatingly, breaking the momentary silence between them. "What made you change your mind?"

"You have the exact same stubborn look in your eyes as your father did," Mephisto answered quietly. "And try as I might . . . no matter what I said or what I did . . . I just could not change his mind."

"And you wouldn't be able to change my mind, either," Dark said, shaking his head.

"No, I can see that now," Mephisto said, patting his grandson's shoulder, leading him over to stand next to the warm fire. "So, after years of trying to find some faërie law that could help me . . . I gave up and turned my attention to helping you."

"Thank you, by the way," Dark quietly cut in.

"Anyway, I thought instead of your one-man-army plan—great plan by the way . . . well thought out," the old wizard began again, the same familiar mocking grin appearing on his bearded face. "I thought I would come up with one of my own. In the summer months to come, from Beltane Eve to Samain Eve, you will be here with me training in the mystical arts."

"And the rest of the time?" the apprehensive little magician asked questioningly.

"The rest of the time, you will be in the care of the same person who trained your father," his voice rolled out as the cavern became slightly darker, as if a large shadow had silently crept over them. "Some say he is not just the Warden of the Stygian Depths, but he is also a warrior . . . a poet . . . a sorcerer and even a smith. In fact, there is no creative skill that he does not only possess, but master. Some say that his face was like a God's, wise and shining, so that no mortal could bear to look upon it. Some say this is the reason his face is shrouded. All I know is, I just call him the Styg."

Dark failed to notice the huge, black shadow that rose up suddenly behind him, detaching itself from the darkness to stand silently. He felt the sudden urge to run, but instead slowly turned uncertainly. The sudden appearance of this ominous figure caused the little apprentice to wheel back in fright, which resulted in his landing hard on his posterior. Dark felt the strong hands of the Styg grip his shoulders roughly and lift the startled boy effortlessly as his feet dangled helplessly above the floor before settling back on solid ground. The cloaked man appraised him curiously and looked back at Mephisto, then back to the lean boy standing in front of him.

"The first thing we need to do is build some muscles on those skinny bones of yours." Styg's voice was chilling, seemingly echoing from deep within the depths of a bottomless pit.

The figure of the imposing Warden of the Stygian Depths now stood before him. A black, expressionless mask that was hidden beneath dark shadows covered his face. A man groomed and hooded in black, he was still wearing the same blackened armor and was wrapped ominously in the same great black cape, just as he had been when Dark had first encountered him years ago.

"Yes sir," Dark mumbled hesitantly and nodded dumbly.

"Does this boy realize this is not going to be an overnight excursion and his training will require years to complete?" asked the masked man, his voice causing the hairs on the back of Dark's neck to stand.

"He does now," Mephisto said dryly with a mocking smile as he looked over at his grandson.

"Years?" Dark spoke, his face puzzled.

"If it is vengeance you truly seek," his grandfather spoke again, his mocking smile gone, "then it must be done this way. . . . You do not have a choice."

Dark knew very little, if anything at all, about this dark assassin from Hell, but his grandfather seemed to have the highest regard for him. After all, his own father did train with him for years, and now he, too, would follow in the old man's footsteps.

"Dark will need to get something straight before I continue," the Styg's voice cut in, snapping the birthday boy's attention to focus back on the macabre man. "I am willing to teach you how to be an assassin . . . not a murderer."

"What's the difference?" Dark again asked hesitantly.

"A murderer kills for some sick gratification or out of passion, while other degenerates kill for what others possess. A true assassin acts out of principle—even though he may kill for money, he does not steal. Of course, it is not as simple as it seems, but that is something you will find out on your own."

"So you are going to teach me how to kill my enemies?" Dark broke in quickly.

"Yes, little one, but it's far more complicated than just showing you how to kill your enemies," responded the mysterious Ward to Hell. "You see, these so-called assassins that reside in your world today are mostly independent operators. They are ambitious and unscrupulous, for they are willing to murder in exchange for a few gold coins, or worse . . . power. I, however, only train those who would assassinate the corrupt and tyrannical or for the common good of your race. Finally, if I were to ever find that you were misusing that which I have taught you or killing for some unfathomable pleasures . . . I would come for you myself."

Dark's eyes widened and his face became ashen as he gulped hard and volleyed back his rebuttal.

"Yes, Master."

The Styg paused and looked back again at Mephisto, who was standing silently, then to his new apprentice, who was listening intently and standing at attention like a young soldier.

"Before we continue any further, I would like to extend my condolence to you and your grandfather on the loss of your parents," his head bowed in respect as he spoke. "Their deaths are one of the main reasons I have agreed to train you, and because I still live by the old axiom of 'an eye for an eye.' So, when you have completed your training and are skilled in the art of assassination, then you will have your vengeance."

Dark watched his new master, his deep blue eyes fixed on the dark speaker while thinking of his parents and the day soon to come when his father and mother would finally be avenged.

"Now, if you are ready, I will make you an assassin of refined skill and subtlety, for killing is an art above the petty and demeaning world of wealth and politics," the Styg began again, his deep voice echoing eerily inside the great room. "You will become a master in poison, acrobatics, martial arts, and swordplay, and will be taught to use a wide variety of deadly devices."

"I am ready," Dark announced quietly.

"Really?" he murmured seriously. "Although . . . all this talk of murder and killing and not once did you cringe or even flinch. That at least gives me something to work with, but you still have one last test to perform before I accept you as my student."

"What is this . . . test?" Dark asked fearfully, shooting a quick glance at his grandfather.

Mephisto, who had been uncommonly silent all this time, now stepped forward, which caused his grandson to frown at him suspiciously, trying to read behind the unblinking visage of the old wizard. In his left hand, a black stovepipe hat instantly appeared. Then, tilting it toward the audience to show the contents to be empty, he waved his right hand. Saying a few magic words, he reached inside. What the old magician pulled out was covered in dense, white fur with long, upstanding ears, large, red eyes, flat back feet, a twitching pink nose, and a fluffy cottontail. It was a cute little bunny rabbit.

"What's the bunny for?" Dark asked suspiciously.

"This is the final test. Dark," declared his grandfather. "You still have to demonstrate to the Styg if you are worthy enough to be his new apprentice."

"What do you want me to do . . . kill the rabbit?" Dark asked fearfully, sounding worried.

"Yes, now do what must be done . . . and kill Cuddles." Mephisto's tone was cold and callous as he held forth the furry sacrifice to his grandson.

"You had to name it, too?" interjected the now irate young magician.

"All those you wish to kill . . . do they too not have names?" the deep voice of the Styg sounded out ominously.

Dark grudgingly took the enchanted rabbit from his grandfather's hands, grabbing the poor woodland creature by the scruff of its neck as gently as he could.

"What am I supposed to use, my bare hands?" Dark asked almost fearfully.

His grandfather spoke a few words and pointed in front of his grandson. There appeared a small, round oak table. In the center and lying on its smoothly sanded top was a weapon of sacrificial malice. The exotic, beautifully styled dagger had an acid-etched silver flame that ran the entire length of its steel blade. Mounted in the hilt, which featured a dragon claw guard in polished silver, was a carved scale handle of ebony with an intricate dragon pommel. Dark looked at the Styg, his lean face scrutinizing the dark figure, shot a helpless look at his grandfather, then looked quickly back at his tiny intended victim. He reluctantly placed Cuddles on the table and took the instrument of death in his hand, its sharp edge twinkling inside the lighted cavern. He raised the dragon blade high above his head, looking desperately at the tiny rabbit, and saw the fear in his own eyes mirrored in those of his helpless victim's. With a sharp pain of regret emanating from his heart, he brought the shining blade down with ferocious force, sinking the sharp artifact deep into the wooden tabletop only inches from the head of Cuddles.

"I can't . . . I can't do it!" came Dark's abrupt declaration as he looked doubtfully at the silent faces staring back at him. "I've failed them."

The Warden of the Stygian Depths silently moved toward Dark, placing a large, gauntleted hand on his slim shoulder, and spoke to his young student.

"No, Dark . . . you have not failed them, for you have passed my test."

"What?" his lowered head rising suddenly upward. "I don't understand."

"If you had gone through with it and killed our little furry friend here, I would not have taken you on as my apprentice," the Styg began again, his voice still fearful to be heard. "But because you did not kill for the sake of the kill, I will train you."

"I still don't understand," Dark said as he stood watching his new teacher in a mixed state of shock and utter confusion.

"The creature before you, Dark, is defenseless, dependent, and alone. Killing it would have been a true act of evil," the assassin answered smoothly. "Instead, you showed great restraint, even knowing the consequences of those actions. I also see that evil does not reside inside your heart and, even though you desperately want vengeance, there is still empathy for those weaker than yourself."

"I just couldn't kill something so fragile and innocent," spoke Dark after a silent moment in thought.

"That is precisely why I am going to train you to be the greatest assassin the world has ever known."

The young assassin's apprentice seemed to hesitate for a moment, then gazed almost fearfully at the tall wizard, trying to judge his reaction.

"And you're really alright with this," he queried shortly.

"The question is, are you alright with all of this?" Mephisto announced blackly. "This is a very treacherous path you are heading down, undoubtedly fraught with great peril and many sinister foes along the way. This journey you are about to embark on will forever change you. So, for better or worse, I will stand by your decision and trust that you made the right one."

Long moments passed as grandfather and grandson looked at one another with broad smiles that reconciled any differences the two had had over the last few years.

"Before we depart for the land of the damned, there is an unwritten code that defines what should and should not be done, and you must agree and abide by it," his black master cut in, breaking the silence. "Breaking the code will cause a loss of face, meaning you will literally lose your face, hence the saying, 'lose face.'"

Dark took a step backward in shock as the frightened fifteen-year-old shot a quick glance at his grandfather and gulped hard.

"Now, let's be on our way," responded his new master, tapping the teen boy softly on his narrow back. He then hustled quickly toward the stairs, motioning for the others to follow him.

"We better get a move on," Mephisto mocked dryly, walking away from his grandson, motioning vaguely toward the stairs. "I don't want to lose face . . . especially since I have grown so accustomed to this one."

As the trio made their way outside, Sommerset was still dark, with only the faint traces of the orange sun filtering through the tops of the Fa'an forest. A thin mist of fog rolled over the surface of Dragon's Mouth Lake, and there on the shore was the *Albatross*, his grandfather's enchanted ship.

"I'll wait aboard the boat while you say your goodbyes to your grandfather," the Styg declared causally, then proceeded down to the *Albatross*, agilely climbed aboard, and stood at her bow.

"You will be back soon enough on Beltane Eve, then we can pick up your studies once again. I will even teach you proper command over Dragon's Breath," the old mystic trailed off sharply, looking meaningfully at his young grandson and suddenly feeling a sense of great loss as the last living member of his beloved family was about to leave him.

"This isn't goodbye," was his grandson's response. "I'll be back before you know it . . . so let's just say 'I'll see you soon.'"

"Do everything the Styg tells you to do." Mephisto's voice broke slightly as the old wizard struggled to regain his composure.

"I will," Dark nodded and managed half a smile. Then, with a hug and a simple wave, Dark left his old teacher and turned to his new one.

Dark quickly climbed into the magical flying boat and sat down heavily in the cockpit. He sat there thinking silently to himself, reflecting sadly on the loss of his parents, and wondered if they would approve of his decision to seek vengeance. He turned to the cloaked assassin, who began to speak.

"If it makes you feel any better, your father was . . ." the Styg's soulless voice paused a moment as he reflected on his old student. "Let's just say he was a little apprehensive like you. Now let us sail to the home of Hades."

From beneath his shadowy cloak, he brought forth a figurative device for the measurement of time. The ornate hourglass was carved from the ivory white bones of a mortal man and flanked by terrifying trimmings in solid silver. The bottom glass bulb, usually filled with fine sand, contained something else—the darkened soul of a horned devil. Upon turning it over, the trapped black essence spiraled toward the center and drained slowly into the bottom container. It was at that point time seemed to come to a standstill. A deep silence settled ominously over the two companions as a conduit opened to the Isles of the Blessed and the entrance to Hell. The shadow cast from the *Albatross* began to change dramatically as it stretched far out and away from them and quickly extended past the horizon. The small, animated boat and her crew sank into and under its own shadow, finally disappearing from view as the inky ebony waters covered their heads. Instantaneously, they were carried across the adumbral tide, their far-stretched shadow coming to a stop in front of a forest-shrouded island as they slowly emerged from it.

"Welcome to the realm of Hades and the abode of the dead, where all mortals go to await judgment day," the Warden of the Stygian Depths declared, placing the hourglass beneath his cloak.

"Is it true that on the far side of the River Styx, the three-headed dog Cerberus stands guard?" Dark asked, almost whispering his question fearful that the beast might actually hear him.

"Yes, and he still does to this day," the Styg replied, turning his broad frame slightly to look at his new student. "He watches the boundaries between the upper and lower worlds."

The long ship glided effortlessly over the Sargasso Sea, the once-tranquil blue colors of the water now deepened to a foul red ichor. Through the sighing wind, Dark heard a strange sound that seemed to surround the winged vessel. He looked about for the source and found it. The sound he heard wasn't random noises, but whispers, voices of the dead who called out from a mass of lean, bloodied corpses writhing among fingers and tongues and other bits and pieces in revelries of sadism.

The frightened apprentice slowly sank back in his seat, trying hard to drown out the now-audible whispers and unwilling to peer over the side of the little ship again. The *Albatross*, still moving steadily above the waves, came toward the unknown shore, unfolded its massive wings, and lifted her crew ever higher over the pebbled beach. They passed over a thick, green forest into the heart of the isle and into a small clearing. In the middle of this hidden clearing was Avernus Lake, and next to its macabre waters a lonely black tower. At its base lay the entrance to the netherworld.

The majestic bird glided smoothly to the ground, landing a few feet from the entrance and folding her giant wings gracefully back along her side. Both master and student disembarked the enchanted vessel and quickly came to stand in front of the gates to Hell. The entrance was beneath a warped and twisted tower made of dark stone. Skulls decorated the outside, with their eyes sparkling in the midst of the gloom. The entrance was made up of two massive brass doors with a large pentagram etched into their surface. Sealed from sunlight, a winding staircase led far into the Eorth.

"Once you enter through these doors, your world will forever be changed," the deep voice seemed to roll out of the shadowy figure.

"Yes, Master . . . I am ready," Dark stammered fearfully.

"Then follow me, my new apprentice."

Moments later, the great doors opened noiselessly, and Dark quietly slipped through and disappeared from view, descending ever downward in darkness until both figures were lost in the depths of Hell.

VIII

For ten years, Dark dwelled in the bowels of Hell with his new teacher, the Warden of the Stygian Depths, not only growing in size and strength, but in skill as well. By day and by night, the young apprentice lay in pitch blackness and longed for the comfort of a lighted candle. As time wore on, he remained in a perpetual state of total darkness. But with each passing day, he became more at ease and accustomed to his dark surroundings. The days turned to weeks and the weeks into years. His once sandy blonde hair turned a sooty black, and his eyes became like the night sky. It was in these days that an enduring bond formed between teacher and student, during which many great deeds came of this dark alliance.

Every Beltane Eve, as flocks of swans migrated in from the south on silent wings, settling in cloud-like drifts on Dragon's Mouth Lake, the apprentice assassin would return to Sommerset. There, his grandfather would tutor him in the truest embodiment of the ancient arts and of the old powers, awesome and unspeakable. During his prolonged studies, Dark uncovered the deepest secrets of the arcane orders and the infinite power of the wand, Dragon's Breath, and mastered them both. Through the mastery of these powerful forces, he could now begin and set about accomplishing the removal of his unsuspecting enemies. The day would come soon enough when he would be lurking among his enemies, waiting for the opportune moment to arise and not just demand satisfaction, but take it. He would decide their fates by the powers of sorcery and black magic or by a sharp blade through the back, the latter of which he liked the most.

At long last, Dark's waiting finally came to an end. His training finished and his term in Hell complete, the assassin headed straight for Sommerset, where his grandfather eagerly awaited his homecoming. Dark's arrival coincided with the breaking of the dawn and within moments found him making his way down the stone staircase, stepping into the great room and quietly into view. No longer a small and frail young boy, he was now a grown man, large and forbidding, with a dark cloak wrapped around his broad shoulders, his lean face hidden beneath the depths of the long hood covering his head. With the nimble silence of a cat he moved gracefully, effortlessly, his long strides covering the cavern floor with ease. As he approached, his grandfather was sitting in his favorite seat at a long table covered in rolled-up scrolls and pieces of white parchment. Mephisto smiled and greeted his grandson with a quick wave of his hand.

"Finally back for good, are we?" Mephisto stood up from his leather chair and sauntered over from the other side of the paper-filled table to greet his grandson. He was wearing a long, silver cloak that trailed on the floor as he walked. His white robes were fashioned from multiple layers of fine silk, and along the hem were strange runes and symbols stitched in silver thread.

"I'm sorry to have to tell you this, but unfortunately my stay here will be a brief one," Dark declared quietly as he stopped before his grandfather, slowly pulling back his black hood to reveal deep ebony eyes. "I intend to start for Duergar in a fortnight."

"Your assault on Duergar will have to wait but for just a little longer," Mephisto explained quickly. "I need you to go and see an old friend first . . . someone who wishes to present you with a gift."

"What friend of yours wants to give me a gift?" Dark asked curiously. "Is it Teigue?"

"No-no-no-no-no . . . it is not Teigue," the wizard in white broke in. "It is Dwaric . . . Dwaric Duergar, son of the fallen king and new ruler of the dwarves."

"I remember him when I was a child; he was just a little taller than I was," declared the cloaked assassin. "What gift does he want to give me?"

"Let's just say it is something that will aid you in your quest," Mephisto continued. "That is all I can tell you."

"When am I expected at his Majesty's court?" he asked, looking quizzically at his grandfather.

"He waits for you now," he began again, turning his head with a slight gesture toward the entrance. "Outside, the *Albatross* awaits your command; tell her you wish to visit Agnarock and she will take you there."

"I shall leave first thing in the morning, but today I wish to visit with the old man for a while." Dark smiled warmly at his grandfather, who stood quietly gazing back.

"Who's this old man you are talking about?" cut in Mephisto sharply.

"Why you, of course . . . OLD MAN!" he mocked heartedly, one great hand reaching over to grip Mephisto's cloaked shoulder tightly.

"I will show you, old man," his grandfather exclaimed, brushing away his grandson's strong hold on his shoulder. He then turned quickly away and walked toward the checkered board on the cavern floor. "Now come play me in the game of kings, where wisdom comes from years . . . not youth."

The next morning, even before his grandfather was awake, Dark quietly stepped out into the morning's first light and boarded the *Albatross*. The air was crisp and cool as a variety of wild birds of all shapes and sizes could be heard singing gay songs from deep within the forest to once again welcome the beginning of another day.

"Fly us to Agnarock, old girl," Dark spoke softly as he told his enchanted flying ship his desired destination.

Even in the absence of any type of breeze, the large seabird easily lofted upward until it was flying high above the clouds. What took most ships weeks or even months took only a few days, for the *Albatross* was highly efficient while in the air. With her gigantic wings, she would repeatedly dive into the valleys of ocean waves then wheel her large frame back up into the air, a technique she used to travel great distances while expending very little energy. The black-and-white feathered boat sailed toward the far fringes of the western world, seeking the land of the immortals and new home of the dwarves.

Two days passed. Dark awoke, his back sore and stiff from another uncomfortable night's sleep in the small cockpit of his flying ship. After crossing the vast Sea of Wonders and passing over wild lands of forests and vast lakes, he spotted the outlined humpbacks of the Ymir Mountains on the horizon. This mountainous region was an awe-inspiring land, from the alpine meadows to the majestic river valleys heavily dotted with spectacular waterfalls. Gliding above a sea of untouched ancient forests, the *Albatross* followed a trail that ended at the flat face of a limestone cliff. The long, winged ship began to circle downward and landed softly on the forest floor in front of the great stone facade.

Dark leaped to the hard ground and moved slowly down the winding, boulder-laden path ahead, casting apprehensive glances about the rugged terrain that surrounded him. The trail ahead wound upward into the very steep and almost vertical overhanging cliff face of solid rock. Dark now stood at the base of the cliff that rose several hundred feet above him. His observant elven eyes scanned its smooth, sheer wall and saw no means by which to scale its slick surface.

"By invitation of the king, I, Dark Solus, ask for entrance to the Kingdom of the Dwarves," Dark spoke aloud. His words seemed to echo back with a ringing sharpness.

There was a brief moment of silence, then suddenly a seam appeared and widened, forming the shape of a thick, stone door that slowly swung open for him. Beyond this magical portal, a tunnel led deep into the earth and the underground fires of the dwarves' forges. Without any hesitation, he headed ever downward through a winding corridor, led by the distant clanging of hammers on steel. The passage opened into a vast underground chamber, and at its entrance two colorless faces watched, rigidly wary, as the cloaked half-elf approached, their dark eyes gazing at him from grey skin. Standing grim and cheerless, they were no higher than

Dark's waist, with rounded bodies and wide shoulders. Both sentinels were encased in full silver-plated armor, and with their stout, muscular arms they gripped firmly in one hand a heavy war hammer, while the other held a large shield embossed with the golden emblem of Mjöllnir, the hammer of Thor.

"Lower your weapons," a voice he recognized from his youth boomed out from behind the two heavily armored guards.

Their steel shields lowered and parted as both of the stout sentries moved aside to make way for the King of the Dwarves. A crowned ruler made his way toward Dark, flanked by courtly attendants and closely followed by a cluster of grim-faced dwarven warriors. These were the elite guard, each one carefully selected by the king. Each one was noticeably larger than the average dwarf male. Completely fearless and loyal, all were dressed in full-plate armor that had been blackened by forge fire. In their steel hands they carried large, brutal double-edged legionnaire axes. He saw the smiling familiar face of Dwaric Duergar, looking fine in feature and showing no signs of aging. His dark eyes were wise and appraising, and his royal dress was regal.

"You know, the last time we met, I was actually taller than you," the diminutive Dwarf King said, tipping his crowned head far back to meet Dark's eyes.

"I could get on my knees if his Majesty wishes," the cloaked assassin replied with a furtive smile while bowing his head slightly.

"I see looks are not the only thing you inherited from your father, but his smart mouth as well," declared Dwaric, also showing a furtive smile.

"You know, I have never heard that one before," Dark began again, flushed and happy at seeing his old friend and clapping the small dwarf warmly on the shoulder. "It's been a long time, your Majesty."

"Dark . . . remember I am still your godfather—so please, address me by my given name . . . all right," the King of the

Dwarves laughed heartily to himself while quickly surveying his godson up and down. "I think your parents would be so proud if they could see the man you have grown to become."

"I like to think so." Dark gave a slight smile.

"But I am curious about one thing . . . why an assassin?" Dwaric asked curiously.

"Magic alone wouldn't be enough. I had to learn to be ruthless and without mercy," Dark answered in quiet earnest. "And sometimes the only solution to one's problems involves someone's death, preferably from the shadows."

"You are like your father!" the little king laughed abruptly.

A moment later, one of the younger dwarves came rushing toward them, waving his hand excitedly, almost stumbling on several occasions in his great haste. Dark looked in startled confusion as the ring of guards parted to let the king's messenger reach them with good news that made the little monarch smile wide.

"Wonderful . . . he is ready for us!" exclaimed the excited King of the Dwarves. "Follow me Dark, if you please."

Dwaric now guided Dark and led him through the stone archway and into a huge cavernous region that sheltered an underground kingdom that no other rivaled in beauty. Every aspect of the miniature city was graced by splendid architecture that had been crafted by true master artisans. Intricately carved statues of past heroes and gods of the old world lined the lamp-lighted streets. Remarkably, assorted gardens were constructed beneath glass domes with exotic green plants and blossoms of pink, blue, and the deepest reds that mantled each pinnacle of the buildings. The great cavern was lighted from the jewel-spangled walls that glittered like a thousand lanterns. The air had a sweet scent and was filled with song that echoed against the tall interior, sung from brightly colored birds that criss-crossed the cavern ceiling. As Dark walked in the domain of the dwarves, he saw that the men wore clothing that was simple, yet functional. Their hair varied in colors of black, brown, and grey, and all were adorned with full-grown beards. The company of dwarven women were garbed in robes of white and blue linen, and all around him he could see that the children were no bigger than a pixie, the youngest even smaller.

"I thought female dwarves could not bear children?" asked Dark curiously.

"Of course they can; that is just a myth!" the dwarf growled irately. "Did you think we just simply sculpted them from solid rock?"

"Well . . . yeah," stated Dark flatly.

The Dwarf King gave his godson a disgruntled look and shook his head in disbelief before speaking again.

"Dark . . . if we could do that, I would have an army as large as this continent and one that could easily take back that which is rightfully mine—my beloved City of Duergar."

"I see your point," the dark assassin acknowledged. "But hopefully, if I am successful . . . you will have that which is rightfully yours; you will have your city back."

"That is what my people hope and wish for, my friend," Dwaric Duergar acknowledged with a smile, looking up at the tall half-elven assassin. "And that is the very reason I have asked you here."

"Why did you ask me here?" he asked with a puzzled look.

"The generous denizens of Agnarock wish to present you with a very special gift, one we feel is needed and one that is best suited for your very purpose," the king smiled.

Dark looked at the little Dwarf King wonderingly, then nodded and smiled his thanks.

"Let us continue," Dwaric said, moving forward.

As Dark followed the company of armored warriors, it seemed the assassin caused whispering among the citizens of the underground kingdom, until their king loudly cleared his throat, which caused the whispering to cease.

"Sorry, my boy. You see, some of them have never seen a mortal man before," ventured his godfather as the procession made its way through the city.

The Dwarf King led him past the royal courtyard of the palace that stood at the center of Agnarock. A nearby display held the skeletal remains of a colossal dragon in the far northeast section of the cavern, its horned head still filled with long, massive fangs too big for its mouth. Finally, he was led into the smoky depths of a mammoth workshop at the southern section of the vast underground cavern. The clang from hammering rang out like explosions that were so loud they triggered tiny avalanches of pebbles to rapidly flow downward from the tunnel ceiling. Veils of blue flame danced and shimmered atop a bed of white coals from the large, well-stoked forge. Pumping the two-chambered forge bellow vigorously was a monstrous brute, a single-eyed Cyclops that stood more than twenty feet tall. A large and heavy-looking anvil sat next to the roaring fire on a large stone block. There, a blacksmith used his ancient ancestral skills to dazzle Dark's eyes in a blaze of sparks of both mortals and gods alike, creating the most amazing treasures the world has ever seen.

"That's Lödd; he is the greatest blacksmith the world has ever known," commented the Dwarf King, a sense of great pride displayed on his bearded face. "Not even the gods have a finer artisan than our shaggy friend here . . . and no one can match his skill with metal."

Silhouetted against the blaze was an extremely muscular dwarf with shaggy red hair and an untrimmed beard that was singed at the ends. The tip of his nose was missing, covered by a fully functioning silver replacement. He wore a buckskin apron that was grey from soot. One hand held large, metal tongs, the other corded arm wielded a stout, short-handled hammer. The smith's power over lifeless metal seemed mystical, his steel hammer glinting from the glowing embers as he struck each piece with superhuman strength. Blackened hands worked like lightning strikes, faster than your eyes could follow, only stopping for the briefest of moments to wipe his sweaty brow. Wondrous marvels began taking shape as the staunch dwarf created a treasure trove of items that quickly began to litter the floor.

Dark was both speechless and amazed and stood there in awe of the master craftsman's restless ingenuity and at the matchless artifacts that now lay at his feet. When the shaggy blacksmith had completed his hammering, he presented his smith work to a flurry of high praise and great thanks from the smiling assassin.

"This armor was crafted from all the secret and impalpable things on Eorth, and its powers are as rare and subtle as its making," he spoke in flattering praise of his own work. "Now, the forge is hot; I am still hungry for renown."

With that said, his stout form turned back to toil at his trade, but was stayed by the quick hand of the cloaked assassin.

"I don't mean to pry, but I must ask what happened to your nose?"

"My mother told me that when I was young, the god Loki was said to be jealous of how handsome I was. So, one night he transformed himself into a gold squirrel and, while I slept, scurried into my room and bit the tip of my nose clean off," the dwarf smiled with satisfaction and turned back to his cooling forge.

"Is that true?" asked Dark, a little bewildered by what he had just heard, his eyes still on the smith.

"Sure it is," the king said with a smirk.

Dwaric ordered the company to move out, and as they were leaving Lödd and his forge behind, he looked at Dark and started to speak.

"Now I will have my servants carry your new armor to your ship, then we will make our way to my palace, where you shall stay as my honored guest."

"I'm afraid I must regretfully decline your invitation, for my need is dire," stated Dark abruptly, gripping tightly the shoulder of his old friend. "Far too long my vengeance has slept abeyant, but now it has awaken inside of me and longs to feed."

"Understandably, my boy. Our hearts and our prayers go with you," Dwaric responded slowly. "And may dwarf steel protect you from your enemies."

Dark was about to speak when he saw that his tiny friend was not quite yet finished with his thoughts, so he stopped himself and held his tongue.

"Before you go, may I ask what your plan is?" interrupted Dwaric curiously.

"My plan is a simple one," Dark responded grimly, a sinister glint in his eyes. "I'm going to kill them all."

There was a moment of ominous silence as the dark assassin's final words seemed to echo back with a resounding, truthful ringing sharpness that made the tiny sovereign smile broadly.

"Next time we meet, I shall present you with a gift greater than the one you have given me," the black-garbed assassin paused and looked directly into the king's own steely eyes. "I will give you back your city . . . I give you my word on that."

As Dark prepared to return to his homelands, he glanced a quick glance back at the underground domain and its people, then turned to the stocky Dwarf King and extended a broad hand. He gripped the smiling king's tiny hand tightly for a brief moment, then with a nod walked silently from the dwarves' company and took leave of the other world.

IX

The morning came quickly to the sleep-filled eyes of the returning assassin. The golden half-light of dawn lighted their descent as they came to rest upon the calm waters of Dragon's Mouth Lake. He wrapped his cloak tightly about himself to help ward off the chill of the early morning. Then, he disembarked from the *Albatross* and quickly made his way to the cave entrance, carrying with him a large wooden chest that he easily flung over his right shoulder.

His grandfather's waiting finally came to an end as he saw his grandson approaching toward him. Mephisto was seated in his reading chair next to the fire, poking the glowing embers idly. Dressed all in green, he greeted his grandson with a sly wink.

"You're back," the smiling magician announced suddenly, looking up at him.

"I am," replied the handsome half-elf, dropping the chest heavily to the floor with a loud thud.

"And here is my gift, bestowed upon me by the King of the Dwarves."

"And what a finely crafted box of wood it is," his grandfather declared jokingly.

"The gift is inside the box, old man," Dark shot back ruthlessly. "Maybe I should have asked Lödd to make me a pair of spectacles . . . to help with your vision."

"You do realize the only reason you have these items is because I asked him to make them for you?" the mystic stated pointedly. "I personally designed these artifacts myself."

"Then you finally got me something good for a change," Dark quickly replied mockingly, trying to hide a growing smirk.

"Well, it was only until just recently that I actually started to like you," was his grandfather's short, sarcastic reply.

Dark stood quietly for a moment and stared wordlessly at an unblinking, straight-faced Mephisto, then gave up and smiled faintly. "I'm just going to open up the chest."

"Good idea," his grandfather stated simply, nodding his approval, inwardly pleased with himself.

Dark bent down, released the latch that held the well-crafted chest closed, and lifted the lid noiselessly open. He rose tall and disrobed to stand shirtless. His muscular body was covered with strange symbols and ritualistic tattoos, each one inscribed in magical, silky black ink. From the handmade dwarven chest, he pulled out and put on a thin, form-fitting black mithril mail shirt made from linked rings of metal that were so fine it could not be seen with the naked eye.

"Wait . . ." Dark exclaimed while he curiously rummaged through the chest. "I don't think I have any boots."

"I almost forgot," his grandfather's tall frame straightened itself as he stood up courteously. "The items you are missing I have in my possession."

Mephisto reached into his green garments, produced a plain black silk handkerchief, sauntered over to the large wooden worktable, and laid it down flat. Amazingly, he placed his hand deep into the circle of the cloth, stopping just short of reaching his shoulder. The first thing the old wizard pulled out was a pair of black leather boots with soft leather soles and a forked tongue that fell from the open mouth of a long-fanged demon.

"These boots will grant you a supernatural nimbleness," Mephisto spoke softly, looking thoughtfully back. "They were your father's; they will help you to run faster and jump higher."

Dark easily slid the enchanted high boots onto his bare feet while his grandfather brought forth two more wondrous relics, the first a plain ring made of silver and set with a single small emerald eye. The second was a small silver pendant that resembled an arrow, broken in half at its shaft.

"The pendant will protect you from any incoming projectiles, such as a single bolt from a crossbow or even a quiver of streaking arrows," Mephisto spoke again, looking sharply at his grandson. "This only works against non-magical missiles, remember this."

Dark took the pendant and pinned it to his armored chest, while his grandfather continued with explaining the rest of the arcane objects.

"When you place this ring on your finger and command the eye to close, it will render you completely invisible," the ancient magus began again, handing over the ring of invisibility to his grandson. "And when you command the eye to open, it will cause you to be visible once again."

"There's a crack in it," Dark noticed, slipping it on his index finger.

"It still works . . . well, most of the time," Mephisto murmured.

"Most of the time?" he paused. "What's most of the time?"

"Oh . . . I do not know," his voice trailed off and remained silent for a few minutes. "About seventy percent of the time. Besides, you're an assassin, you don't need to be invisible all the time. Just try sneaking around a bit more . . . you're good at that sort of thing."

"Whatever you say," Dark gave a deep sigh. "Is there anything else?"

Mephisto once again reached into the black hole and this time pulled out a black wooden baton with strange, foreign markings carved into its smooth surface.

"This device extends to unimaginable lengths with only a mere thought . . ." Mephisto's words stopped short. His features tightened and grew dark with anger as the tall magician seemed to be fighting to contain a building rage within. The baton in his grandson's hands had extended instantaneously, with the ebony pole barely missing the old man's head, instead striking the bedrock behind him with a shattering impact before contracting back to its original size.

"And I see it contracts in the same manner." Dark gave a dumbfounded half smile back at his obviously angered grandfather and quickly sheathed the pole into its scabbard, then strapped it firmly to his thigh.

"Next time, try and warn me before you almost skewer me like a piece of meat . . . okay?" Mephisto said smiling coldly at his grandson, walking several paces away and scratching his head. "It's all fun and games until someone loses an eye, so use your head next time."

"Yes sir," Dark said sheepishly.

Hurriedly, he ransacked the chest for the next piece to adorn himself, hoping to avoid any further confrontation with his grandfather. From the bottom of the container, Dark lifted out and quickly donned a gruesome-looking breastplate forged from a black mithril alloy with fortified pauldrons, one spiked while the other an open-mouthed half skull. The front was designed with the image of a large demon face that was grinning with malicious intent. The creature's large, unsettling blinking eyes glowed with an evil, unholy crimson light, and a throbbing, shadowy form floated eerily beneath its black, lustrous surface. Over his hands he placed a pair of jet-black, articulated clawed gauntlets adorned with dwarven runes and pointed spikes encompassing the entire forearm that ended with two hooked blades at the elbow.

"Your armor has the ability to heal itself of any damage sustained during combat," Mephisto announced softly, his look showing he was still not over nearly being impaled by his own grandson. "There are never any repairs to be made, for it has its own capacity to magically regenerate itself."

"That's amazing. Lödd is truly a genius," Dark declared smoothly, flexing his steel hands, trying to break in his new gauntlets. "Now let me show you the mask."

The final piece that completed the collection was a garish mask made from magically hardened obsidian with large, glowing eyes lit by a supernatural light. The demonic façade conformed perfectly to fit his angular face, transforming to a thick tough leathery skin that bonded to his own, with the mask mimicking his facial expressions. Upon placing this hellish semblance on, red demonic eyes shone with the power of Hell, and the fanged mouth of his breastplate smiled wickedly with glee.

Mephisto nodded his approval, a huge smile visibly displayed on his jubilant face, inwardly pleased at the frighteningly designed guise of his grandson.

"If this does not instill fear in your enemies . . . well . . . then you're screwed."

"It is my actions that will instill fear, not my armor!" Dark exclaimed boldly.

"Have you given any thought as to what you might call your new persona?" Mephisto asked after a moment's silent thought.

"Demon Raider." As the name rolled out of Dark, the eyes on his mask flashed a brilliant red.

"That is a great name, and I see you chose to honor both your parents by taking each of their aliases," the old mystic commented warmly. "Nice touch. I am sure they both would have been very pleased, if not honored."

The temporary moment of silence was broken as Mephistopheles moved with purpose toward his cluttered work desk. In his hand, a rolled-up piece of leather parchment suddenly materialized. He untied the silk binding and motioned for his grandson to join him as he unrolled it flat onto the tabletop next to the black handkerchief.

"This is a rough map of the known and unknown Eorth; it will help guide you on your scavenger hunt for these much sought after and needed artifacts."

"The Styg said you two came up with a plan," Dark said, taking his mask off and laying it beside the map as he came to stand next to the old historian.

"Both of us figured to even the playing field, so to speak. You would need to equip yourself with powerful magical items," Mephisto began again. "These weapons will assist you while you hunt down your enemies, because once you pass through the city gates of Duergar, you will truly be on your own."

"That makes sense, but where do we begin?" the handsome half-elf asked quickly.

"That is the problem; we don't know where any of these items are or even who has control over them," the silver mage spoke, looking at his grandson with little hope. "But we know who does, and better yet, we know how to find them."

"Great . . . who are they?" Dark broke in curiously.

"Three of the Norns," his voice had an ominous tone to it.

"The three sisters of fate—but isn't reaching them impossible," he cried.

"There is one way," pronounced Mephisto, pointing to an island on the map that Dark knew only from the stories his mother told him as a child. "Here is the Island of Turning, and there you will find the Horn of the Norns and its new owners, the Harpy Sisters."

"I remember them as frightening bedtime stories that Mom used to tell me, to make sure I didn't wander off from the house or the sisters would carry me away, she would say," Dark replied, remembering the horrific tales about the three sisters he was told as a child.

"Now, once you have the horn in your possession, it can then be used to transport you to the Isle of Skye, the home of the Norns," the wizard spoke.

"How are the Norns going to help me—or the better question would be why?" Dark cut in short, staring at the old wizard blankly.

Mephisto gave a silent, sour look in response before finally speaking, his face showing visible signs of frustration.

"Just like your mother. If you would let me finish, I will tell you," the surly answer came at last. "Once there, you will be afforded one question, and only one question. Ask for the location of Finders Keepers . . . and that is all, or you will be bound in servitude to them."

"What's . . . Finders Keepers?" he asked quickly and without hesitation.

"I thought you would never ask," was his grandfather's sarcastic reply. "It was said to have been created by a powerful sorcerer who was hell-bent on finding the brazen thief who had stolen from him a large, clear-cut diamond that he used to track down and find his prey, and no magic can hinder its clairvoyant vision."

"You've done quite well, old man," the motley-looking assassin spoke evenly as he picked up his demonic mask and placed it over his handsome face.

"You are not leaving now, are you?" came his grandfather's short, direct question.

"I've waited a long time for this!" Dark declared vehemently, flames erupting from the red eyes of his demon face. "I wait no longer."

Before his grandfather could utter a single word in response, the assassin called Demon Raider silently slipped away from the great cavern into the stone stairway and made his way to his waiting winged transport. The *Albatross* turned her bulky frame into the headwind, its enormous wingspan easily allowing her to gain height, and with an additional boost from the windy lake, glided off into the distance. Flying a few feet above the tops of blue waters, the majestic vessel leveled out and began a long, curving flat flight, staying perpendicular to the rushing wind.

As the giant sea bird traversed the vast, watery expanse, Dark quickly recalled all he knew about the Harpy Sisters and their protected isle. The Island of Turning, he vaguely remembered, was so named because any who attempted to land on the coastal dwelling was repelled. The Harpy Sisters were protected by their sister, Iris, Goddess of the Rainbow and messenger of Hera. He remembered there were three sisters, Aello, meaning storm swift, Celaeno, the dark, and Ocypete, the swift wing—all winged female monsters associated with death, fate, and the torment of all races. Known as the hounds of Zeus, they were dispatched by the god to snatch away or Harpazo, as the Greek would say, people and items from Eorth. Dark's mother used to tell him that when a person suddenly disappeared from the Eorth, it was said that he had been carried away by the sisters.

The *Albatross* propelled them both skyward, with just a few swift, powerful up and down strokes of its massive wings, until the home of the Harpy Sisters came into view. The island was a great temptation to sea travelers, with majestic, mountainous landscapes and a coastline with a multitude of beautiful beaches and rocky caves. Below him, Dark spotted a small ship gliding smoothly on the sun-burnished sea and unwisely heading toward the tiny island. The vessel's black sail was furled, her many oars gleaming in the sunlight, rising and falling in perfect synchronicity to the beat of a loud and steady drum, its sound even reaching the assassin high in the heavens. Before the crew could reach the safe harbor of the isle's sandy shore, a huge, black tentacle rose monstrously from beneath the waves to the surprise of the astonished, unsuspecting sailors. Beneath the boat, he caught sight of something huge, its bulk covered by the hull of the ship. Then, several more of the blackened arms shot out from the darkness. The encircling dark appendages came crashing down like freshly fallen trees, knocking the panic-stricken men sprawling. The wooden frame of the boat moaned and creaked before finally snapping. The shouts and screams of the crew were forever silenced. Sinking sluggishly beneath the waters, the sailors were carried downward to their watery graves.

This would not be Dark's fate as he sailed over the sandy shore and on toward the cave where the repellent Harpies made their nest.

"Go home, Alba, this time I'll find my own way back," Dark shouted as he exited the moving vehicle and fell like a stone to the Eorth.

With a few simple words, the horned assassin instantly changed the rate of his descent only a few feet from impact, gliding safely to the ground like a feather falling. He landed near the forest at the edge of the grasslands, then closed the eye of the ring, making him invisible, and began marching rapidly northward. He followed along the edge of the Tantris River as it wound its way through the Strophades forests. Dark plodded on, moving noiselessly over the rough ground until he caught the sound of female voices. The invisible assassin found a pair of large pines to get behind and crawled under the shelter of some low-hanging branches.

The cave of the Harpies was actually part of the bed of an old underground river that formed three different cave levels. Near the side of each cave was a name inscribed into the rock, which read to say, "Aello," "Celaeno," and "Ocypete." There was a loathsome stench to everything—scraps of rotten food and even bits and chunks of human flesh littered the ground, emitting such a smell that not even animals could bear to come near. The smell was so intolerable, it was almost enough to make the demonic assassin turn around and head back. In the center of all this garbage and standing out of place in this horrific scene was the exquisite marble sculpture of Iris, the Rainbow Goddess, carrying a staff of two intertwined snakes and a jug of sweet wine.

He listened intently for several long moments, staring into the blackness of the caves; then he heard it again, only this time it was the clear sound of an animal sniffing about.

"That's strange, sister, but I'm quite certain I smell something."

"What is it you smell, sister," another voice similar to the first rang out.

"I believe that's the unmistakable scent of man flesh, sister."

How these two foul beasts were able to smell his presence from so deep within the cave was truly amazing to him, especially with the toxic odor that permeated the air about them.

"I really don't mean to be pushy, but might I hazard a guess?" one of the voices politely asked.

"Oh, but certainly, sister," the other politely responded.

"How nice, thank you," the first voice said.

"Not at all, not at all," the second voice responded again.

What Dark heard next wasn't so much a sniffing sound, but a loud smelling sound like someone had buried their nose directly into the back of his head and inhaled vigorously.

"I think I have it, sister."

"By all means, do tell, do tell."

"I wager it's a human, and freshly bathed, too."

"No, sister, I think not," the voice interjected quickly again, wildly sniffing the air. "I'd say this was a half-blood, wouldn't you?"

"I would indeed, indeed I would," the other voice spoke with glee.

"Apparently, someone has wandered lost into our home."

"Apparently, very apparently," the other voice spoke, sniffing the air again.

"He seems to be outside, sister."

"Well, well, what are we waiting for? Let's go."

"Come then, let's go see to our supper."

"He's ours for the taking," the Harpies' cackling echoed from out of the cave.

"Should be a bit unnerved when he sees us," one chided.

"Really should, I'd say," she laughed maniacally.

Dark heard the chilling scratching of their clawed feet on the bedrock floor as the two sisters came to exit the cave.

"After you," one sister laughed.

"No, please, after you," the other insisted.

"No, no, no, no, no, no, no, I insist; age before beauty, you know," the sweet voice laughed casually.

"Oh no, sister, don't be silly, go ahead," the other sister soothed.

"Oh no, no, no, let's be sensible about this. You first, please," the other sister insisted.

"I have it, let's go together," the other sister answered back.

"Shall we?"

"Surely, sister, we shall."

The two shadowy figures stepped forth from the dank darkness of the cave and came to stand in the warm, basking glow of the noon sun. They were fair-haired winged maidens, not homely creatures or even disgusting monsters as described by writers, bards, and storytellers. These lovely haired creatures with beautiful faces had long, slender, swan-like necks and broad, feathered wings. However, what was accurate in their description were the razor-sharp teeth that they savagely displayed, the claws on their hands and feet, and their faces that shone pale with hunger.

"I've come for the Horn of the Norns." The voice was Dark's, still hidden from the Harpies' view by his place of concealment and protected by the ring of invisibility.

"Who dares demand of the sisters, Aello and Ocypete?" yelled Aello.

"Our supper demands of us, sister," Ocypete acknowledged.

"Show yourself, demander!" the first one exclaimed.

"Yes, show to us, demander, show to us!" the second demanded.

Dark had actually hoped to avoid any confrontation with the sisters and to maintain his advantage of stealth and secrecy, but with his presence known, he had no choice now. He moved without hesitation and silently edged himself toward the winged maidens, unseen by their searching eyes. A moment later, the eye on his ring opened, revealing the demon assassin and startling the squawking pair, as they now could see his sharp horns glinting dully and his red eyes glowing brightly.

"Oh, look at this one, deary. Isn't he luscious?" Aello quickly turned her head and asked her sister.

"Oh, he's lovely, lovely, just the thing for a half-elven pie," chided Aello, grinning savagely, her wicked teeth showing.

"Oh wonderful, wonderful suggestion," declared Ocypete.

"Do you really like it?" Aello asked of her sister.

"It couldn't have been better if I thought of it myself," insisted Ocypete again.

"Ah, thank you, sister," a bowed Aello responded in kind.

"Where could he have come from, you suppose?" asked Aello curiously.

"Maybe from the gods, sister?" explained her sister with uncertainty in her voice.

"Shall we ask him, sister?" she whispered cautiously.

"Yes, let's do," exclaimed Ocypete.

"My name is Demon Raider and I have asked you for the Horn of the Norns," Dark cut in sharply, his voice now angered. "I shall ask a second time, but no more."

"Then ask us, Demon Raider, ask us."

"Yes, Demon Raider, ask."

"Go fetch me the horn and I shall spare your lives. But be quick, for my patience is wearing thin," the dark assassin demanded.

Both sisters turned their winged backs to the enraged assassin and huddled close together in conversation.

"He did ask us twice, sister," Aello whispered in her sister's ear.

"Yes, sister, he did. This is true," Ocypete agreed slowly.

"Then shall we oblige him, sister?"

"Yes, let's do something nice for him."

"Most definitely, most definitely," continued Aello, inwardly musing over the prospect. "But first, you must meet Celaeno."

"Oh yes, sister, he must, he truly must," Ocypete concurred.

Dark paused for a moment and looked at the two sisters who waited patiently for his response. When he finally spoke, his voice was furious and his steel hands clenched tightly.

"You foul-smelling creaturessss . . ."

Before Dark could finish his rant, the third Harpy, Celaeno, swooped down from out of her place of concealment from behind a low-lying bank of clouds and carried him off toward the heavens.

"Look, sister, now we can truthfully say we raise our own food," Aello exclaimed mockingly with a slight, refined laughed.

"Raised food—oh my, my, my, you are a clever one, clever indeed," responded Ocypete in sudden understanding.

Celaeno's sharp claws held tight the struggling assassin, climbing higher and higher until they both were lost behind a large cloud formation. A deathly silence settled over Aello and Ocypete as long moments passed with nothing happening, both searching the cloudy sky for any signs of movement. Their waiting ended rather abruptly, when movement finally came in the shadowy form that hurtled toward them, then impacted with the hard ground in a chorus of cracking bones. Loud screams and weeping sounds of unforgettable agony erupted from Aello and Ocypete upon seeing the lifeless corpse of their sister lying mangled at their feet. Celaeno's twisted form lay broken in a pool of feathers and blood, her body riddled with small, black bolts.

"Oh, my sister, it seems we're in a precarious predicament," Aello cried mournfully.

"Oh yes indeed, very precarious . . . very." Ocypete fearfully looked over at her sister, nodding in complete agreement.

The remaining sisters froze in fearful silence as the sound of wings flapping interrupted their mourning, their eyes darting furtively about, frantically searching the sky. Their sharp eyes came to rest on the winged dark form of their sister's assassin as he emerged from the clouds and swooped gracefully down to land nearby.

"He did not tell us he could fly." Aello's voice shook as she clutched her sister's arm.

"No, he did not, sister. No he did not," Ocypete's voiced rasped slightly.

They stared at him wordlessly as he moved noiselessly into their midst, his eyes wreathed in the flames of perdition with shadowy wings as black and soft as smoke. There was no time to fly away, no place to hide, and definitely no longer any chance for any possible escape as the assassin known as Demon Raider closed the distance between them. He smiled grimly as he considered their fate, when the sudden animation of the marble statue rippled with movement.

"Hold, mortal, and stay your hand against these, my sisters," the stone statue spoke, slowly delivering her commanding message in the voice of the Rainbow Goddess. "If you do not, I shall exact a god's vengeance upon you."

Dark paused for only a moment, turning his fiery demonic gaze briefly toward the two Harpy Sisters, then slowly back at the divine intervention of Iris before he causally raised his left arm upward in response to the statue's threat. In one smooth motion, he held forth the faintly glowing dragonhead of the wand; the power locked within flared up immediately. "Piss off!"

With a roar, a ball of flame burst forth from the mouth of the dragon, leaving his hand trailing wisps of smoke. An instant later, the blazing ball slammed into the stone torso, bursting into a bright flash of flames, leaving only the charred, smoldering base intact.

"Might I suggest we make a hasty exit," Aello spoke up quickly.

"Oh, you are the epitome of wisdom," Ocypete encouraged her.

"Thank you," Aello said, thanking her sister.

"Not at all," Ocypete said.

"For the last time, get me the horn . . . now!" the enraged assassin screamed, followed by a chorus of foul oaths. Dark stood rooted in place as they moved quickly in fear across the rocky floor toward the cave and momentarily brought back with them the lost Horn of the Norns.

"If you ask me, sister, I'd say he's very rude."

"Agreed, he's an unmitigated scamp," she protested, quickly glancing over at the assassin.

Dark paused and sighed deeply, shaking his head resignedly, his long arms folded in angered pose against his black armor.

"Give me that!" he growled, his fangs gleaming as he snatched the horn from the clawed hands of the startled Aello.

The artifact was a large cow's horn that had been sanded smooth. The characteristic rim was riveted to the horn, constructed from three pieces of metal—gold, silver, and bronze—and etched with detailed pagan symbols. It had a strange bit of metalwork in the center, reminiscent of a human eye. The mouthpiece consisted of a decorated opening carved from a single large crystal of gallium that was only found in the cave of crystals.

"Iris will be most displeased, and punishment for defying our sister will be swift and severe," Aello exploded defiantly.

"Yes, punishment will be swift and severe," the other warned shortly, sticking out her long tongue like a child.

"Remember well the name of Demon Raider!" he cut in darkly, turning on them in fury with the demonic image of his armor grinning menacingly. "For I am an assassin from the very depths of Hell, and no one shall stop me from my appointed task . . . not even a god!"

"Then are we too to suffer the same fate as that of our sister?" Aello's voice broke slightly, her eyes riveted on the assassin's own glowing eyes.

"I will allow you to live on one condition," he glowered fiercely at the cowering maids. "You shall never again taste the flesh of a man, woman, child, or beast that runs, walks, or crawls upon the face of the Eorth."

"Then what will we eat?" Aello cried hastily.

"Yes what will . . . ?"

"You will eat the plants and fruits provided by Mother Nature, along with the fish that swim in her sea. This and this alone shall be your only sustenance," Dark cut her off with a quick wave of his hand.

"And what if we refuse?" Aello spoke defiantly, but still frightened of the power the stranger possessed.

"Then you both will suffer the same fate as your sister," the dark assassin cautioned, pointing to the bloody carcass lying silent on the cold ground.

"We will obey Demon Raider," both sisters sang in unison, showing visible signs of being afraid of their new master, each knowing what would happen if they disobeyed him.

He glanced at the two shaken sisters who nodded dumbly, then stuffed the horn into the gaping, open, fanged mouth of the demon from his breastplate.

"Obey you shall . . . and to make certain you are true to your word," he commanded venomously, his eyes lighted by an unholy glow as flickering blue flames wreathed his steel, clawed hands, "I leave you with this!"

With an undisguised fury, he fiercely gripped their heads and let loose a series of foul incantations, causing the flames surrounding his hands to erupt with a mighty roar. The two winged sisters let out sharp howls of pain as Dark released the energy of the spell, their blood boiling inside their veins, a soft scarlet glow appearing on their chests. Thin wisps of black smoke rose from the newly placed sigil, branded painfully into their breasts just above the heart as both went limp and fell heavily to the ground.

With the Horn of the Norns safely stowed away and the sisters held with a binding spell, he bade them both farewell and simply vanished.

X

With a gentle shaking of his shoulders, Mephisto managed to bring Dark slowly around, his eyes opening to see the old magician standing silently over him.

"What happened?" Dark asked wearily, closing his eyes momentarily, allowing his tired mind to lift the grey haze that clouded his muddled thoughts.

"I take it this is the first time you have ever used a teleportation spell," Mephisto queried.

"Yeah," he responded, removing his mask with a grunt.

"Now you know why magicians and wizards alike seldom use teleportation as their primary mode of transportation," the old mystic said, smiling.

"I feel like somebody just hit me with a giant hammer," the weary assassin declared shortly.

"That is because the power for the spell comes solely from the caster," Mephisto clasped the gauntleted hands of his grandson and easily helped pull him to his feet. "And it requires a tremendous amount, so naturally it leaves you feeling weak and disoriented. And if you are not used to the effects, you could easily black out."

"Well that's going to be a problem."

"Not necessarily," Mephisto cut in quickly. "I know someone who can help."

"Who?" Dark shot back with a puzzled look showing on his face.

"Vanora," Mephisto declared unbelievably, standing tall before his grandson, meeting his gaze squarely and unblinking.

"Grandma . . . you're kidding me!" Dark interrupted quickly, not quite believing what his ears had just heard.

They both remained silent for a few minutes, Dark's grandfather brooding in his own thoughts. Finally, his face calm and relaxed, Mephisto began to speak again.

"Yes, your grandmother has something that will help you. But let's not get ahead of ourselves. Did you get the horn?"

"Of course, it's right here," he responded smoothly, unnervingly reaching his hand into the horrifying mouth of his demonic-faced armor and bringing forth the fabled Horn of the Norns.

"Oh, that is just wrong," Mephisto muttered in disgust, his mouth distorted.

"Yeah . . . I know. But I'd like to see someone try and pick my pocket now," Dark spoke, laughing in amusement and sporting a broad, maniacal smile.

Suddenly, the old wizard froze for a spellbound second, his nostrils flared, and his large brown eyes began to water. "You stink!"

Dark inhaled briefly, stopping himself short, the look on his face showing visible signs of distress. "Those damn dirty birds. They had garbage scattered everywhere, not to mention other things! . . ."

"Nasty, foul creatures," his grandfather advocated.

"I couldn't move an inch without stepping in something disgusting," he exclaimed heatedly. Even smelling his demonic mask made his head turn away in nauseous disgust. "The smell was so bad you could literally taste the rotten stench in the air."

"How nice for you . . . now go wash up," concluded Mephisto, holding his nose with his fingertips. "And don't come back until you no longer smell like a troll's arse!"

Without even a word or a gesture, Dark turned away from his grandfather and disappeared into the shadows of the stairwell that led to the bathing chamber. Dark didn't make it out of the bathhouse until late into the evening; his grandfather had already turned in for bed and was asleep almost immediately. He ate a light supper, looked one last time at his first prize, the horn, and then he too retired for the night.

Daybreak found Dark awake early, his solid frame rising gingerly from the warmth of his feather bed to dress hastily in the dark garb of the assassin Demon Raider. He was eager to start early, believing his grandfather was not yet awake when he made his way downstairs. The great room was silent, or so he thought when he spotted Mephisto lighting a fire in the great stone fireplace that was quickly started with the snap of his fingers.

"You're up early," the lean magician spoke softly, the fire snapping at the wood as he relaxed in his high leather chair, pulling his grey robes tightly about his body for warmth.

"I thought I'd get going as soon as possible," Dark announced quietly.

"I totally agree. It is, after all, the early bird who gets the worm," Mephisto murmured gently, chuckling to himself at what seemed more than just wisdom from the old adage.

"Am I missing something here?" he asked in an almost quizzical manner.

"It is just that your grandmother . . . nothing," the large smile that showed on his face was suddenly lost, his thoughts were now found in sudden realization.

There was a moment of awkward silence as both just stared at each other wordlessly. Then Mephisto, trying to relieve the tension, let out a jumble of words that slightly resembled a question.

"Tell me . . . uh, the horn . . . any problems with the Harpies?" His grandfather shifted around in his chair uncomfortably and gazed absently into the crackling fire, feeling unexplainably trapped.

"You know, she . . ."

"Don't . . . not another word about . . . you know who," the old wizard cut in sharply, pointing his finger threateningly like a dagger at his grandson. "Now, just tell me how things went and nothing more."

Dark looked sharply at the old man and uttered a deep, low laugh, then pulled up the stone bench and sat next to the fire with his grandfather. He took the better part of the morning to recant his tale of the Harpy Sisters and the incident with the Statue of Iris.

"I don't think you should have done that, Dark," his grandfather scolded. "Maybe I can send Teigue to have a talk with Zeus."

"Teigue knows the King of the Greek gods?" Dark asked in amazement.

"I don't think there is a being that our little friend does not know." He turned toward Dark, and a slight smile played across his lean features. "He is a charmer, that one."

"Does he know the Norns?" he paused slightly and asked in jest.

"No, but I do," the wizard's face nodded as the familiar mocking smile crossed it fleetingly. "Well . . . not really. I don't exactly know them per se, but I do know of them."

"Funny," Dark's face turned hard. "Well why don't you just tell me what you know then?"

Mephisto looked up at him thoughtfully and bowed his head in mocking amusement. "As you wish, your Majesty," he said, his face softening with another musing smile. "These maidens, mighty in wisdom, weave the web of fate that is twined with the flow of time. The three Norns are the daughters of Erda, the Eorth Goddess, and of the Frost giant Norvi. Urd is the oldest; she is always looking back into the past, which she oversees. Verdandi is young, and her only concern is with the present, and she is very beautiful. Skuld has her face covered by a veil, and she is the one who determines the length of each life, since the future is not for anyone but her to know. From my references in the Eddas, they dwell in Asgard at the base of Yggdrasil, known as the world tree. Their primary jobs are to weave the web of fate and time and to care for the great ash tree along with the Well of Urd. They take water from the well every day, and with it the white clay that lies about the well, and they sprinkle it over Yggdrasil so its limbs shall neither wither nor rot. The water is so holy that all things that come into contact become white as an eggshell."

"How is this helping me again?" he asked finally after a brief pause.

"The Norns can see into the future and even predict events for those who consult with them," the old historian began again, "which is exactly what you are going to do."

The enlightened assassin nodded and smiled slightly.

"They will tell you where the items you seek are located, and that will be your first step taken in what will be a long journey ahead," the ancient sage acknowledged.

"Then I guess it's time to know my future," Dark declared, eager to begin his journey.

He hastily jerked away, stretching his steel-clad hands toward the large cow horn that sat on top of the table where he had eaten his supper the night before. Bringing the instrument around in front of him, he looked curiously back at Mephisto. "So what do I do?" he asked a moment later.

"Well, you just purse your two lips together and force a burst of air through the small end," directed the sarcastic music teacher simply, making a blowing gesture with his mouth.

Under the astute observation and guidance of his grandfather's vast knowledge of musical instruments, Dark drew a deep breath, his hand under the bell. He brought his lips to the mouthpiece and sounded the horn. What was produced had a distinctive moaning, mournful tone, the scale clear and mellow, yet disturbingly beautiful. In the distance, a sound that mirrored their own echoed back as if to return an answer to their call. Just then, Dark's body began to stiffen like a statue. A white glow so bright his grandfather had to shield his eyes protectively spread out from his torso. One moment the strange glow filled the entire room and the tensed form of Dark was lost in the light. Then, in a brilliant flash, it was gone. Dark, no longer stiff, slowly slumped to the ground, one hand pressed to the floor, the other still holding the horn. He climbed shakily to his feet, still weak from the strain of magical travel, then stood quietly for a moment as he quickly surveyed his new surroundings.

Yggdrasil, an immense ash tree, towered over him, with long, massive branches extending far into the heavens, with the tall tree being supported by three roots that extended far and away to other distant locations.

His keen elven eyes spotted a giant golden eagle perched high on the branches of Yggdrasil, and below the wise, majestic bird sat a staring black hawk. A brown, bushy-tailed squirrel scurried up and down the ash tree's large trunk, with four large stags that darted deftly between the broad branches, only stopping briefly to consume its nourishing foliage. Lying beneath the world tree was the well of Urd, also known as the Well of Fate. It wasn't so much a well but a lake that was the color of milk, with two swans gliding gracefully over its mirror-like surface.

Drawing water from the well and taking the white loam that lay around it was Urd, a maid old and haggard. She poured the water and sand over the roots of the evergreen ash tree so that its limbs would neither wither nor rot. The second sister, Verdandi, a maiden in the middle of her years, was busy attending to the task of weaving the rope that measured individual lives as well as the destiny of the universe. The third that rounded out this trio was the young and beautiful Skuld, her youthful features covered by a veil. Her work of carving the destinies of people into a wooden staff came to an abrupt halt as she turned to the black-garbed assassin.

"Cast off thy shoes from off thy feet, for the place where on thou standith is holy ground," Skuld spoke, her voice loud and scolding.

Dark sat down the horn, quickly removed his leather boots, and stood barefoot on the cool grass.

"My name is . . ."

"We know thy name, Dark Solus," the Norn broke into his thoughts. "And the coming of this day, for Giallar horn has been returned this day."

Before the words could escape from the mouth of the youthful seer, the holy horn faded, never to be lost again, and from this day forth it would only serve as the drinking vessel for Odin, the one-eyed god.

"What thou seekest, ye shall find in the land of the rising sun, a gem that will help thee locate the objects thou seeketh," the soft declaration from Skuld was almost lyrical to his ears. "The Nameless knows of thee and thy meeting soon at hand, for the power of the gem shows him thusly."

"Nanashi, that's just great, and he knows of my coming before I even knew," the angered assassin stormed. "Any other good news?"

"Yes."

There was a long moment of silence.

"Well . . . what is it?" Dark asked, a little bewildered.

"I cannot say," the veiled sister responded in a sharp whisper as she neared Dark. "But I can speed thy travels . . . if thouest art ready?"

"I am," Dark bowed in gratitude, remembering to not forget his boots. "And thank you for all your help."

An azure glow began to surround the barefoot assassin as Skuld had completed her spell with nothing more than a simple motion of her wooden staff. In the time it took for a single blink of Odin's good eye, Dark arrived fatefully to stand in front of a house he had never seen, but knew to be the residence of Nanashi, a Sheol assassin who lived in the largest city of the Khan dynasty.

The enormous City of Nye is the pride of the Khan's massive empire and the center of a thriving opium trade. Most who venture to this treacherous city return home a little poorer and lucky to be alive, while the unlucky do not return at all.

The house was located in the Musashi district, which was widely known as the samurai area, so there were not many, if any city guards patrolling here. The house itself sat at the end of a long, spotlessly clean street lined with high stone walls that shielded the gardens and gracious homes of the upper class from prying eyes. It was late in the night, so the wide streets, shaded by dozens of weeping cherry trees, were beautifully lit by street lamps that gave the whole place a soft, magical glow.

After quickly pulling his enchanted boots on and strapping them tightly about his feet, he took forth the horned mask from the black confines of the demon's mouth to once again don the guise of the assassin Demon Raider.

"Close," he spoke softly to himself, but instead of vanishing from view, nothing happened.

He tried again and, like the first time, nothing happened. Again and again he tried, but as before he was unable to obtain the magical effect of invisibility.

"Damn it," was just one of the many oaths of blasphemy uttered by the upset assassin. "No matter, I just need to be quick."

He noiselessly and easily ascended the stone wall and took a sly peek from behind a large, red paper lamp that went out when Dark's long shadow stretched out to extinguish its flaming candle. What he discovered was a place that put as much emphasis on art, beauty, and refinement as it did on swordplay. The garden here, which featured an idyllic pond with a waterside teahouse, had many secluded nooks, ancient trees, and a wide assortment of colorful, fragrant flowers.

Then he heard something. It was only faint at first, from somewhere in the darkness beyond the little teahouse that caused him to look over alertly, listening intently for something further. It took several moments, but finally a lone guard emerged at the edge of the small pond, stopping only briefly to stretch loudly in boredom. The guard was clad in a scarlet kimono and a pair of wide trousers that looked rather like a long, divided skirt. A long sword, called a katana, was housed in a beautifully decorated sheath that he carried in his kimono belt fastened around his waist.

Fate smiled on the demon-looking assassin as not one, not two, but three more scarlet sentinels came to stand next to the first, talking and joking in low tones among themselves.

"This is way too easy," his eyes rolled back in disbelief.

At last, he rose to his feet and swiftly moved from his high perch as silent as the shadows about him. Like a graceful cat, he began to move toward the unsuspecting sentries, his small hand crossbow suddenly appearing on the back of his clawed gauntlet. It only took an instant for each to realize that death had come for them as the silent, accurate arrows of Dark dropped all four with single shots, each one falling down dead in small, bloodied heaps. He paused only long enough to hide the bodies behind a thick cluster of green shrubbery before he began to creep forward toward Nanashi's home, his movement as soundless as a child's smile. Dark's shadowy form darted covertly in quick, bounding leaps, weaving furtively between blossoming cherry trees and low-lying hedges. The horned assassin was just a dark blur against the faint moonlight on the garden grounds, his keen elven eyes searching carefully for any sign of more patrolling guards.

For long moments he remained completely undetectable as he moved steadily toward the main entrance, making certain there were no guards close at hand. The large, shingle-roofed mansion had two floors; the golden walls were set off with intricately carved and brightly painted wooden latticework. Upstairs, above a pillarless veranda that faced the garden, were a few lighted windows that broke through the misty blackness. In a quick dash, the demonic figure sprinted for the cover of a huge, spreading cherry tree growing beside the structure, whereupon he instantly melted into the shadows. Sticking to the wall, he soon had his nimble hands working the locked door latch until it opened with an audible snap; the sound seemed loud as he froze, peering cautiously around to see if his forced entry was heard. Without hesitation, Dark slipped hastily through, then closed the sliding door silently behind him.

Inside was symmetrical, and each room was connected with long hallways. On display was a small collection of samurai armor and weapons, as well as beautiful, black-ink drawings and illustrations. An elegant stairway led to the upper floor, and a low cough from someone upstairs told him where Nanashi would be found. He moved toward the open stairs, making his way guardedly up the narrow steps, always staying alert for any sign of a trap. Dark studied each step as he went, his keenly trained eyes searching for any trip wire or hidden device ready to be sprung with one careless mistake. A small landing came into view as he stood at the summit of the staircase, from which a short hallway led to the source of the light.

He began to creep forward, his movement noiseless as he peered in through the open doorway to the large room. Immediately, he spotted Nanashi, his lean form kneeling in front of a low-level table, practicing what looked like calligraphy, with a large paintbrush in his left hand that moved gracefully over the top of a large piece of white rice paper. He wore a traditional green kimono; the wide-sleeved garment reached well below the knees, held about the waist by a long, sash-like belt, and thrust in the front were his long katana and shorter wakizashi. His black hair was long and straight, falling well past his shoulders, and he had dark, almond-shaped eyes that carefully studied his own writing art form intently, each stroke perfectly exact.

"So how many of my men did you kill?" the Sheol asked quietly, his eyes still focused on his artwork. "Or should I even ask?"

"Just a few," Dark stated flatly as he entered the room.

"How generous of you. I guess I should thank you for leaving some alive," ventured Nanashi quietly, still applying the ink to the paper while using his whole arm in making the stroke.

"It's the least I could do," the demonic assassin soothed, with the mask mimicking his own sly smile. "Especially after what happened the last time."

"Yes, I remember . . . and so does the emperor," Nanashi whispered harshly, his eyes finally looking up to stare at his silent intruder. "He still mourns the loss of his son, and has even quadrupled the bounty on your head."

"Quadrupled . . . wow . . . I'm flattered," he laughed shortly. "That's why I was surprised when I didn't see the royal guard waiting for me . . . especially when the gem made you aware of my coming."

“Ah yes, the gem of location, the reason for your foretold intrusion into my home.” Extending his small hand inside his voluminous kimono, he quickly produced a large, deep blue diamond with a faceted girdle that gave off a faint luminescent glow as he brought it into view. “Isn’t it beautiful?”

“Yes, it is,” Dark declared quietly. “And I should thank you.”

“Thank me . . . for what?” still kneeling, the Sheol asked curiously.

“Well, I thought I would have to spend the rest of the night searching for its whereabouts, but here it is, gift wrapped like a present,” he laughed in amusement. “And it’s not even my birthday!”

“Silence!” demanded Nanashi furiously, his lean face distorted in sudden anger, the constant smug smile suddenly villainous. “You are a cocky one, assassin.”

“I am a cocky one, and do you want to know why?” Dark’s voice cut through Nanashi’s anger, the slender black baton once at Dark’s side now pointed menacingly at Nanashi. “Because I can be!”

The hieroglyphics etched into the wooden baton began to glow, instantaneously extending forward, catching Nanashi off guard and striking him squarely in the chest. The rapidly growing pole pushed the surprised, green-garbed man forcefully back, smashing him through the cypress-studded wall amid a shower of wood splinters. The hapless aerialist flew wildly through the air and crashed with an audible thud onto the flagstone pathway below. Like a shot, Dark was upon him and with magical dexterity leapt forward through the shattered opening from the upper floor, firing his black hand crossbow with blinding rapidity. Even after Dark landed, he continued his assault, releasing bolt after bolt with audible twangs from the taught bowstring, each arrow flying almost invisibly to its target. It happened so fast, it seemed like every arcing slash of Nanashi’s blade was nothing more than a silvery blur, with each speeding projectile exploding into tiny, black splinters.

They both paused, breathing heavily amid the cool night air; Nanashi chuckled inwardly, a slow, arrogant smile spreading over his clean, smooth face.

"I see we've been practicing," the masked assassin declared quietly.

"Whatever I can see, I can block," the arrogant fellow spoke with an unshakable confidence in himself, motioning for Dark to continue with his futile assault.

The fiery eyes of Demon Raider flared brightly and stared at Nanashi, watching the grinning face of his skilled adversary, and for a moment no one moved. With the coming of the new day soon upon him and weary of this prolonged struggle, Dark began to intone the words of power to release the ancient spell on his unsuspecting victim. A mass of thick, black clouds began to swirl, rapidly drawing together, forming a huge, clenched fist that hung ominously overhead. With a simple downward gesture, the power of the spell was unleashed, sending the giant fist of arcane energy smashing down upon Nanashi. The powerful crushing force squashed the tiny man like a bug; the loud, horrible crunching sound of bones snapping rang out sharply.

"Didn't block that one . . . did ya?" he muttered angrily, and with a wave of his hand the huge fist dissipated.

He strolled silently over the grassy grounds until he reached his shattered foe. One gauntleted hand rummaged through the bloodied kimono and came forth holding the large blue diamond. Suddenly, Dark halted and looked cautiously around as if sensing someone's presence, then looked back slowly over his spiked shoulder to see a small figure standing motionless behind him.

"I was wondering when you were going to finally show yourself," the half-elf declared knowingly, turning to stand before the true owner of the gem of location, meeting his gaze squarely.

From behind the cover of a small grove of trees emerged the long figure of Nanashi, arriving in secret. This ninja-like agent was clad from head to toe in black garb, slightly tainted with red dye, his flesh completely hidden all except for a small slit around the eyes and a long cloak draped across his shoulders and head.

"Demon Raider, it's been a long time, and I see you've upgraded your armor," the voice rolled out of the Sheol assassin, pointing to the silent remains of his mirror image. "So how did you know that wasn't me?"

"I noticed he was holding his brush in his left hand," Dark informed his host with a smooth reply. "And I know you are not left-handed."

"You are a clever one, Raider . . . and well informed, too." The cloaked man swaggered forward a few paces with an arrogant, unshakable confidence in himself. "But no matter; clever cannot kill."

"No . . . but I can!" Dark cried vehemently.

The demonic assassin attacked immediately, his flaming red eyes burning with the fury from the flames of Hell, his long, sharp fangs gleaming dully in anger. A semi-solid black shadow stretched forth from his clawed, gauntleted hand, forcing to his will and coming to coalesce into a shadow-formed sword. Dark brought the darkened spectral blade sweeping downward for the kill in one quick, precise slash with wisps of shadowy threads following the weapon as it moved. Unfortunately, his victim was too quick, as Nanashi rolled deftly away from the deadly strike—but not quick enough, as Dark saw his blow catch a small portion of the cloaked shoulder, drawing first blood. Then, in a totally unexpected move, the lean Sheol swirled his dark cloak, wrapping it over the top of his head, and dissolved into nothingness just as Demon Raider's shadowy blade was about to cut him in two. Invisible, the eastern assassin stung Dark with a series of puncturing strikes from every direction, causing large, gaping wounds that spurted massive amounts of blood. With superhuman dexterity, the wounded half-elf sprang backward and landed with cat-like ease, escaping the deadly blows and coming to his feet in an instant.

"I don't need to see you to kill you!" Shouting defiantly, Dark whirled about in a cry of hatred.

Dark thrust the blade of his shadow sword deep into the ground and, with a rushing surge of power, thin streaks of the purest shadows exploded violently outward in all directions like thin, sharp rapiers of darkness. Only when he felt the slender blades bite into his invisible adversary's flesh did the Sheol reappear, mortally wounded, his black-cloaked body shuddering once abruptly until he finally crumpled lifeless to the Eorth.

For many a long minute, Dark sat exhausted in the slowly fading twilight of the night, at last forcing himself wearily to his knees as he waited for his strength to return, then climbed shakily to his feet. Bleeding profusely from several nasty deep puncture wounds, he called up the spell of teleportation and in an instant was back home in Sommerset.

XI

Dark collapsed slowly to the worn stone floor of his grandfather's cave, his heart beating violently, as he finally succumbed to the poison from Nanashi's invisible blades.

"Mephisto!" exclaimed Teigue excitedly. "It's Dark. Come quick!"

"What is it now . . .?" The old wizard's voice went silent upon seeing his grandson lying on the cold ground, his still form motionless in a pool of his own blood.

"I just came by to see if I could get a rematch, then I stumbled upon Dark . . . just lying here amid all this blood," the tiny faëry sputtered desperately, his breathing laboured.

"Quickly, we must get him to the sanctuary at once," Mephisto responded calmly.

Bending down to kneel on one knee, he carefully lifted up the still form of his grandson's bloodied body in the cradle of his two strong arms. Teigue retrieved the wounded assassin's horned mask and quickly followed the vanishing magician, who had already proceeded to the healing waters of the sanctuary. Within seconds Mephisto carried Dark's unconscious body into the magical healing waters of the shimmering pool. The blue glowing liquid became muddy as blood flowed out like red clouds, but almost immediately dissipating and restoring once again to a crystal clear fluid. Mephisto quickly examined him, seeing numerous cuts and bruises, with large gashes about his back, shoulder and neck. The healing waters would take care of his wounds, broken bones and even any internal damage, but the ugly, swollen black marks indicated something else. Poison!

"I don't think I can treat this," Mephisto declared worriedly. "This is a very unusual poison, personally made and very unique with the only cure coming from its maker . . . and I am guessing that he is probably dead."

"So does that mean that Dark is going to die?" Teigue asked in a barely audible whisper.

"No, I won't allow it!" the ancient healer exclaimed boldly, shaking his head faintly in hushed defiance.

"But what can you do?" the distraught faëry asked anxiously. "You yourself said the only cure died with its maker."

"There may be . . ." his voice trailed off, with deep vacant eyes that looked lost in thought. "First thing I need to do is slow this poison."

In the blink of an eye he was gone, leaving Dark just floating there, his head barely above the water; with the next blink he was back, a small black bag held tightly in his hand.

"What's that?" Teigue asked sharply.

"This is the Wallet of Perseus," Mephisto said quickly. "From this, Dark will have what he requires."

Grasping the cloth bag he immediately rummaged inside and from its contents he removed a large plain wooden sand timer.

"Is that what I think it is?" asked Teigue, incredulously at the sight of the black hourglass.

"It sure is," declared the lean enchanter quietly, smashing the timepiece into the tiled chamber floor and spilling out the contents of the glass bulbs.

"And how will this help?" the tiny faëry flew forward.

"This darkened soil will not only slow down the spreading venom, but stop it completely . . ." Mephisto trailed off despondently, as he pushed the timer's sand into his grandson's already healing wounds. "Unfortunately, the time stopping effects will only last for one day and one night."

"That's genius, pure genius!" Teigue perked up upon hearing what he thought was good news, but then another question came to form in his tiny mind.

"I do have my moments . . ."

"But wait . . ." Teigue paused, asking absently. "Won't you know who, be a little mad or something?"

"Death . . . oh, he won't mind, we go way back," Mephisto said in a nonchalant manner, still attending to his unconscious grandson.

"You know Death?" the little faëry whispered apprehensively.

"When you live this long," the ancient silver dragon began again, "you eventually get to know everyone."

He glanced down at his young grandson, his face still ashen and covered with a heavy sheet of perspiration, still floating unconscious and breathing erratically.

"And after the twenty-four hours are up, what then?" the little faëry asked fearfully, breaking the momentary silence.

Without waiting to reply, Mephisto faded and disappeared without even so much as a word and before Teigue could voice any further questions.

"Mephisto . . .?"

Teigue stared unblinking at where the mystic had stood a second ago, then turned to the still floating figure of Dark, who stirred slightly and was beginning to awake. The son of Solus opened his eyes slowly and looked up at the small smiling face of the flying faëry, his hands clapping together excitedly.

"I'm in the pool . . .?" he groaned painfully. "That can't be good."

No it's not I'm afraid, you were poisoned," declared Teigue abruptly. "Your grandfather saved your life."

"Again . . .?"

"Yes . . . again," Mephisto's voice rang out with his sudden reappearance, his warm face smiling as he made his way over to Dark, in his hand an extremely large leather bound tome that he had opened to a specific page. "I see that you have come back to the world of the living."

"Well, I very well couldn't leave you all alone . . . could I," a sickening cough interrupted his laughter, as the armoured assassin rose weakly to stand waist deep in the cool waters. "Who would take care of you?"

"Yes, who indeed, I would truly be lost without you," the tall magician smiled to himself as he ran his finger down the page, finally stopping with a loud triumphant exultation.

"What is it?" Dark asked curiously, removing his clawed gauntlets and setting them down in front of him on the tile floor.

"I take it you know you were poisoned . . ."

"By a Sheol," he informed his grandfather, cutting him short.

"I thought so," the old magus began again, his face grim. "Your wounds will heal, but I could not extract all the poison . . . it just keeps reproducing, but I did manage to stop the venom from circulating any further throughout your body. However, you have less than twenty-four hours; therefore it will eventually kill you."

"That's it then . . . it's over before it's even begun," the brooding assassin spoke sourly through gritted teeth, his face lowering in a sombre silent morose. "I've failed them . . . I've failed them both."

"No, you have not failed!" he explained to his sullen grandson, the old historian's words echoed off the solid walls with a resounding sharpness that caught everyone's attention. "The Cup of Wonders is the next of your items you must now acquire, for with it, you will be made whole again."

"And what exactly is the Cup of Wonders?" Dark asked a moment later, no longer brooding.

"The Cup sadly, is a drinking vessel made from a single unicorn horn," he answered dolefully. "Blessed with the powers of purification and healing and they say those who drink from the horn are immune even to the foulest of poisons."

"That's great news, but where can it be found?" the colourful little faëry broke in unexpectantly.

"That's a good question," his grandfather was speaking again, closing the large book softly. "And one for which I have no answer."

The grimacing features of the assassin, still wading in the healing pool, relaxed briefly and a faint smile crossed his lips as he turned to his grandfather. Mephisto's serious countenance was suddenly put at ease when Dark's hand emerged from the open fanged mouth adorning his abdomen, in his hand the large blue gem of location.

"We'll find the cup's location with this," he promised tossing the multi-faceted diamond at his grandfather who easily caught the precious stone, then examined it closely.

"The gem of Finders Keepers, this will not only show us the location to the cup, but to all the items you need!" yelled the old conjurer.

Mephisto dropped the large leather book and suddenly made a quick rush toward his grandson who had just stepped awkwardly out of the pool and dropped heavily to one knee, a little dizzy from trying to move about too quickly.

"You're not going anywhere," his grandfather ordered in a stern voice, a small cot suddenly appearing in the room, then he helped Dark to the little bed where the assassin collapsed in exhaustion. "Now, Teigue will stay here and attend to you while I go in your place and retrieve the cup myself."

"Yes sir," was Dark's quiet response, pausing wearily to catch his breath.

"But we still don't know where it's located," the emissary for the Faëry King cut in soberly.

"We will as soon as I use this," replied Mephisto, his hand squeezing the deep blue stone, his emerald eyes closed in focused concentration.

In his mind's eye vivid images flashed of a magical animal with the body of a horse, its coat snow white and a large spiralled horn resting in the middle of the creature's forehead. Mephisto also watched, as suddenly branches crashed and the beautiful beast sprang from the trees, followed by the shapes of huntsmen and hounds, twisted faces that plunged blades into throat and heart. Finally he saw the master of the hunt raising his lips to the ivory horn, undisturbed by the destruction of the unicorn.

"King Magh has the Cup of Wonders," came the slow growling response, his wise face grim.

"King Magh . . . he is a corrupt and evil ruler," the tiny faëry stammered fearfully. "They say that when famine hit his land, the cruel king silenced his hungry people by allowing them into a food storage building, then locked the doors and set the place on fire."

"Yes and his fortress lies to the west on the Plain of Wonder, unfortunately a great distance away," Mephisto remarked quickly. "So I must take my leave if I am to return in time."

He turned abruptly and walked back to the old book that still laid on the tiled floor, picking it up he turned back to Dark to wave goodbye.

"Hey . . . thanks for everything," Dark spoke, a broad smile showing on his handsome face.

"Don't mention it my boy, I . . ."

"No . . . I mean thanks for everything," with deep sincerity, his grandson declared after only a moment's pause. "For without your help none of this would be possible. Even now you are going off to a distant land, against unimaginable odds, so that I may live."

Mephisto smiled briefly and nodded, pausing in silence before speaking again.

"And live you shall, for nothing shall stand in my way . . . NOTHING!" vociferated the tall magician, his features fierce, his emerald eyes bright with determination. And he left them.

"So what exactly do you call that thing?" Teigue asked curiously, pointing at the grinning mouth on the assassin's abdomen.

"Faëry Muncher," responded Dark seriously, with the little emissary gasping in shocked horror, his tiny eyes wide in fright.

Mephisto appeared outside, greeted by the first light of an early Sommerset morning, suddenly afraid that his worst fears would be realized and he would not make it back in time. For what he didn't reveal to his grandson was the country he needed to reach is bordered by an enchanted river where wind and water go completely awry. You cannot fly across it nor can you swim or even sail across it; but quickly clearing his mind of such thoughts, he already started to form a plan for the impossible crossing. Silently, he knelt next to a small oak tree and from his silver silken robes, he pulled out a small black pouch and emptied the contents onto the grassy eorth, small ivory figurines tumbled out in a heap.

"Where are . . . there you are," he mumbled to himself.

Scooping up the remaining tiny toy animals, he mechanically placed them back into the little bag, then safely stowed them away. Stepping several paces back, the aged mystic snapped his fingers twice, causing the ivory figurine to instantly grow in size, then magically it came to life with a loud ferocious roar. This mysterious creature resembled a massively oversized black panther nearly twelve feet in length, with a wingspan that was doubled in size. The wide-bodied beast had glossy black fur splattered with red markings that covered its muzzle, paws and just the tips of its dark feathers. It had fierce glowing red eyes and when it roared, its large teeth glinted and gleamed in the morning sun; his long tail whipping constantly side to side. Patting the great beast on his massive shoulder, the big cat laid down flat, allowing Mephisto to grab a handful of fur and haul himself upward to climb atop his wondrous flying mount.

"Let's fly, Red," before he could finish his thought, the large black panther shot far upwards until they were soaring among the large snow white mountains of clouds.

The large beast soared out across the sea flying at an unimaginable speed and journeyed westward until meadows and forests shimmered beneath the racing shadow of the tall mage and his winged mount. Late in the afternoon he reached the river that marked the border of King Magh and Lochlann, the waters having a life of their own and the wind suddenly began to blow. When Mephisto attempted to cross, strong winds began to bluster; a vertical wind shear caused him to deviate his course forcing them through the clouds towards the Eorth's surface. The river that flowed south reversed its current and with a white explosion of whirlpools and spray, the water ejected turbulently, throwing up jets of gushing water skyward. He set the black panther down on the bank of the rolling river, a bit perturbed he paused before easily dismounting, his body a little worn and sore from the constant travel.

The tall traveller observed that the river was broad at all points up and down the shoreline, forming a natural barrier against any would be enemies. With an unrivalled determination in his heart and mind, Mephisto strode forward, even as geysers erupted in a flurry of activity and steam sprayed out of the water's surface. The ancient sorcerer began calling upon the divine powers of nature, his hands turning cold and numb as he completed his spell. A bank of freezing mist began to form over the flowing river and the ground at his feet turned white with frost. When the thick frigid mist dissipated, the rolling river turned into a solid block of ice and with the river's barrier nullified, he quickly mounted Red and both crossed without further incident.

Mephisto flew with great haste across the grasslands, flying over small trees and clumps of dense brush that was dotted throughout the panoramic emptiness. The Plain of Wonder was smooth and open, its surface like a thick grassy blanket and all around the fertile plains were farms and croplands that not only fed the city, but made its King wealthy from trade. From here he passed by the poor people of Lochlann and by their homes that were scattered throughout the countryside, then turned onto a broad roadway until he finally came within sight of his destination.

Calmly the lean magician dismounted and with a sharp snap of his fingers, the great black beast began to shrink until it came to be a tiny ivory figurine once again. Placing the wondrous little item in his pocket, he strode forward onto the barren Plain of Wonder and stood before the fortress of King Magh. The castle was bristling with black towers, the gate bolted and the stonewalls loomed high above the grassy plain.

"Give me the Cup of Wonders or warriors to defend it!" Mephisto flung back his head and loudly shouted his challenge.

The answer he got was warriors. Shouting war cries, a large company of men burst forth from the opened gates, all had murder in their voices and evil in their eyes.

"Wrong answer." Mephisto's breath became cold and frosty, his eyes glowing faintly blue with his strong voice trailing off into a whisper as he unleashed his spell.

The air around him quickly cooled and a rumbling from beneath the ground began to build until finally the soil from under the feet of the charging troops broke open and thousands of razor sharp ice crystals erupted upwards. Their needle-like tips easily punctured the thick metal armour of the rushing vanguard, causing hundreds to be killed by the field of icy stakes. The deadly frosted lances cruelly impaled each victim, leaving them dangling in horrific positions, some even protruding from out their mouths and eyes. Those not killed instantly suffered greatly, screaming helplessly in pain until finally succumbing to a slow and agonizing death. The second wave came almost instantly, with archers quickly launching a flurry of burning arrows towards Mephisto, the concentrated barrage somehow just missing the unmoving and steadfast wizard. Armed with long swords and hooked pikes, the sustained enemy assault broke through the terrible frozen carnage at the base of the fortress and were only moments from reaching Mephisto.

Speaking his own name aloud caused his eyes to flash with a brilliant silver light that quickly flared into a steady white pulse. A cloak of flickering flame surrounded the powerful spell caster, then it began to slowly rise until finally resting above his head in a wreath of orange fire. The silver energy writhed and twisted, shaping into the form of a huge semi-transparent dragonhead, the flames shifting in various colours of red, orange and yellow. When the last wisps of arcane energy flowed over his lips, a powerful explosion of hot flame burst outward from the dragon's open mouth, creating a deadly raging heat that left nothing but a path of ash in its wake.

The gate of the fortress lay in smouldering heaps of metal; a crowned King Magh stood several yards beyond the blackened archway, gazing gravely back at Mephisto. In his hands he bore the legendary Cup of Wonders. The unicorn horn was ivory white at the base and black in the middle with a sharp gold tip and star-like jewels that blinked in the reddening sun.

"Who is it that kills my finest men?" the purple robed King spoke as he walked across the blackened plain toward Mephisto.

"I am Mephistopheles, the Silver Mage," the words sounded with a slow burning hatred. "And I am here for the cup of healing that you bear."

"I have heard of your name and more, I have heard it prophesied that you would slay my warriors," the bearded King pleaded, his cruel eyes fastened intently on Mephisto. "But without the cup I would no longer be immortal."

Mephisto advanced on the King and quickly snatched the horn from his weak grasp and began to turn, but stopped and abruptly spun back around.

"If immortality is what you desire, then I shall grant you this gift!"

Suddenly leaves began to sprout from King Magh's slender fingers and his smooth flesh hardened to rough bark until finally he stood as a tall oak tree, his branches waving in the gentle breeze. Without even a glance at the charred bodies of his fallen enemies, the silver sorcerer set off for home with the healing Cup of Wonders in hand.

XII

It was mid afternoon when Dark finally opened his eyes again, and he found himself resting comfortably in a long cot made of stretched cloth, his demonic armor still on. Hovering nearby was the faithful little faërie, in his hands a moist cloth that he used to wipe the feverish forehead of the bedridden assassin. It had been several hours since his grandfather left to seek out the Cup of Wonders, and even he had to wonder if the old wizard would make it back on time. Yet, somewhere in the recesses of his dulled mind, was the lingering belief that Mephisto would never fail him, even against what were seemingly insurmountable odds.

"That's why he can teleport without feeling the effects that I do. Now it all makes sense," mumbled Dark, trying to clear his sleep-filled eyes.

"What makes sense?" Teigue asked.

"Why the old man is able to teleport without his energy being drained," Dark began again, his words slightly garbled. "And why he is able to do it at will."

"Yes, those of us with this natural ability are able to control the side effects, but constant use of this power would drain us to the point of no return," Teigue said, smiling with a wink. "Now . . . if there is something else you wish to know, ask it quickly before your grandfather gets back."

"Well, there is something I always wondered; it's bothered me ever since my parents' death," Dark spoke again, his breathing labored and his voice lowered. "When they died, why didn't he just go back to Duergar and destroy them . . . just kill them all?"

Teigue sighed deeply, pausing for a brief moment before responding to a melancholy Dark. "First of all, don't think he didn't want to, because he wanted to show them his true form and consume them all with fiery vengeance," Teigue continued. "But he could not do this, for all of Duergar believed him to be the Shadow Lord, and even the good citizens of the city would come to defend her against such a hated foe. And being a silver dragon with a lawful nature makes him unable to do any harm to any creature, man or beast, who are pure of heart. So you see, Dark, things are not always as they seem."

"No, now I get it. I should have never doubted him," Dark concluded, feeling slightly ashamed.

"Now, is there anything else?" Teigue asked.

"As a matter of fact, there is. . . . No one ever told me what happened with he and my grandmother."

"Well . . ." Teigue never got the opportunity to finish his thought as Mephisto suddenly appeared, and in his hands he held the Cup of Wonders. Without even so much as a hello, the old conjurer hurried over to the shimmering pool and plunged the drinking vessel deep into the cool waters, filling it full.

"I see you took your sweet time, old man," Dark smiled slyly, amused by his own comments, but his voice was still subdued.

"Well, I had a few things to do," Mephisto turned with cup in hand and, standing tall, he strode toward his bedridden grandson. "I saw a few old friends, went fishing for a couple of hours, then flew to the city of Nye for a new silk shirt . . . just to mention a few."

"Wow, I'm surprised how you can even carry that heavy horn. You must be exhausted," Dark's laughter quickly turned into uncomfortable coughing.

"I just hope I don't . . . OOPS . . . spill any," his grandfather jested, purposely spilling some of the precious curing contents onto the tile floor and shooting back his own furtive smile followed by a festive wink.

All Teigue could do was shake his head and watch in silence, hypnotized by the comedic play being performed at stage level by these two jesters.

"I think we had better stop our foolishness. Poor Teigue here looks like we have driven him slightly mad," Mephisto laughed in amusement. Tilting his grandson's head forward, he brought the Cup of Wonders to his lips to drink.

Dark drank slowly, savoring the contents of the horned cup like an excellent wine, feeling the strength immediately returning to his body. A moment later, with the sleep dispersed and his rested mind fully awake, he climbed out of bed, an astonished Mephisto rising with him, his arms held out to catch him if he should falter.

"I did not expect it to work that quickly," his grandfather responded, examining him more like a protective grandmother than a physician.

"You look like you're back to your normal self again," Teigue smiled.

"I feel like new, like I've been reborn somehow," he smiled roguishly, as his thoughts again focused back to his ultimate goal. "And soon I will have my revenge."

"Well, how about we eat first and start on the revenge tomorrow," Mephisto spoke shortly as growls of hunger erupted from his empty stomach. "I am simply famished."

Minutes later, the three were seated around a long wooden table laden with a great array of savories, sweets, and drink to rival that of a feast fit for a king. The light for this banquet was provided by hundreds of tiny lit candles that floated high overhead, gently bobbing up and down on what seemed like invisible waves and traveling clockwise on a circular sea.

"Now that you have the gem of location, you will have no problem finding the rest of the artifacts you need," Mephisto exclaimed, waving a large chicken leg in the air at his grandson.

"Speaking of which, what is the next item?" Dark asked casually as he sipped red wine from a silver chalice.

"The Belt of Heroes," the old historian replied quickly. "It is said to be made with the severed heads of nine legendary heroes, each one endowed with magical strength. All were attacked and slaughtered by the Drow King and his band of dark elves. In drow folklore, the belt was made from their skulls and the shackles from their hellish prison. Then one day the belt he wore around his waist somehow mysteriously disappeared, lost for centuries or stolen, I'm not sure; probably locked away in someone's treasure vault."

"They also say whosoever wears the belt shall be given their strength . . . or so they say," Teigue interrupted sharply, both hands holding a thimble full of wine that he quickly drank.

"Then I shall leave first thing in the morning," Dark declared, quietly turning to meet his grandfather's gaze.

"You'll need this," Mephisto produced from his pocket the large blue diamond, setting it down on the table in front of Dark with a wink.

When Dark awoke the next morning, the sun, with its light bright and warm, had already cleared the horizon of the eastern forest. The early morning mist slowly rolled across the lake waters, with the sky to the north appearing dark and forbidding as the black-armored assassin boarded the already waiting *Albatross*. Once again, he reached into the open mouth of the animated fanged demon face that adorned his breastplate and, like a performing circus act, pulled out Finders Keepers. In silent concentration, he thought of the Belt of Heroes, and suddenly his mind was bombarded with images of the Drow King, his dark elves, and a thief in the night dressed all in black. He had seen the thief become a victim of a large, dark shadow in a strange land of flies, but the gem did not reveal the truth concerning the whereabouts of the belt.

"What the hell do I do now? . . ." Dark trailed off in stunned silence. "Oh, wait, I know what to do."

He shook his head in silent disgust and held the large, cut stone out slightly in front of him, this time knowing exactly what he should do. "Find me the Belt of Heroes!"

The instant Dark finished barking his command, the blue diamond came to life in an aura of pulsating blue light that suddenly began beating rhythmically like a pumping heart. Then, from within its very core, rose a shimmering white star, not unlike the ones you would see twinkling overhead in the night sky. Higher and higher it flew, trailing behind it a translucent tail of light as it ascended into the heavens.

"Alba . . . follow that star," Dark exclaimed, pointing a clawed gauntlet finger at the rapidly flying star.

The *Albatross* cocked its head back in acknowledgement; her great wings snapped out and seized the wind, sending them both soaring skyward in hot pursuit of the quick-moving beacon. The streaking light shot far upward and, with a sudden burst of energy, the large seabird followed close behind until they were sailing among snow-white, mountainous clouds. For many hours they traveled in a southerly-east direction, until finally they angled down through a large cloud mass and out into the sunlight once again.

Dark was swiftly carried over the Mountains of Marm, west of the Xanthos River, passing by several distinctive rock-cut tombs that were carved into the sides of the purple cliffs in this region. The Eorth slid quickly past below them as they reached far and deep within Asia Minor until they arrived at a city he knew only from stories told from his grandfather's extensive travels. Lycia was an independent kingdom, ruled by a Sarpedon, a Cretan exile and brother of King Minos. He remembered from the tales that Mephisto told that the city and the surrounding countryside were being ravaged by a fire-breathing creature. The ancient traveler also spoke of screaming in the night, of small children gutted by sharp claws, and even of stone houses utterly destroyed in explosions of fire. His grandfather also told him of how the king had sent warriors to the mountains to slay the monster—but of those who went, none ever returned.

They sailed past large stretches of forest before reaching the valley floor, where the shimmering star descended and was lost from sight as the trees of the forest obscured everything from view. "Alba, stay close," he spoke quietly before he leapt over the side and landed softly on the ground with the grace of a cat.

The *Albatross* took to the sky at once and tirelessly circled in among the clouds until she was needed again by her young master. Noiselessly, Dark followed the quick-moving star into the forest and, after a short time of traveling, he came to an area where the Eorth was blackened and flying above were circling vultures. The half-elf assassin now followed the glowing light of the gem, its faint flashing pulses becoming faster as he came closer to the absent star. Finally the gem of location led him to a gorge that was dim with hanging smoke and loud with the sound of flies feeding on the swollen, headless rotting cattle that lay scattered about, its rank odor filling his nostrils.

Dark froze as something moved among the shadowed rocks below him and fire flashed upward in long streaks of flame. Then, the huge beast came into clear view, and upon seeing this unwanted interloper, the creature surged swiftly up from the stony floor of the gorge and lunged forward. This monstrous hybrid was a lion, furred and clawed with protruding ears and a ruff of black mane around its thick neck. From one shoulder grew a horned goat's head, long of tooth and with eyes glittering blood red, its head twisted upward as frothy foam fell from its rabid mouth. From the Chimera's right shoulder protruded a fierce red dragon's head; two massive horns swept backward and flames flared from the scaled nostrils. Arising from the monster's back were two large bat wings; its hindquarters were that of a giant goat; and instead of a tail, a writhing snake protruded with an open mouth that bore fangs as it hissed at the masked intruder.

Dark stood and remained solidly before the huge, rushing abomination. He had never seen a creature of this size and ferocity, so any hesitation at this unexpected assault would most undoubtedly result in his untimely death. It swiped at Dark with the huge, clawed paws from the forequarters of the great lion, but the agile assassin leaped to safety by only scant inches. Rolling quickly to his feet, the bowstring from his hand crossbow sounded off in harmony, with several bolts burying themselves deep in its thick skin with audible thuds. The Chimera rasped in fury, its serpent tail raised upward to strike; the lion's head roared and the dragon's head spat gouts of fire, while the goat's head spewed a venomous black gas.

The flame strike and gas cloud had no effect on Dark, and so he was left unharmed, but was momentarily blinded, which left him wide open for another attack. With surprising speed and agility, the bizarre beast set himself once again on its slippery prey. The lion's open mouth struck with stunning force, its sharp teeth cutting deeply into Dark's armored shoulder, striking bone with a loud crunch. The three remaining heads also struck ferociously; the goat head unsuccessfully tried severing the arm of its prey, but Dark's armor was too strong. The dragon spewed hot flames directly into the face of the masked assassin, and the serpent coiled tightly around his leg in a deadly grip.

Dark now acted instinctively, his steel fist striking the goat with uncanny precision, raining down blows on the side of the creature's black head with bone-shattering force. The lion's head roared in agony, causing the nightmare attacker to release its vise-like grip on the armored assassin's wounded shoulder. Falling backward, Dark summoned one last desperate surge of power from his left arm that held inside an equalizer within . . . Dragon's Breath. A thin blue ray of intense cold surrounded by clear ice streaked out from the wand's open mouth; the sound of cracking ice followed in its wake. The icy blast struck the surprised and unprepared Chimera as large crystals of clear ice formed around the creature until it became encased in a thick sheet of ice.

The fallen half-elf climbed dazedly to his feet, his breathing labored; even his thoughts were weary as he tried to recuperate. He was bleeding profusely from his shoulder, the pain excruciating; the large, open wounds exposed a break in his clavicle. The pain and swelling at the area of the break made it difficult to move his arm or shoulder. To ease the discomfort, he fashioned a sling out of a piece of silk rope and used it to hold his shoulder back. Shock slowly spread over his battered face as he gazed fixedly toward the ground, his eyes concentrating on a winged shadow that was growing larger. Within his scattered thoughts his mind had gone numb, but his years of training prevailed, and with the swiftness of a blinking eye, he moved as the maddened creature swooped toward him. Once again, he had come close to death, but somehow managed to evade its fatal touch.

Within seconds, Dark rolled to his feet with the skill of an acrobat. The figure of a second Chimera stood before him, its features identical to the first except for the lion's head that was maneless. It hesitated for a brief moment as its attention was directed at the frozen statue of the first Chimera, tinged with frost and encased in clear ice with cold air wafting off its crystalline surface. The creature took a cautious step backward, its huge bulk posed to strike, its many eyes fixed on the tiny man that stood before it. A rasp of fury came shrieking out of the monster's three heads before it charged wildly across the stone foundation to attack the black-garbed assassin.

Dark, mustering every ounce of strength he possessed, called upon the divine spirit of Mother Eorth, quickly made an arcane gesture, and, with the last of his words, activated the power of the spell. His left hand began to illuminate slightly, his flesh turning an ivory-grey, and with a touch, Dark transferred the flow from his hand onto the ground. The energy of the spell burst forth and with a thunderous noise the ground before him tore open. With his winged foe ready to pounce, a colossal rock-formed arm erupted from the large, gaping crevice and grasped the rushing beast, holding it fast in its stony, ruthless grip. In one final arcane gesture, its howls and screams were forever silenced as the Eorth closed silently behind it, sealing the Chimera in a stony grave, buried for all eternity beneath a mound of stone and rubble.

Dark, still in great pain from his multiple wounds, could think of only collecting the fallen gem by the first Chimera and of obtaining the Belt of Heroes. With his arm in a sling and the pulsing glow from the diamond Finders Keepers directing his way, he slowly moved out of the gorge, up a gentle slope, and down a winding path shrouded by tall trees. He reached the top of the valley and continued on through the forest that stretched out ahead of him, pausing only occasionally to catch his breath.

The fading rays of the late afternoon sun slowly caressed his armored frame in faint glimmers, his shadow cast growing long and lean as his search for the belt of strength came to a weary end, or so he hoped. The gem of location had brought him to a hillside on which stood the long-forgotten Temple of Artemis, said to contain the bones of the legendary Greek hero Theseus. Built of white marble, in the Doric style, it had columns entirely surrounding the central, enclosed cella, adorned with the figures of the exquisite frieze still decorated with paint. The temple still had all its columns and pediments intact, and even had most of its original roof. However, the other decorative chiseled features had inevitably been badly damaged by thieves, looters, and of course, through the ravages of time.

Dark crept cautiously inside, halting momentarily in the large, open entryway; his searching in the near blackness for any signs of potential danger revealed no one in sight. Inside the ancient interior were a stone altar and a statue of a goddess facing the entrance. Lying on top of the altar was the Belt of Heroes, caked in layers of dust and covered in cobwebs with the shining star riding over top.

"Finally," he muttered to himself.

Trailing drops of blood as he walked, the tired assassin stood wearily before the sacrificial Altar of Artemis and, picking up the belt, he tossed it causally over his left shoulder. The broad belt was made of pitted and scarred iron chains, said to be made from the shackles of the dead. Nine small obsidian skulls were attached; each one seemed to whisper softly. A silver inlay of horrifying scenes of death lay in between each gruesome head. As he lifted his red demon eyes with a parting glance at the Statue of Artemis, he saw movement in the shadows and froze instantly. For long moments, he stood motionless in the darkness of the temple, his one good arm slowly raising upward and pointing the housed wand toward his new foe. Then, abruptly from under the cover of darkness, he was set upon by a third Chimera, the multi-headed creature sliding from concealment behind the statue. Poised and more than ready to rid the world of a third abomination, he stopped as the ghastly beast began licking at his feet—it was only a baby!

"Now what am I supposed to do with you?"

XIII

Mephisto woke early in the morning, the air damp and cold, as he made his way to the great room where he quickly started a fire in the great stone hearth. The cavern was silent as he moved quietly from the warming fireplace to relax in his high, straight-back leather chair. The still-sleepy wizard leaned back and folded his arms, ready to close his eyes for a quick nap, when his eye caught a trail of blood that lead toward the secret entrance to the healing pool. Mephisto put aside his thoughts of sleep and hastened to the secret chamber, hoping to find his grandson with all his body parts intact. He appeared quite suddenly with a worried look that quickly turned to a wolfish grin as he spied his grandson relaxing beneath the shimmering liquid canopy of the watery tree.

"You know I would say I am surprised, but somehow I'm not," mocked Mephisto a moment later.

"What now, old man?" asked Dark suspiciously, his eyes narrowed.

"Just that I am not surprised to see you here, lying in the healing pool . . . injured . . . again!" his grandfather started.

Dark groaned audibly. "Here we go," he muttered.

"I'm just saying, next time try sneaking up on them for a change," laughed Mephisto. "After all, you are an assassin. You are an assassin . . . right?"

The weary half-elf nodded and smiled slightly.

"You know . . . if you want, I could just hire an assassin to do the jobs for you. . . . I'm just saying," the old magician jested, glancing down at his grandson, chuckling deeply to himself, which made Dark turn to look. "I am quite wealthy, you know . . . so it wouldn't be a problem. But that's your call, not mine."

"I'll think about it and let you know," Dark was grinning wolfishly himself. "Anything else?"

Dark continued to lie motionless, his back against the wall of the pool and his head resting on the edge, waiting for the inevitable response from his mocking grandfather, who stared upward for a few moments more, grinned smugly, and nodded. His mocking smile changed to one of astonishment, for from the corner of his eye he spotted something crouching under the wooden bed, the darkness concealing it fully except for the many glowing eyes that stared eerily back at him.

"Just one more thing—what . . . is . . . that?" Mephisto asked in unabashed amazement.

"That's the Baron," admonished Dark, grinning.

"You named it?" he asked in bewilderment.

"Of course, he's my new pet," he answered casually.

Long moments passed before the old wizard spoke again. "Fine, but you feed it and you pick up after it," exclaimed his agitated grandfather. "Now, when you are ready, come down to see me. I have news of your next item." And he left without even a parting word.

With Mephisto gone, he could hear the creature moving, the scraping sound growing louder as the small Chimera inched forward in a half crouch until it sat behind Dark's head and went to sleep. Almost an hour later, he decided to go looking for his grandfather and headed for the great room. When Dark finally made his appearance, he saw his grandfather relaxing in his favorite chair absently munching on the remains of a small breakfast he had prepared for himself.

"Come sit down and eat; you must be famished," the tall wizard looked up sharply at Dark and smiled warmly. "And tell me of yesterday's adventure."

Magically, a second chair appeared, along with, on the table in front of him, a large breakfast platter complete with strips of bacon, sausage, stacks of fluffy pancakes and syrup, buttered bread, and two kinds of eggs, scrambled and sunny-side up. With his meal completed, the two of them talked for quite some time as Dark related the story of his encounter with the baby Chimera and the incident with its two terrifying parents.

"And that's why I brought him back here," Dark began again, pushing his finished plate away and stretching himself. "I couldn't just leave him."

Mephisto nodded in approval, his lean, bearded face turned hard, and he paused in thought, putting his finger to his lips before speaking. "Do you know a place called Black Abbey Bower?"

Dark knew of this name—it was a name synonymous with all things evil, a name used to frighten little children, used as threats to keep them from straying. A name that sent shivers down the spine of grown men and women, of ghost stories told before a late evening fire, tales of the feared trolls from the far north. "No . . ." he said, looking sharply at his grandfather and uttering a low chuckle. "Just kidding. Actually, Dad would say if I did something wrong, the trolls would come and get me, then eat me whole."

"Those were not just stories, but detailed accounts of actual events," replied Mephisto quickly. "No doubt they embellished the tales to make for a better story, but in their portrayal of Og 'the man eater,' there was literal truth in all those narrations. Word of this hated creature spread throughout Vandringar, carried by bards, minstrels, and wandering knights who luckily managed to escape the fiend's deadly clutches. Those not so lucky would be found horribly mutilated the next day."

"So the stories about the children are true?" Dark broke in, his voice muffled with rage.

"Yes, unfortunately it is true; his preferred victims of choice were the children. These he would flay alive with his sharp, curved claws; their tender, pink flesh he would eat savoringly," the grim historian answered. "The skins and heads he would take back to his lair in the hills, known as Black Abbey Bower, to have mounted on stone walls as trophies of his triumph over man."

"And what item does this monster possess?" he asked curiously, rising to add more wood to the fire.

"The Chalice of Cerridwen," Mephisto continued quickly. "He who carries the goddess' emerald talisman is given the strength, after being dealt a death blow, to rise once more to strike down his enemy. And somehow it has fallen into the merciless hands of that foul beast."

"Let me get this straight. As long as this murderous bastard possesses that magical artifact, he cannot die," declared Dark absently, turning toward his grandfather after pausing for a few minutes, lost in thought.

"That's correct. So while he carries that cup, he is impossible to defeat," the old wizard frowned and shook his head, a look of consternation registered on his lean face.

"So all I have to do is somehow take the emerald chalice away from Og and then kill him . . . no problem," Dark stated simply. The broad smile on his face turned into a hearty laugh, and the assassin looked over sharply at the grim face of his grandfather.

"You make it sound so easy," the old wizard's features showed he felt this was no laughing matter and the whole of the situation should be taken more seriously.

"It is easy . . . in my head, it's already done." He looked back to reveal a brash smile that played over his lips, clapping his grandfather on the shoulder, then turned quickly from him and followed the trail of his own blood to the hidden entrance of the secret room.

"Where are you going?" Mephisto called after Dark.

Dark, without stopping, walked through the opening in the rock wall and up the stone steps, his response echoing back down to his onlooking grandfather. "To get my armor . . . for on this day I dine with a man-eater!"

Dark soon returned, dressed in his black demon garb and with his latest prize, the Belt of Heroes, wrapped securely around his waist. His grandfather was slumped down in his chair and gazed resignedly into the dying fire, the cooling embers still glowing faintly. He greeted his grandson and called him over with a wave of his hand.

"I forgot to tell you—Teigue dropped off a letter for you," Mephisto informed him, holding out a thin, white folded sheet of paper. "It's addressed to you."

"Who's it from?" he asked curiously.

"It's from your grandmother," muttered Mephisto. "That will tell you where and when to meet her."

Dark ripped open the sealed paper and hurriedly scanned its contents. "She wants to know why I've been hiding from her," he laughed. "And she also says where to meet and how to contact her."

"Hiding, she's one to talk," came the quick comment. "That woman has been hiding for over five hundred years!"

"And that's my cue to leave," Dark announced suddenly, donning his mask once again. "I'll see you soon and with the cup in hand."

"I'll be waiting," Mephisto smiled knowingly.

The dark assassin turned away and was gone. Dark took to the sky, flying high on the massive wings of the enchanted *Albatross*, and sailed in the same direction the star had taken. They voyaged for some time, over a day and a half, before the streaking star led them to a land he did not know and past a place of high, pock-marked cliffs, loud with the cries of seabirds. He turned inland and sighted a fair country, flat and green and dotted with tall woods and misty meadows. Vandringar was a realm where giants roamed and elder gods still held sway—and also home to the bravest of men, the warriors of the North, the Vikings.

By late afternoon, Dark had left his faithful flying friend and began his march northward toward Black Abbey Bower. He walked for what seemed like hours as the pulse of the beating gem told him that the beast had changed directions several times, but now picked up again toward the northeast. The rain began to fall in a slow and steady drizzle through deep grey skies and heavy wind. The bad weather persisted throughout the remainder of the day as the rains fell unchecked; the air was cold and at times almost bitter.

He remained on the move, constantly keeping a close watch on the gem of location and on his surroundings, always alert and ever ready. In the shadows of the late afternoon and the greying of twilight, the half-elf assassin moved silently through the thick woods, then paused, his progress abruptly halted as he sank down into a low crouch, disgusted at what he saw. Here was a place of horror, not meant for mortal eyes. Long, wooden stakes stood along a pathway, each topped by a blackened human head, the relics of unfortunate earlier victims, it seemed. In the distance up a treeless slope were the crumbling walls of the ancient monastery known as Black Abbey Bower.

As night descended into darkness, the persistent rainfall finally began to taper off, and a low, rolling mist moved in like a wool blanket. Dark's sharp mind knew this would be the best time to strike. As long minutes passed, still searching through the black shroud of the mist and the rain, he did not see the troll pass, but the sound of savage, hungry munching did reach his straining ears. Cautiously he advanced, feeling his way carefully, not making a sound; even his breathing was a steady, noiseless whisper. He risked moving a few feet farther, then, with a single word, he vanished, becoming invisible, his eyes still working madly as he glanced about for any signs of movement. Dark spotted him quickly, his huge form seated upright on a carved stone statue only a few feet from a roaring open fire.

Og was a large, fiendish-looking giant, about two and half times as tall as a human. He had huge, powerful sagging shoulders and long, thick arms that reached well past his knees. The creature's tree trunk-like legs ended in huge, yellow-clawed feet; its hide was like the rough, moss-green bark of an old, dying tree. The beast's hair, if you could call it that, was a long broom of oily, black, bristly strands that no comb could pass through, and its yellow eyes stared cold and malicious. He was feeding hungrily, his long, sharp teeth carefully gnashing at the still-warm flesh from the leg of a dead man and chewing loudly as spatters of blood caked his face. Amid the gruesome spectacle, Dark noticed the emerald chalice was nowhere to be found. With the behemoth's back turned for the moment, he knew that such an opportunity might not come again, so he slowly continued forward.

With agonizing slowness, he moved like a stalking cat hunting its prey, navigating his way through the rising cloaking mist until finally crouching behind the still-feeding troll.

He smiled faintly, then like a black, soulless instrument of death, struck out with his shadow sword, cutting the exposed flesh of the troll's thick neck.

Og, staring in fright and with his throat bleeding freely from the gaping wound, tried vainly to stem the flow of blood gushing from his slashed artery. The beast continued to struggle violently for a moment more, then, before he even had a chance to defend himself, fell lifeless into the bloodied Eorth.

Dark passed by some crumbling walls and quickly made his way toward the broken Gothic arch of the abbey's gateway, thinking to himself that the ancient talisman would be found there. A moment later, his preoccupied mind jerked sharply awake, alerted by his highly keyed sixth sense that urged him to leap clear from some unknown danger that would have ended in his death. He rolled to his feet, only to be forced back a moment later by a repeat assault, finally bounding deftly onto one of the oddly shaped, large crumbling stones that dotted the ground.

He caught the dull white flash of the sudden sweeping blade as it whipped past his masked head, and his own translucent blade came up skilfully to ward off the fatal blow. There stood the massive figure of Og. In one massive fist he carried a vicious-looking bone spear, barbed with a saw-toothed head, purposely fashioned to shred its enemies' flesh.

"I know what you desire, little thief," an angry and surprisingly alive Og growled, his large, fanged teeth clenched in hatred. "But you will not find it there."

"It speaks," declared Dark mockingly, with a hint of confidence sounding in his voice. "Then tell me, slayer of children, where is this chalice that I seek?"

"Hidden . . . within a riddle!" snarled the taunting voice of the troll.

"Tell me your riddle so that I may claim my prize," the assassin responded quickly, smiling back with a demonic grin.

The giant troll paused momentarily, his spear still pointing menacingly toward the cocky braggart. Og then grinned back in satisfaction and nodded his answer.

"Answer my riddle and find what you seek," the chilling, hoarse reply came at last. "It lies within a container with no lid, within a pot that never needs washed, and one that cooks without fire."

Dark then shot a sharp look at the monstrous face of Og; a nefarious grin spread slowly across the face on his breastplate and his large eyes glowed red.

"I'm surprised someone as slow and stupid as you can even speak, let alone comprise a conundrum."

Abruptly, the huge troll attacked with blinding speed, slashing out with the barbed bone spear and slashing wildly at the agile assassin. His blows, however, were easily parried, and in his maddened fury, he dropped his guard, leaving himself momentarily vulnerable. Dark fought violently back, battling his way through a mass of clanging blows from the heavy spear, then twisted sharply to one side to avoid the striking blade that buried itself deep into the damp Eorth. At the same instance, he countered with his own weapon strike.

Amid a howl of wild cries, down came the troll's severed arm, the clenched fist still clutching the bone spear as it fell with a splash into a large puddle. Their eyes locked momentarily, and then the huge beast let out a roar of laughter, stooped forward, and picked up his still-twitching arm, quickly reattaching it to his bloody stump. Speechless, Dark stepped back and stared, but his quick mind began forming a new plan of action, and maybe one further test was required before he could answer the troll's riddle.

In a quick dash, Dark sprang forward and swung his shadowy blade with expert precision, slicing through the giant's neck, sending Og's head spinning in a bloody arc while great gouts of blood spurted from the trunk. When the head fell, he smashed it under the heel of his leather boot. The head cracking open like an egg, brain matter and pus oozed out and spread onto the wet grass. The black-garbed assassin slightly retreated and stared in dumbfounded amazement as the monstrous body rose to its feet, picked up the bloody pulp that had been its head, and restored its devil's form, making the creature whole again without so much as a mark on the troll's neck.

At that moment, Dark knew the answer to the riddle and also what must be done to slay the beast once and for all. The shadow sword he held firmly in his hand faded and vanished, and with grim determination, he stood rooted in place to meet the inevitable attack. As predicted, huge fingers closed around his armor-clad body, jerking the passive assassin into the air as he stared at a palisade of crooked, yellow stained teeth and into the crimson cavern of a hungry mouth.

A surge of arcane energy erupted from Dark's glowing eyes, sending out red bursts of fire. With a mighty exhalation, a flickering red flame exploded outward from his open mouth, shooting a powerful fountain of fiery liquid that engulfed the troll's massive head. Dark was immediately released as the deep, haunting screams of pain rang out from the troll, shattering the night's silence. The upper portion of the animal's body suffered severe burning; the head was almost completely destroyed with part of the skull being reduced completely to ash.

The dark assassin did not hesitate. Moving quickly and with superhuman effort, his clawed gauntlet slid swift and deep into Og's tough belly. His bark-like flesh was ripped open, and his intestines spilled out. Wrenching the emerald chalice free, Dark pulled the talisman of Cerridwen from the beast's stomach, revealing the answer to the troll's riddle. Og's garbled moans died quickly in the night with one faint gesture of Demon Raider's steel hand. Invisible forces of magic slammed into the creature's chest and, with a bloody pop, the troll's small heart burst out of its back and skipped along the ground several times until finally coming to rest next on a crumbling block of stone marble. The troll slowly dwindled and sank to the floor, amid a spreading pool of scarlet blood. This time, when the massive troll fell, it did not rise again.

Dark stood silently next to the fallen man-eater and, an instant later, the lifeless, bloodied body exploded in a blinding flash of fire that erupted from out the mouth of the dragon wand. Columns of crackling pyres blazed skyward like giant, flaming pillars that thrust through the misty darkness to brighten the night sky in a dazzling array of light. He watched until the fire subsided to flickering tongues of flame and then slowly died to ashes, the blackened smoke disappearing in a silent hush.

Suddenly, Dark turned sharply to the left as his keen elven ears heard the approach of someone or something behind him. From out of the floating mist emerged a giant black shadow flowing toward him. He instantly recognized the massive form as it passed before him. It was the *Albatross*. Within minutes, he was resting comfortably in the cockpit, as the hulking silent seabird soared gracefully away and, moving swiftly, it settled into a large glide until it could no longer be seen.

Moments later, the once still and lifeless tiny heart, left lying alone and forgotten in the darkness, began to beat once more.

XIV

Dark flew across Vandringar until the persistent rain had disappeared, to be replaced by a fresh, clear sky and a full moon unhidden by a vast, dark ceiling of storm clouds. Gone was the dark, impenetrable mist that made it difficult to navigate, replaced by shining stars that lit his way as he came to the sea. Out over vast waters did the seabird soar, aided by the warm summer winds at their backs, far across a rolling plain of blue until Vandringar dwindled to a line on the horizon and vanished altogether.

With his lean frame weary and exhausted, the youthful assassin breathed deeply and settled back in the cockpit of his flying ship, his eyes closing momentarily as he allowed his tired mind to drift into a sleepy haze. The rushing of the wind and the periodic flapping wings from the *Albatross* faded into a faint drone of sound that not only soothed him, but lulled him toward the comfort of sleep.

Dark was on the verge of slipping away entirely when his mind snapped awake, suddenly realizing the forgotten treasure that lay in the dark void behind the demon's teeth of his armor. Removing his gauntlet and setting it aside, his lean hand slipped beyond the long, sharp fangs of the creature's open mouth and emerged, gripping the emerald chalice. It was a large, primeval emerald cup that was decorated with polished emerald stones with two twin dragons encircling the bowl, belching flames against the stem and lower portion of the cup. The interior of the elegant vessel and rim of the chalice were graced with two stylized roses on opposing sides, and a beautifully interwoven pentagram was designed in brushed metal. In the bottom of the drinking cup was the shimmering star from the gem of location, still glowing faintly until Dark returned it once again to rest within the confines of the blue diamond.

On the morning of the second day, with the sun rising from its restful slumber, so did Dark, while his faithful flying companion tirelessly sailed on. Their voyage was coming to an end as he sighted land off in the distance, a place he knew well and a place he had seen many times as a child. A fair country was Umberland, flat and green and dotted with woods, comprised of great lakes, canyons, wide rivers, and mountain ranges. This enchanted land was home to hundreds of species of mammals, birds, and fish as well as various dark and immoral creatures that lived within the vast forests and wetlands. Umberland was home to Kingdoms of the First World; lands not meant for men, ancient realms ruled by the old races. To the west, the dwarves ruled beneath towering mountains; to the north were the forests of elven clans; and to the east a dark and windy wasteland was home to the most ancient of races, the dragons. South Umberland was a magical place ruled by the Witch Queen, his grandmother, and there her rule was absolute.

They sailed on for a few more hours until at last the *Albatross* glided down a winding river with a wall of trees pressing close to the water's edge. The river coiled and turned inland through an impenetrable forest into a mist-covered clearing surrounded by gigantic elm trees. At one end, a single tree stood noticeably taller than all the rest, with a thick trunk and heavy of bough. Standing stones rested atop its serpentine roots, and at the base of one of the large, flat stones lay a well of clear water so limpid that it seemed to give off light. A treasure resided inside the well, a king's golden diadem. It was a magical treasure that protected the entire realm from what Dark knew not, nor did he ever get a straight answer whenever he asked.

To this tree Dark walked, on the ground beneath his feet a carpet of leaves freshly fallen from the circlet of trees that surrounded him. A drinking horn of gold hung beside the well, and Dark picked it up, filled it from the golden waters, raised it to his lips, and drank heavily. From the hedgerows beyond the clearing, the scent of lavender drifted in on the wind, the same lavender smell that permeated throughout his grandfather's home. Then a strange sound floated on the air toward him, sounding strongly in his ears. Harp strings issued a series of beautiful notes, and through the genial melody of music sounded the ringing of belled bridles, heralding the approach of a great company.

A moment later, a splendid column rode out of the forest, and leading the procession were gold-clad knights mounted on white horses. Behind them was a bevy of beautiful women cloaked in scarlet, their hair shining, and around their necks great torques of twisted gold and the bridles of their horses glittered with gems and golden bells. Colorful servants carried tall standards; the insignia on the pennant was a golden crown of pearls seated over a large, spreading tree surrounded by a wreath of ancient, dark symbols. The surrounding company parted, and out rode a crowned rider on a white horse, bridled and draped in gold, but it was not as golden as its rider. She was a strong, beautiful elven woman with a proud bearing, her skin paler than a swan on a wave of blue, and eyes as green and clear as dew on blades of tall grass. Golden hair hung with gold rings, and she seemed clothed with the dawn, for her draperies were the color of rose petals. Around her neck, a small amulet was worn on a fine chain of silver, blackened by an unnatural fire. The jewel was made from a pale white crystal carved in the likeness of a full moon with a smiling face sculpted on its surface.

Before dismounting, the crowned woman turned to her elven host and, in a language Dark could not understand, she whispered her royal command. Her escorts turned obediently, with the golden knights trotting alongside, and riding in procession made their way through the trees and into the sunny meadows that lay beyond. The Witch Queen now stepped lightly down onto the soft, grassy floor, then walked toward Dark until she stood before him.

"Hello Vanora." The air around him was laden with the scent of lavender.

"Oh, Dark, don't call me that. I am after all your grandmother," she spoke in a voice like the sighing of the cool wind through the trees. "And I don't care how old you are now or even how old you will get, I will always and forever be your grandmother. Now come give me a hug."

The ruler and queen of the witches moved forward, approaching her grandson with arms opened wide, finally putting her slender arms around him in a loving embrace as a tiny teardrop rolled down her rosy cheek.

"Now you must promise not to stay away from me for so long." It was more of a command than a request, even though her words were softly spoken. "You must promise."

"I promise . . . Grandmother," he responded with a mocking smile.

Vanora, still holding Dark close to her, stopped, reluctantly released her grip, and took a step backward to view him more closely for inspection, her face showing displeasure at his demonic attire. "That's a different look . . . it's . . . um . . . nice."

"It's not meant to be nice, it's supposed to be scary," he continued quickly. "I want them to fear me."

"You look scary to me . . . and I am your grandmother," she exclaimed. Her creamy hands reached to touch the smiling demon face from his breastplate; its fanged mouth snapped, causing her hand to jerk back sharply. "Friendly guy you have there."

"That's nothing, you should see him when he's angry . . ." He immediately straightened with his thoughts left unspoken, for his attention was drawn to the slight movement high atop the leaf-covered branches of a giant elm tree.

"We have company," Dark calmly remarked in a hushed whisper.

"Witch Slayers," Vanora announced curtly, her face showing great disdain for her hated nemesis.

The thick foliage granted concealment to creatures in their branches, with the canopy of leaves also being an excellent vantage point for snipers. No sooner did the thought enter his mind than several streaking black arrows flew unhindered in a blurred line toward his grandmother. Before Dark could even react, the slender Witch Queen had already moved forward. Holding her arms aloft, she began uttering a low lyrical chant. Quickly, a warm glow began to spread out across her hands, projecting a blue radiance in the shape of a giant eagle that opened its enormous wings, shielding both of them. The giant shield, glowing with magical energy, hovered only a few feet in front of them and was able to easily block the speeding projectiles from hitting their intended target.

Anger flashed red in Dark's eyes, and with the rage of a caged beast, he let loose a flurry of bolts with a dramatic sweep of his muscular arm. The arrows flew almost invisible into the dense covering of leaves, with each one finding its mark, striking their unseen targets, which gave agonizing howls before falling to the ground in unmoving heaps.

It was in that instant that a dozen elven warriors began to detach themselves from the thick carpet of green leaves that lay scattered on the ground. Camouflaged in armor made from the large foliole of the giant elm trees, the Witch Slayers, waving their exotic swords with grand flourishes, rushed wildly toward them, shouting death to the Witch Queen.

Dark spotted them first and took a step forward, but Vanora put out a restraining hand, stopping her grandson, then directed a withering glance at the charging assassins. The slender queen was quicker to realize what was happening. Dark stared incredulously at his nearly eight hundred-year-old grandmother, then reluctantly lowered his weapon and stood fast.

For one split second, time itself seemed to come to a complete standstill as the slender queen began to call upon the forces of nature, speaking the ancient words that carried with them the power of the spell. Tendrils of writhing green light began to encircle her small form, with her call causing the light to be dispensed to the surrounding vegetation, enveloping it in a soft, green corona. For a few seconds, all living plant life radiated light before being absorbed, then finally faded, causing a massive awakening in the circle of greenery. The grass and small shrubbery began to overgrow the grove, rushing toward the advancing elves like a surging tidal wave.

The creeping plant growth curled and coiled around the elven intruders, tightly ensnaring them, rendering their weapons useless against the toughened growth. A glimmer of magical intelligence shone in the knotted eyes of the giant elm trees as they lurched forward, trapping the Witch Slayers like caged animals, their thick branches like the wooden bars of a jail cell.

His grandmother moved toward her captives, her light frame held erect and in her eyes the undisguised glint of burning fury. Dark felt a chill run down his spine that made him glad a thousand times over he was not the enemy of the Witch Queen. She moved from one captive to the next as their wooden confines were now aligned in a row, the elm trees standing behind like giant sentinels. The elven queen stopped suddenly before one of the prisoners, a big man—well, big for an elf—with long, blond hair and two very noticeable criss-crossed scars on his pale cheeks.

"I shall ask you this only once," Vanora's features hardened as she spoke, her voice cold and menacing. "Who informed you of our rendezvous?"

There was an impossibly long and agonizing moment of unbroken silence as the tiny queen waited expectantly for a response from the silent defendant, but none came.

"You wish to remain silent," she again spoke icily, her patience now gone. "Then forever silent you shall remain."

Reaching down, the angered Witch Queen picked up a large handful of soil, then, slowly rising, she flung the rich Eorth, with sprinkles of dirt falling on the jailed slayers.

"As this soil returns from whence it came, so too do I return you to the Eorth. Now rest and walk no more."

The held elves shuddered, their flesh becoming swollen until finally it split and shredded so the muscle and bones showed through. With a faint crackling, the bones began to crumble as their bodies decayed into a light brown soil until finally their decomposing remains slowly fell and returned to the Eorth.

Suddenly, the queen's guards, led by their captain, thundered forward behind them with swords drawn and at the ready, arriving a little too late to help their ruler. The mobilized elven knights came to a halting stop in a sentry line several feet from the pair, dismounted, and stood at attention, waiting expectantly for further instruction from their ward.

"Thank you, captain, your help is most appreciated," the queen spoke in a dry, mocking voice as she walked toward him.

Grandmother and grandson strolled directly between the captain and his men, looking neither left nor right as they moved past the trees and into the sunny meadow that lay beyond. Without a backward glance, they strolled across the meadow through tall birch trees to a clearing ablaze with wild, colorful flowers where he saw a pavilion in the most beautiful embroidered silk, adorned with gilded lavenders and crowned with an eagle of burnished gold. Within were piles of white fur and rugs of Asian silk, the likes of which Dark himself had never seen, even in his many travels abroad. A blazing fire filled the tent with a safe and cozy warmth, lamplight shone on vessels of silver and gold, and laid out on a low-level table, a feast fit for a king, or in this case a Witch Queen. Beautiful elven maidens were busy with final preparations, and the murmur of their sweet voices could be heard like birds singing. But with a simple wave of his grandmother's hand they left, and he was alone with her.

Dark dropped his horned helmet onto a large pile of fur next to the opening and sat down on one of the large, fluffy cushions next to the wooden table, stretching himself before he spoke.

"Remind me to always stay on your good side."

"I will," came the quick remark from his grandmother, still standing and sipping wine from a jeweled cup of gold. She looked over at Dark and smiled the same devilish grin his mother used to give when she had caught him in a lie and yet would say nothing.

"You know, I could find out who it was that informed those slayers of our private meeting," remarked Dark soberly.

"No need, for there were only four people who knew of your arrival here this morning," responded Vanora coolly.

"Your grandfather being the first, with myself being the second, and you, of course, the third, and lastly Famon Fane, my longtime friend and chief advisor and someone who is mysteriously absent on this day."

"Then I should like to meet this Famon Fane and introduce him to my blade," exclaimed Dark angrily.

"If I can find him, then I shall gladly introduce the two of you," came her slow, growling response after only a moment's hesitation.

"Why do the elves hate you so much, anyway?" he asked curiously.

"You mean you don't know?" the elven queen spoke up quickly.

"No one was ever allowed to talk about it, or you for that matter . . . ever," Dark replied quickly.

She paused, shaking her head resignedly. "Then I shall tell you," Vanora began again, her face softening as her slender hand reached over to grip Dark's shoulder. "Better yet, why don't I show you."

As her words fell on his elven ears, the lighted lamps began to dim and her soft, whispering words created an illusion so real he almost believed he was in the actual forested city of the elves. The City of Eldred was like a white diamond amid encircling mountains of green, built upon a series of small lakes with forested islands filling the placid waters. Graceful wooden bridges spanned each one; their grounds were flat and there were no stones for building, so platforms were constructed, built into the thick and colossal trees to house the elven population. On these platforms sat mansions of pearl, with many beautiful flowers entwined in their branches with carven figures of beasts and birds that ran upon the railings. High atop the branches of the living towers were countless lights gleaming in colors of gold, silver, and platinum.

"Now I shall spare you the details of how we met and start off where I was still ruler of the elven clans with your grandfather by my side." As she spoke, the scene flashed to the queen's lavish bedroom overlooking the entire city in front of a wall of windows. "Your grandfather was scolding me for taking one of his magical tomes, a witches' grimoire of the blackest magic, something that was strictly forbidden in elvish society. You see, Dark, elves are the purest form of magic there is, so because of this, certain laws were instituted to ensure its purity. Even though I was the queen, I was still subject to her laws, and a High Council of elder elves was put in place to help enforce those laws. So the study of black magic was strictly forbidden, but I paid no heed and delved deeper into the dark arts. Many years had come and gone, and around the time when your mother was still in her early youth did my secret studies become known once again. However, this time Mephisto informed the Elven High Council; angry that I had gone behind his back, he felt he couldn't trust me anymore."

"If it's any consolation, I know to this day that he regrets his hasty decision," Dark broke in, his voice heartfelt.

"No matter, what's done is done; he made his decision, right or wrong," she spoke with an almost cold and callous attitude. "Now where was I . . . oh yes . . . the banishment. I was to leave the City of Eldred forever, never allowed to see her beauty, her magnificence, or her splendor ever again."

Dark didn't have to see her face, streaked with tears. He only had to listen to her shaken, quivering voice to know the pain she felt and the sorrow and sadness of not just losing her home, but losing her daughter as well as her husband—and all on the same day.

"On that day, my true followers and those still loyal to my crown revolted and tried to block my forced expulsion. Your grandfather stepped in to subdue the caustic situation and suppressed what would have been a terrible civil war within the race of elves. At that time, there was a division of countries, and those who followed me settled in the warmth and comfort of the Southland, with its mild climate and dense, green vegetation. Historically, South Umberland was born, and we were beginning to rebuild a new civilization, with new ideas, new laws, and many new cultures and practices. Do you follow me so far Dark?"

The young half-elf nodded and smiled slightly, still staring at the play that proceeded in front of him.

"Well, during this period, the Elder Council appointed a new successor to the throne. Ollen from the House of Greyfell became the new Elf King, and with his first new proclamation he instituted a new order. That's when the first Witch Slayers appeared in history, a group highly skilled in many of the lost arts of the old world, bound and determined to establish peace and order. They devoted themselves to hunting down and capturing any and all binders and practitioners of black magic; to seek out and destroy any being who gives command of their soul to what they deem as evil forces. The king's own daughter, Nysarra Greyfell, is one of these fiendish prosecutors. The Grey Elf, that's what she calls herself, tried to end your mother's life on numerous occasions, becoming her nemesis that relentlessly hunted her almost day and night. I'm even told she has worked for Kalifen on more than one occasion."

"I'm sorry, Grandma. I had no idea you went through so much," was all he could say as he sullenly bowed his head, feeling ashamed how he had treated her growing up and wondering how he could possibly make amends, or even get back the time he spent not getting to know her.

"Now you know," her voice died away in a broken murmur. She turned to look away from him and stared off into the distance, then abruptly turned back, her beautiful features tightened and black with anger. "Now there is something I ask of you. When you find those responsible for Leynorr's death, I don't want you to just kill them . . . I want you to hurt them. Make them pay for what they have done. . . . Make them all pay!"

Dark's head jerked up, and he looked at his grandmother. His cold, black eyes locked on hers. "I promise you, every last one will suffer, and no mercy will be shown."

"Good!" cut in Vanora sharply. She closed her eyes in thought, and when she finally opened them, she finished the last of her wine before turning to her grandson.

"My spies in Duergar have some disturbing news for you. It seems a glass egg was crafted by Janus, a glass artisan still friendly to our coven, made for the dark mage Kalifen, the use of which there is but only one—to replace one's own heart with that of a soul gem, a ritual intended to give immortality by placing your beating heart inside a special glass talisman. Once placed inside the egg, you can no longer be killed by any means except by breaking the glass, which in turn breaks the spell. Once broken, you must give the heart back to its owner, but remember—break the egg only in the presence of the true owner, or he will stay immortal with his living heart turning to an unbreakable stone."

"And where is this egg now?" he asked her eagerly.

"My spies do not know," spoke up Vanora quickly. "But they did overhear something about the Giant Bran; that is all I know."

"That changes things. Hopefully Grandfather will know what to do," Dark muttered under his breath and then quickly came to stand up with a puzzled frown showing on his lean face. "Thanks Grandma . . . for everything, but I have to go."

"Wait, this is what you came for, isn't it?" interjected the little queen, removing the necklace from around her slender neck and handing it to her grandson. "Just think about the place you wish to be, the greater detail of the surroundings you have inside your mind, the better. Then close your eyes and, when you open them again, you will instantaneously be teleported to your desired destination."

"Just like that?" he asked.

"Just like that," she answered.

He balanced the pale white crystal gently in his hand, then held it up high and peered curiously at the full moon amulet that glowed slightly in the faint lamplight. He fastened the fine chain around his neck and, picking up his demon mask, he hugged his grandmother one last time and casually waved farewell.

"Wait!" the tiny elven Witch Queen broke in suddenly, her slender hand held up to stop him. "Just until you get used to it, stick to open spaces first . . . alright?"

"Okay, I'll see you soon."

"Make sure you come see me before you go to Duergar," she broke in again. "Or else I'll come see you."

"I promise I will." As Dark spoke the last of his words, he closed his eyes and vanished.

XV

When Dark opened his eyes, it was a little after midday, and he found himself standing in front of his grandfather's cave. Instead of going directly in and down the stone steps, he found his way blocked by the giant limestone boulder that usually sat adjacent to the opening. Not wanting to waste the power of the Necklace of Teleportation, the returning assassin instead opted to test his strength by using the magical properties of the Belt of Heroes. His lean muscles strained under the massive weight of the huge rock, but slowly and with great effort, the once-thought-to-be-immovable object suddenly began to move, until the opening was finally clear.

Seconds later, he made his way down the smooth stone steps and was greeted by the angered voice of his grandfather yelling, "Stop! Stop! STOP IT!"

Dark stepped quietly into the great room, and to his shock, there were torn and ripped pieces of parchment, broken jars of glass, and tiny splinters of wood with blackened books of magic still flaming on the ground. Besides the paraphernalia of reading and writing that was strewn and scattered about the floor, other articles littered the area as well. Among such articles, the long, wooden worktable was capsized with a leg missing; the skeletons used for study lay broken in small heaps alongside the flasks, crucibles, and retorts of the practicing alchemist.

A moment later, the distinct sound of heavy boots reverberated along the trail of debris that sat on the stone cold floor and, from in front of him, scurried the little Chimera out of the darkness from the adjoining room with his grandfather chasing close behind. The Baron came running in, surprisingly quick for his small size, carrying the Key of Solomon, an ancient and rare manuscript of formulas and spells, with each mouth gripping a different section. The Chimera finally stopped when he came to rest behind his master, crouching in hiding from the infuriated wizard. Three sets of eyes turned straight ahead and squinted through the legs of the surprised assassin, still chomping loudly on the ancient pages, its small tail darting back and forth in play, the snake head covered by one of Dark's wool socks.

Mephisto came forward screaming a flurry of loathsome oaths, stopping quickly, his face flushed and angered and his fierce eyes full of rage. The old wizard's burning gaze fastened hatefully on the black creature, his fist clenched as if ready to strike a blow. He was about to vent his anger and frustration on his grandson, but suddenly was unable to continue. His breathing was labored as he took a moment to catch his breath before finally speaking.

"That . . . THING just destroyed about a hundred years of diligent, painstaking, mind-numbing work!" an irate Mephisto boomed aloud, his finger pointing menacingly at Dark's newly acquired pet. "And some of those spells have no duplicates . . . NO DUPLICATES!"

"I'm so sorry Grandfather," Dark remarked upon removing his horned mask, trying hard to hide the growing smirk showing on his handsome face and trying even harder not to laugh. "Bad boy, Baron, bad boy. We don't touch Grandpa's things."

It took him several tries, but he managed to wrest the remaining pieces of the torn book from the toothy grins of the goat, dragon, and lion's head. Finally, he passed the soggy, teeth-marked pages that dripped black spittle back to his grandfather, who was no longer angry, but instead had his mouth open in shocked disbelief.

"Wait a minute . . . who are you?"

"What . . . what are you talking about?" he asked quietly.

"Who are you, sir, and what are you doing in my home?" exclaimed the old mystic, his eyes narrowing in suspicion.

"It's me, you senile old fool. It's your grandson, Dark," he declared pointedly.

"My grandson, no . . . impossible, you liar," ventured Mephisto abruptly. "For if you were my grandson, you would have broken bones, cuts, bruises, or some type of horrific, life-threatening wound. But you clearly have none of these, not even a scratch or even a blemish on your skin. So, you see, you cannot possibly be my grandson."

Dark stood for a moment in mute silence. Mephisto chuckled inwardly at the sight of his grandson's face, a slow smile spreading over his own lean face. Dark's smug smile vanished as he pushed past Mephisto. The maddened assassin did not bother to even turn around, but began to quickly climb the stairs to his bedchamber.

"One more thing—he's been staying in your room," the mocking magus called after the brooding assassin.

"Yeah . . . so?" he shouted back.

"Well that's not the only thing he's been doing," Mephisto, pinching his nose, echoed his response. "Pee yew, if you know what I mean."

"Holy crap . . . Baron!"

The rest of the day was spent cleaning, not with magic, but with a mop, bucket of water, sweeping broom, and dustpan. His grandfather was down on hand and knee trying desperately to salvage anything legible—even the smallest piece of scrap was saved so long as it had written word inscribed on it. Dark, however, carried what seemed to be an endless amount of little flaming presents from his new pet Chimera. Every time he went back up the steps and into his room, there always seemed to be somehow one more added to the pile of stinking gifts.

"You know, someone would be wise to invent some spell that disposed of little messes like this!" he shouted down to his grandfather.

"Someone did!" was the loud response.

"Yeah, where is it?" Dark shot back abruptly, his own response even louder.

"In Baron's belly . . . you jackass!" The only answer that came down to Mephisto was the silent, foul odor of flaming sulphur.

Shortly thereafter, just before the sun dropped behind the horizon completely, the trio were gathered around the three-legged table, the missing leg replaced by a long-bristled broom. The quickly prepared meal was leisurely eaten as Dark retold his encounter with the Witch Slayers and the news about Kalifen and the Giant Bran's possible involvement. Mephisto sat quietly listening, but still muttered silently to himself, occasionally glancing over at the now-sleeping multi-headed mongrel.

"From what I remember, the giant known as Bran the Blessed once ruled the Island of Albion in the early days," Dark began speaking again. "He was an ancient and just guardian king on the Island of the Mighty who watched over his people even after death. So then, why would he help Kalifen with anything?"

"I know Bran, and he wouldn't," Mephisto broke in shortly. "I suspect foul play, but of what kind I know not."

"I guess I'll get my answer when I find this giant from the north."

His grandfather nodded in agreement. The two sat and talked for several more hours, both pondering the information provided by the Witch Queen's spies until finally turning in for the night. Dark was asleep in moments, but it seemed he had slept for only a second when his grandfather awoke him. Around midnight, the ancient mystic approached his bed without a sound and informed him that he was leaving to see the Styg on urgent business and he would see him when he returned from Albion.

When Dark and Baron awoke again, it was dawn. He promptly took outside his baby Chimera to take care of its morning business. In the faint reds and yellows of sunlight, he saw the tiny faërie Teigue flying toward them, dressed in a fine suit of green and yellow leaves. The minute, dark figure seemed almost a part of the forest, his suit a natural camouflage for his surroundings. Dark knew that Mephisto must have asked him to come and watch over his place and keep it safe from the many mouths of his new three-headed nemesis.

"Hi Teigue, you here to watch Baron?" Dark asked, although it was not so much a question but a statement of fact. "I really appreciate it."

"No problem, my friend," Teigue stated, sighing deeply. "I'd just much rather be going on these adventures with you, traveling to distant lands and fighting fierce creatures, but instead I end up babysitting them."

The half-elf looked at the little faërie humorlessly, shaking his head in mild amusement; the assassin then chuckled softly. He quickly stopped, the amused smile on his face suddenly gone as he paused in thought a moment, staring at the little man's attire. He particularly noticed the steel thread used to weave the leaves together, the same weave of steel he saw was used in the construction of the Witch Slayer's armor.

"I just want to be able to help you . . ."

"Where did you get your new suit?" Dark cut in short, his voice sounded smooth.

"My suit . . . ahhh, you noticed. Exquisite, isn't it?" the proud voice rang out. "And the genius associated with this little number is Boddeker Stitch, a fabulous tailor in Duergar."

"Teigue, my little friend . . ." he smiled faintly in the spreading sunlight. "You helped me out more than you could possibly know."

Teigue nodded in understanding, then stopped suddenly, shaking his lean face in confusion and glanced questioningly back at Dark.

"What . . . I did?" was his confused remark. He then quickly flew after the half-elf, who was already heading down to the cave.

Dark ate a quick breakfast and, before long, was sailing into the clear, blue skies, once again on the wings of the *Albatross*. About mid-morning, the guiding star of Finders Keepers led them eastward for several hours, then steadily north for the remainder of the day. Albion lay northeast of Faëroes, through miles and miles of the roughest, most treacherous waters of the Eorth's largest ocean. As they rode high over the crashing waves, gone was the humid heat from the day's sun, blown west by the cooling night breezes, and with it came a peaceful solitude. It was late evening when the weary travelers finally reached the shores of the mighty island and, with his keen elven eyes, Dark gazed out at the huge forests beyond. The island itself was made up of low, rolling countryside in the east and to the south, while large hills and scenic mountains dominated in the western and northern regions.

Lost in private thoughts, Dark followed almost carelessly the unseen trail of the guiding star, which had disappeared into the black forest below miles before. When it became too dark to continue, the horned assassin directed the *Albatross* into the bordering forests below, where he looked for a place to make camp for the night. In the midst of a stand of trees, near the jagged ridge of a mountain, he found a well-made hide shelter that had a central, cave-like chamber with five long, branching rooms. A pungent smell drifted from its wide, dark opening. Quickly, he built a small hearth fire near the entrance to help drive away the dank smell. The weary assassin ate then slept, well shielded from the cold night winds of the mountains. When Dark woke the next morning, the sky was growing lighter and the stars had disappeared altogether. It was a dull, sunless day that followed when he gathered up his belongings and sent the giant seabird home to Sommerset. The day was damp and chilling to the bone, and he found it devoid of any warmth and comfort as he journeyed farther north. The second day wore on quickly, and the sun never appeared during his long march as heavy clouds completely blotted out the sky. The world he traveled through was a cheerless, hateful grey land, and the tall, black oaks that surrounded him were a dense mass of forest, standing like a great wall between him and Bran.

It was late afternoon when the traveling half-elf finally came to a secluded and remote valley that was surrounded by steep and rocky strewn crags. The mountainside right above a giant peak looked like a stranded whale made from a huge layer of sloping limestone. On the right side, in the flank of the mountain and below a set of limestone cliffs, Dark could see a huge entrance, but blocking the pass was a mass of large rock with an accumulation of loosely packed rock fragments that sloped outward from the entrance—in other words, a rockslide.

With a simple flick of his wrist, Dark sent three flaming balls of fire hurtling toward the avalanche of immovable rocks and sand. The fiery spheres, roughly the size of a human fist, struck with such a tremendous force that they erupted in a shower of golden sparks and red flame. The surrounding sky lit up in a bright flash of light that was followed by a large explosion so powerful it even caused the nearby trees to rock back and forth. Chunks of flying debris whistled past the steadfast assassin, who stood firmly planted amid a rising plume of crushed gravel and dust.

Once clear of rubble, the entrance was more like a huge hall, a portal right in the middle of the cliff face. The cave seemed to narrow a bit as soon as weathering from the outside no longer had any influence, but the passage was still impressive in size, being at least one hundred feet wide and nearly double that in height. There were numerous speleothems, with most of them on the cave floor as stalagmites, flowstone, and even rimstone pools. The main passage seemed to flow up and down with several pits along the way; one was a long shaft that the agile assassin easily leapt across. He walked along in total darkness, noting how the cave was very impressive in both size and beauty, then minutes later stopped, shooting a quick glance skyward. The cavern was enormous; a vast, towering section of the cave, the ceiling overhead was at a height of twelve hundred feet and nearby was a spring of life-giving water. Next to the clear water, the surface smooth and glasslike, sat a giant boulder with a frowning face dimly lit by streaks of phosphorescence that ran through the walls of the ancient chamber.

"Finally," he spoke aloud.

"Who's there?" a deep, booming voice sounded out of the darkness. "What does the Shadow Lord require of me now, Kalifen? How about my ears or maybe my nose? Speak, damn you!"

"No, Bran the Blessed, it is not Kalifen," Dark's voice broke through the momentary silence; his red, glowing eyes were all the giant could see. "I am the son of Solus and Grandson of the ancient silver mage."

"Mephisto's Grandson?" the shadowed giant asked of his unseen visitor. "Is your name, perchance, Dark Solus?"

"Yes, but I now prefer to be called by a different name." With a single gesture and a silent word, the black-shadowed cavern was illuminated by hundreds of tiny glowing orbs of light. "I am Demon Raider."

In the light, Bran's head was massive, standing, or in this case just lying there, but it was still well over two stories tall. Just a single tooth of his was larger than Dark's entire body, and he quickly mused to himself that he could actually live inside the enormous head as a home, with his eyes being the windows and his wide mouth the entranceway. Bran's broad, placid face was deeply lined, giving it a wise appearance, with magnificent chestnut hair. A large, braided beard outlined a wide mouth, and his deep, pond-like blue eyes were set beneath shaggy eyebrows.

For a brief moment, Dark hesitated in awe of the huge, hulking apparition seated across from him. But with stoic resolve, he walked closer toward the forbidding figure.

"I have to admit I am a little disappointed in your overall size." Coolly, the black-garbed assassin began again, "I guess I just expected there would be a lot more of you."

"Well, it seems Kalifen has taken my body to the frigid wastelands of the north, home of the white-furred bear," the lowered voice of the Blessed echoed off the cavern's ceiling like ringing church bells. "On an island of ice surrounded by a ring of fire, my torso stands guard over a smooth box of onyx, a square container with no opening but a single hole, just big enough to fit your finger into. What is contained in the box I do not know."

"How do you know this?" came Dark's quick question.

"On my cloak is pinned a broach of silver and amber," he murmured, "an ancient item of legacy with the ability to confer on me a gift for seeing visions of the present and future, the ability of second sight."

"Then how is it that you ended up here?" Dark interjected quickly.

"It foretold only of the island and my body magically controlled to protect the contents of the box," Bran announced after a moment. "How I ended up here in my present condition is still a mystery to me. The last thing I remember was sitting down for an afternoon meal near my home. I drank a cup of wine that a may fly flew into and I swallowed it. Then . . . I'm here—that's all I remember."

"And how will you get your body back," laughed the dark assassin.

"Why you, of course," the giant smiled knowingly as Dark looked quizzingly back. "You are, after all, seeking the precious cargo locked within, or is this just a meeting of chance?"

"And just how am I going to accomplish this task?" gasped Dark. "Sail it back like a floating barge?"

"Remove the amber broach that holds my cloak, and my body will transform to that of a colossal bird I've called a Roc," the giant ordered firmly. "Do this, and he will be yours to command."

"Why does that sound easier said than done?" was his muffled reply.

"Oh, it is, I'm afraid," the big head replied softly, "for you will most likely be swatted like a fly before you can even get close enough. And, besides that, it will take the strength of a giant to undo the clasp. But if you can do this, I will reward you with a prize worthy of a god."

Dark thought a moment and finally nodded hopelessly, raising the glowing blue diamond in his clawed hand, and thought of the giant's lower half. From deep within the giant's enormous brain popped out the guiding light of Finders Keepers, just above the nose, which caused Bran to stare cross-eyed to see the star. Then, not a moment later, the shining star sprang skyward and headed toward the high cavern ceiling and vanished beyond.

"The gem of location, if I'm not mistaken," Bran mused thoughtfully, gazing in the direction of the shooting star as he spoke. "I heard a high-ranking Sheol in the Kahn's empire stole it from a female Dogai assassin after killing her in the most gruesome and savage of ways." He looked questioningly at the silent assassin, then cast one final look at the heavens, then back with curious eyes at the horned, shadowy figure.

"He did," Dark declared dryly. "Then I took it back . . . in the most gruesome and savage of ways."

Dark then turned and spoke softly, stretched forth his arm, holding open his right palm, and recited the ancient words, "*Adfer chan'r ffagla*." As the last of the words fell from his fanged mouth, white-hot fire burst forward from his outstretched palm, like a writhing and swirling tornado. The blinding, fiery glow spread outward in a field of twisting flame and finally spiraled into a fading cone of fire, and there stood Nightmare wreathed in the unholy flames of Perdition.

"Now don't wander off, I'll be back before you know it," he laughed in amusement, then leapt onto his horse called Nightmare, pulled hard on the reins, and galloped away, while all Bran could do was roll his large eyes in quiet despair.

Northward his faithful mount took him, traveling fast over the land, past the towering mountains that framed the Highlands of Hadding, past Scotland and Wales and into the vast bluish mists of the ocean that encompassed Albion. There, the horse from Hell's stable shook its fiery mane and leaped onto the water, riding high atop the crest of the waves where the sunlight sparkled and shone. Out over the surging surf the black horse galloped, quicker than a retreating shadow it sped hastily above the rolling and battering waves of the great mother sea. Far across the plain of blue they went until the mighty Isle of Albion faded like a distant memory and was lost from view. They passed by the movements of several schools of fish and the flights of the seabirds that soared high above them, leaving a flickering trail of fire as they continued steadily north. The reddened sun finally faded into the west, and the only light besides the glimmer from Nightmare's trailing wake of flame came from the stars shining brightly overhead. When he had finally reached a point where no fish swam and not a bird cried in the sky, he knew he had entered the realm of eternal night, ruled by creatures who were not mortal and definitely no friend to man.

The black-garbed explorer passed into the Polar Circle and beyond. Still, they continued farther north, no longer riding atop shimmering waves, but a huge frozen plateau of cracking ice and white snow. They sailed over a frosted continent of diamonds until they stood on the fringes of a wall of mist into which they smoothly rode and vanished. Time disappeared almost entirely as the soundless black haze that encased them seemed to endlessly stretch on forever. Finally, they pushed ahead through the limbo world of eternal darkness and back into the world of living as the dark abyss faded and the wall of mist was left far behind.

A blue ocean once again lay under flaming hooves where they sailed among enormous icebergs under the light of the midnight sun, which cast a unique turquoise glow on the giant perpendicular walls of frozen water. Within minutes, they came at last before the frigid isle of ice with huge, snow-covered mountain peaks that pierced the clear night sky and encircled by a raging ring of fire that stormed skyward. The gigantic crystal mountains stretched upward, reaching high enough to pierce the clouds as they stood guard over the rising and setting of the sun.

The black rider and horse plunged resolutely into the burning ring of fire, coming out the other side unscathed, then finally coming before a wall of mountains that blocked their path. There was no way around; the passage to the boundary of the mortal world lay through the heart of darkness, a tunnel filled with the gloom of a dug grave. Beyond it laid the black box and the end to his journey as well as the unknown world where Bran's body now dwelled.

"This is where we must part company, my friend." Dark dismounted and sent his fiery companion back to his home in Hell.

Unflinching, the armored assassin marched into the empty blackness of a wide mouth that yawned in the mountainside. Through the cold and damp darkness he walked as the tunnel walls oozed with slime and crawled with small scurrying creatures. Off in the distance, a pinpoint of light suddenly appeared ahead of him, followed by a refreshing breeze of fresh, warm air. A moment later, he was greeted by the light of the sun, and it was then that the contours of another world took shape before him.

He was in a wondrous land where no mortal had ever walked before. The flowers were the color of pearls, the bluest of sapphires with clusters of ruby reds and faint pinks like diamonds. Overhead, silver grapevines sagged under the weight of large bunches of sumptuously colored dark red and blue flavorsome grapes. The lush gardens were thickly planted with every kind of tree; the many varieties of trees fascinated Dark with their great size and beauty. Close to the gardens and the entrance was a large river, a stadium in width, flowing directly through the middle of this hidden otherworldly realm.

The demon-garbed assassin watched in amazement as something enormous took shape beside the river. There stood the headless body of Bran the Blessed, the ageless, deathless guardian that now watched over the locked-away heart of the Shadow Lord. The giant's torso was taller than the tallest tree, so tall it could wade through the sea and, if it had a head, it would ride above the water's surface. The body was dressed in the silks of some fine court, and a tartan kilt was worn about its waist with a kilt pin of silver attached to the front flap purely for decoration. His cloak was a finely crafted garment of a dark blue material with the seam sewn with silver thread, and fastened around his shortened neck was a broach of silver and amber. In the giant's gloveless hand he held a sword, the blade pointing downward, whose hilt glittered with jewels.

Without eyes to see or ears to hear, the mountainous body sensed the assassin's presence, how it did Dark never knew. Then the hulking form turned and came lumbering toward him. Dark, unmoving, watched as the terrifying spectacle thundered forward, the thudding of booted feet shaking the very ground with each step. The young assassin stared out at the awesome assault; his masked, lean face coolly impassive, his demeanor calm and steady, as the wild charge grew closer. The black-garbed defender's eyes turned instantly skyward, for surprisingly the looming tower of flesh and bone passed by overhead, then went several hundred yards behind him before stopping abruptly. Once again Dark braced for the massive charge, crouching in a defensive position—well, as defensive as one can get while facing a rushing headless giant's body. And once again, the lumbering mass passed over top and this time ended up wading deep into the river. The wondering half-elf stared unblinking as time and time again the gigantic torso regularly drove by him, until finally growing tired. As the day wore on, he simply walked over to the black box lying unprotected and scooped it up in his arms.

At the river's edge, Dark stood in silence and watched the rather comedic spectacle unfold in front of him while eating several large and ripe apples from a nearby tree. A smug smile crept over his demonic features, thinking to himself that Kalifen had greatly overestimated the headless body's effectiveness. Like a clear ringing bell, Dark had an epiphany; he knew the only way the spell-quickened bottom half of the giant Bran could be animated was by someone schooled in the sacred text. He also knew there must be a piece of parchment inscribed with the name of the one true God and a passage from the sacred scriptures pinned somewhere on the body. A particular true ritual or some sort of spiritual exercise would have to have been performed to demonstrate the power of the written word in order to control the massive physique.

Instantly, Dark saw what he was looking for; there, in one of the many folds of the giant's fine garment, was a piece of paper barely visible. He quickly closed his eyes and, when he opened them again, he was high in the sky snugly tucked away inside a voluminous pocket. Pulling the white parchment free from a securely fastened pearl-headed pin, he recited backwards the scripture that had started the enormous torso in motion. When Dark had finished his recitation of the passage, the gigantic frame stopped its movement and stayed frozen in time like a statue of stone. Moving swiftly and with great dexterity, he removed himself from the spacious, buttoned-down shirt pocket and quickly ascended the steep summit of the behemoth's massive upper chest.

With the magical strength of a giant, his nimble hands forced open one of the stiff and heavy clasps of the silver and amber broach. Once undone, the finely made blue cloak that rested about the body's mammoth shoulders became a flickering field of archaic energy that wrapped around the towering torso. The magic formed into a mantle of large feathers shining pure white around his broad shoulders and huge back. The head of a giant bird, its beak of pure silver, sprouted up from between his shoulder blades. His body and arms became completely covered in thousands of iridescent feathers that changed color, becoming an icy blue hue.

Dark had landed silently and rolled clear of the transformation and now stood and gazed in wonderment at the unbelievably huge Roc. It was truly a thing of beauty and delicacy to behold. Then he casually walked over to his beautiful new charge and, managing a cheerful smile, he quickly climbed onto the thickly plumed back of the waiting Roc that would convey him back to White Mountain. As the gigantic bird drew away, the assassin's winged mount had already reached the height of clouds and was soon lost from sight, its thunderous flapping drifting into silence.

The voyage back to White Mountain took only a few hours as leagues were covered in what seemed like only seconds.

On the back of the giant Roc, the assassin clung securely, his clawed, gauntleted hands gripping tightly the central shaft of one of the bird's prodigious feathers. When they arrived back in Albion, it was a cool, cloudy day lighted by a shining sun. Ahead in the distance, the towering mountain stood clearly outlined against the sky. As the massive bird swung down to enter the capacious entrance in the middle of the cliff face, Dark felt the welcome coolness of a friendly breeze blowing smoothly over his armored frame. The black rider glided easily through the spacious portal and down the dark passage, finally flying into the vast, oversized cavern and settling over beside the dimly lit head of Bran.

Moments later, after Dark dismounted and with a few unknown words from the giant's mouth, the great winged beast began to undergo a transformation that twisted its body. Feathers swelled into shadow, and from that penumbra a standing, headless torso emerged. Then, while the dark assassin stood staring, the mighty body knelt down and, with one huge hand, lifted his own severed head; rising slowly, he turned to face the half-elf.

"Follow me outside and I will present you with your gift," the giant's mouth moved. Then with a long, rolling laugh and still holding his massive head aloft, he strode off into the dark.

Outside, the giant replaced his missing head as mighty legs once again rose among the tree trunks and his large blue eyes peered down at Dark through a canopy of trees. He smiled at the black-garbed assassin and made a graceful bow.

"A thousand thanks, my young lord," he said. "But if not for your kindness, I might have been trapped in White Mountain for all my days. And these certainly would have been long and many."

He handed Dark a sack that was made from a fine, creamy-white wool, then added, "This is for rescuing me and returning my body. Only open this in the center of any cloud of your choosing."

"Do what now?" was his dumb remark.

"If you are truly the grandson of the silver dragon, Mephistopheles, then you have the ability to tread on the soft surface of a cloud," Bran remarked absently. Then, bending to one knee, he held out his palm flat and waited for his tiny rescuer to stand in the middle of his hand.

Like a flying balcony reaching into the heavens, he ascended steadily upward, higher and higher, occasionally glancing down only to see the ground growing smaller. Above his head the flat, wide hand reached into a heavy cloud, passing through its grey wetness and emerging into yellow sunlight and a sky of the purest blue. Clinging to the hand, Dark stepped out onto a rolling field of murky film, cautiously putting one foot on the cloud floor. It was springy and solid as turf and, after testing it several more times, he let go of the giant's hand and set out to find the middle point where the mass of fog was the thickest.

In the middle of the misty nebula of smoke and water particles he stopped, setting the bag on the ground. He opened the wool sack, which revealed a large gold key and a miniature castle, like that which is made for little boys to play with, but more exquisitely perfect in detail than any toy could ever be. Taking the tiny novelty, he set it on the moving ground and almost at once the little castle began to swell. Skyward the towers soared, the stone walls pressed outward, and each block and mortar joint gained in size. As the building grew, every wall became sharp and true, every turret was crowned with golden tiles, and two huge, gold chains lowered the drawbridge. As the building grew, tree trunks, crowned with the greenest of leaves, began to shoot up through the smoky floor. Before long, a full-scale fortress stood solid before him, its turrets flying banners marked with his own symbol, its walls climbing with heavy-laden orchids in a wide assortment of colors and shades.

In the castle's gateway, Dark inserted the gold key and unlocked its large wooden doors; the key iron spoke aloud.

"Master!" it said, its words drifted through the corridors of the castle.

XVI

Upon entering his newly acquired abode, Dark discovered wooden panels done in elaborate woodworking detail lining the walls of every room, along with every door panel also being delicately carved. The interior of the regal palace gave off a majestic aura as the keep was filled with quite a unique floral décor, cornices and beautiful artwork with large Gothic ceiling paintings scattered throughout. The courtyard he found contained blue ceramic-tiled granite seats with a large, circular fountain that spouted multi-colored columns of water high into the air. Directly adjoining the courtyard stood a golden ballroom, and inside music could be heard, made by an invisible orchestra that played under moving chandeliers of light. Connected by a staircase covered by paintings on its walls, the first floor's main attraction was the spectacular grand hall, which was ornately decorated with statues of glass and stone. The huge room was dominated by a mounting of a sinister-looking black dragon's head with long, curved horns. Every square foot was home to beautiful scenic art displays, each one a different scene that told a themed story. Lying above the wainscoting were multiple sets of exquisite stained glass windows bearing transparent portraits of every type of dragon. Sweet-smelling herbs such as chamomile, rose petals, daisies, fennel, and one he recognized immediately, the familiar fragrant smell of lavender, added a robust flavor throughout the castle. In the fortress, he found many kinds of rooms from a solar or private sitting room to a lady's bower room, along with a tiny chapel for praying and twenty eight bedrooms of various sizes, each one lavishly furnished. A kitchen at the far end of the stately manor came complete with cooking ovens for baking and huge fireplaces for smoking and roasting food. The part of the castle that fascinated him the most was the dungeon, dark and foreboding and filled with secret passages. Finally, he found his favorite by far was the throne room with two large thrones placed under a circular dais that also rested under a canopy upholstered in black and red silks with silver accents, detailed in jewels and strange symbols.

Dark sat down in the larger of the two thrones and suddenly, echoing all around him, he heard the same deep voice that greeted him when he first entered the magical fortress.

"Yes, Master."

"Hello?" was Dark's slightly startled response.

"Yes, Master," the hollow voice replied again.

"Who or what are you?" he asked, slightly stirring in his kingly seat.

"I am Mur Manor, and your wish is my command," the castle's large voice seemed to enter his thoughts. "And wherever you wish to go I will deliver you."

"Then take me to Dragon's Mouth Lake in the land of Sommerset," the new Lord of Mur Manor exclaimed after a moment's silent thought.

"As you wish." The command was instantly obeyed, as slowly and silently the cloud and castle began to move.

Dark smiled broadly and, after taking off his mask and placing it on the chair next to him, he began thinking of the benefits of owning a flying cloud castle and how it could help him in his quest for vengeance. Just then, his heightened senses alerted him to the sudden approach of someone from the other side of the room, and he quickly turned to face the silent intruder, but to his surprise saw nothing.

"Who else lives here?" the assassin asked evenly.

"Only you, my Lord," the voice assured him.

"Do I have any servants?" he queried shortly.

"Yes, my Liege," was the toneless response.

"How many?" the stocky half-elf breathed a sigh of relief.

"One hundred and twenty-two," the castle answered.

"And how many are in this room right now?" Dark cut in quickly as he peered around his throne room quizzically.

"Ten."

Over the next several weeks, Dark became more familiar with the castle and its many unseen servants, invisible spirits who once lived as he did. They had lived hundreds of years ago as loyal and faithful servants to Mur the Magician, a great wizard and guardian to the lesser folk around him. In later days, the enchanter's deeds became the stuff of legend, and his name would forever be remembered.

It seems one day long ago, in a time when heroes still ruled the lands, a black dragon of immense size and stature came to his Kingdom of Cadmus. Terrible in its fierceness, a fire-breathing, water-poisoning predator and a dreaded foe of man, this scourge was a source of plagues, bringing only starvation and violent death. The creature soared on great wings toward Mur's Kingdom; over every settlement it flew, its strikes were terrible and swift as it spewed gouts of flame until finally disappearing into the distance. All dwellings, made from either stone or wood, were all but tinder for the dragon's flame. All that remained were charred ruins covered by a pall of black smoke, echoed with the crying of children and the wailing laments of women.

Mur was not only the king, but he was also the champion of his people, and only he could slay the dragon. Accordingly, he armored himself in a magical shield to protect him from the dragon's fiery breath. He came at last to the beast's lair. There, in a mass of smoke shot with flame, the two ancient powers fought. The old magician roared, then the ground shook as the beast fell and the sound died away into silence. Mur's people honored their king and built him a castle befitting their hero. So enormous was it that it could be seen by sailors far at sea. But nothing about dragon lore was simple. Unfortunately, the slain creature was a descendant of Tiamat, a goddess of the saltwater ocean and a monstrous embodiment of primordial chaos. Tiamat gave birth to dragons and serpents; these were her own offspring, and upon hearing the news, she flew into a rage when she learned about her child's death and she wanted revenge. Her tears poisoned the wells of Mur Manor, and all who dwelled there and drank of the spoiled waters were cursed to remain in servitude for eternity. Such was the fate of Mur the Magician along with his one hundred and twenty-two servants.

The cloud castle eventually reached Dragon's Mouth Lake in the early morning, just as the golden half-light of dawn lay breaking. Dark woke with sleep-filled eyes in the splendor of his royal bedchambers, in a king-sized bed filled with the softest of feathers. The half-elf quickly dressed himself in his assassin's garb that was provided by the Dwarf people, and with his horned mask deep within the void of the demon mouth on his breastplate, he closed his tired black eyes. When he opened his eyes, he was standing inside of the great room of his grandfather's cave. His long travels finally came to an end as he approached Mephisto, who was sitting in his favorite chair. It was tattered and torn and missing large patches of leather with long, deep fang marks indented into the wood. Without stopping, he bade him good morning and directed him to stand. Then, grabbing the old wizard's shoulder, Dark closed his eyes and activated the power of the necklace around his neck.

"Nice to see you too, Dark . . ." Mephisto paused in mid-sentence, his hazel eyes opening wide in instant recognition as he surveyed familiar surroundings. "Isn't this Mur Manor?"

"It used to be," came Dark's quick reply.

"What's it called now?" his grandfather asked, looking over at his grandson.

"Why Dark Manor, of course." The broad smile of the castle's owner grew even wider as he was feeling quite pleased with himself.

"You know, it actually has a nice ring to it," the ancient mystic nodded in agreement. "I actually like it."

"Me too, but we can discuss this later. Right now, I need you to tell me how to open that."

His grandson was pointing a slender finger at his latest acquisition. Sitting on a large, round oak table was a square box with a smooth-textured surface made of a semi-transparent black gemstone and marked with metal inlays. Upon each of its sides and perfectly centered were delicate engravings of interwoven pentagrams skilfully sculpted into the dark surface. It also possessed a small hole big enough for a finger to fit into.

"That is a chest of the Dogai," the old historian exclaimed assuredly, looking sharply at his grandson. "A secret sect of assassins even older than the Sheol. They would fashion these cubed containers using ancient shadow magic, said to be impossible to open by any means—a near-perfect vessel for hiding their most valued and prized possessions—and the only way to open the unbreakable chest is with the key, the forefinger of its maker."

"How am I supposed to get Kalifen's finger?" Dark asked with a questioning curiosity in his voice. "Although it would be fun to try."

"You don't," his grandfather interjected coolly. "You simply use Sleek."

"Who or what is a Sleek?" he asked with a bewildered look.

"Sleek is the name of a small shape-shifting creature," the eternal sage began again, relaxing into one of the plush and very comfortable chairs that were available in the great hall. "He can mold his body into an exact replica of Kalifen's unique finger key."

"Okay, so where can I find him and who do I have to kill to get him?" Dark spoke disconsolately.

"You can find him in the Tower of Woe to the south, surrounded by the Sleeping Seas," the practitioner of the mystical arts concluded with a smile. "The creature's owner is a warlock called Vainamöinen, and you need not kill him, but only ask for the creature and it will be given to you. He was one of my first students and belongs to the order I created to help serve and protect the City of Duergar from the evil that to this day still dwells inside her."

"Isn't that the same order that Taliesin was a part of?" Dark cut in short, his look one of great mistrust and suspicion.

"The Order of the First Circle . . . how can you know we can trust him, or any of them, for that matter?"

"I trust Vainamöinen as I trust you, but to be sure travel on the *Albatross*, and she will know if he is indeed friend or foe," the wise historian suggested.

Dark looked inquiringly over at his grandfather and nodded slightly.

"Well, this should be a simple trip for me, then," the assassin's voice was sarcastic as he smiled brightly. "I should be home by nightfall."

Mephisto stood up quickly, paused momentarily, and stroked his beard, his steady gaze fixed on the stuffed and mounted trophy head of the dragon that hung on the wall in front of him. "You know I think I used to date her."

The rest of the morning was spent giving Dark a guided tour by his grandfather. Side by side, the two companions walked and talked as Mephisto carried most of the conversation, explaining in great detail all he knew about the castle and its rich history. It was midday when the pair stopped and visited the huge dining hall, where a small feast had been exquisitely prepared by the ghostly kitchen staff. There, they ate their fill until even Mephisto was unable to take another bite. Then, both stood up slowly from the long dining table, moved out to the hallway, and started for the grand hall.

"I must be leaving Dark. I have business of my own to attend to," his grandfather spoke, placing a hand on his grandson's armored shoulder. "Before I go, I'll tell Teigue he must stay a little while longer. I think both he and the little guy have become quite attached to one another."

"All right, then I go to see the Warlock and ask for his aid," declared Dark abruptly, pointing his finger again, this time at Mephisto. "But when I get back, you're going to have to tell me what it is you are up to, old man."

"Of course I will," the tall wizard promised.

Without further word, both left the richly decorated grand hall, each one traveling by magic means, with Mephisto ending up in his cave standing next to Teigue and the baby

Chimera. Dark appeared outside under a brightly shining sun and a clear blue sky and quickly entered the awaiting *Albatross*, which drifted above the placid blue surface of Dragon's Mouth Lake. It took only a few minutes for them to reach high into the cloudless heavens and soar far beyond the gaze of men until they were just a tiny dot on the horizon. The giant seabird was extremely efficient in the air, traveling many thousands of miles using very little energy from flapping. Repeatedly, the *Albatross*, with its massive wingspan, would pull up into the wind, exposing herself to a rising headwind, then suddenly turn into the other direction and dive back into the shelter of a wave.

In the late hours of the waning afternoon, amid an oncoming cold front that caused the formation of dark clouds, they sailed where no islands lay on the horizon or loomed near. In the distance, he saw a gleaming tower and toward this the *Albatross* flew. When he finally drew near, he was struck in silence. The Tower of Woe was a column of silver, rising straight from the rippling waters; it rose so high that he could not even see the summit. It even appeared to Dark to somehow be holding up the sky as the greying clouds obscured the true height of the towering silver pillar.

Dark's gauntlet-covered hands fastened tightly to the feathered boat as he guided the ancient craft across the swaying waves and, with an abrupt surge, nosed upward. Moving in a sharp arc, they raced for the concealing wall of smoke, oblivious to the hail of silvered arrows that showered down from the top of the monolith. Like a bolt of shimmering moonlight, the arrows streaked toward him, with two stray arrows catching him squarely in the chest, knocking the surprised assassin from his flying mount and into the cold waters of the Sleeping Seas.

"Get out of here, Alba!" Dark exclaimed heatedly, which his faithful flying ship obeyed instantly, wheeling about in the opposite direction toward the safe haven of Sommerset.

Muttering angrily to himself, Dark began to alter the flowing water in the area surrounding him, causing a deadly vortex to form that suddenly exploded him upward in a massive surge. The twisting body of water safely carried Dark atop a frothing wave of thick, blue seawater that rose up like a whirling, cylindrical column. With two silver-shafted arrows still embedded in his chest, he struck back viciously with projectiles of his own. With a circuitous pass of his hand through the air, then whipping them forward with the last words of the spell, he launched a concentrated barrage of sharp-tipped blades of white, hissing energy. With a rush, thousands of deadly missiles filled the sky, sweeping upward through the hazy void to the ramparts of the tower walls and finding their target.

At the summit of the high tower, Dark quickly saw his wounded attacker lying helplessly on the floor of the open landing. It was a woman! She was strikingly beautiful, her slim, graceful figure perfectly proportioned and her skin a creamy white. The female was unmistakably elven with long, dark hair and ears that swept upward to pointed ends, with striking silver eyes that helped define her elegant face. Around her graceful head she wore a silver circlet with matching necklace and armbands, the design light and airy. She was suited in leather armor tanned to a fine grey, and pinned to her white lace corset, now streaked with blood, was a silver broach shaped like a bird in flight. Her cloak, beautifully decorated, was dyed greenish-grey to blend in with the forest and was wrapped tightly around her slender shoulders. In her leather-clad hand was a silver bow embossed with emblems of the moon, while the shaft was engraved with intricate runes that glowed and pulsed with a soft light.

Dark stood motionless, riding atop his churning watery perch, his keen elven eyes quickly running over her small countenance, then he spotted it on his second pass. There, around her neck, dangling delicately from the thin silver necklace, was a pendant with the unmistakable symbol for the House of Greyfell. This was no ordinary Witch Slayer, but the daughter of the ruling King of the Elves and the hated nemesis of his mother's, the Grey Elf. At that moment, hatred ruled him as the anger he held deep inside spewed forth in a leap of rage. His shadow sword's sharp blade extended downward, hunting for warm elven flesh, but instead finding only the bitter taste of cold stone. With the spell broken, the vortex of swirling liquid swayed slightly and then collapsed back down to the sea. As he landed with the agility of a cat, his focus was now turned to his hated enemy. The nimble figure of the Grey Elf had rolled clear of the falling doom and sprang lightning quick to her feet. Trailing large drops of blood behind her, she leapt over the side of the tower's walls and disappeared through the clouds. For a split second, the enraged assassin considered chasing her, but realized immediately what a foolish decision that would be.

The wind whipped bitterly across the exposed landing with a cold numbness that made him feel if he remained outside he would be frozen solid. At the top of the tall spire, an exposed staircase was visible, and through this landing he gained entrance. Dark cautiously and carefully crept down a sweeping stone staircase that led to a great round chamber with the scent of sandalwood that perfumed the air. The circular room was filled with racks holding various scrolls, stacks of dusty books, and ancient grimores bound in black leather. Around the room, hanging on the walls, was a collection of old paintings, and on a large desk, a pile of papers, an inkwell, several quills, and a thick-lighted candle flickered. The ceiling rose some thirty feet overhead, which gave the chamber an open sense of majesty, and painted on its surface was a mural depicting the goddess of death and magic. Glowing orbs filled with blue fire hung on black chains, providing ample light from exposed wooden rafters. An altar stood at the far end of the room, and inscribed on a silk banner hanging behind it was a strange seal; on either side were brass braziers filled with sweet-smelling incense. An impossibly tall, ornate mirror stood in the very center, and next to it, on the floor, a recently deceased body lay twitching with two silver arrows protruding from both eyes amid a growing pool of blood surrounding the grisly mass.

The fresh corpse was an aged man, heavy-browed and white-bearded; it was the Warlock Vainamöinen. Dark paused only an instant to glance down at the two arrows still buried in his broad chest and slowly withdrew the deadly bolts, casting the weapons away in disgust, then moved on toward the altar. The lingering echo of booted feet on rock was the only sound made as he moved around the dead wizard; his eyes wandered briefly to his own reflection in the tall mirror. Finally, he halted before the hand-carved wooden altar, his eyes traveling instantly to the object of his pursuit—the small, shape-changing creature that rested atop a silken pillow.

Sleek sat as a figure of a woman made from gleaming bone. Her hair was curled in the finest of tendrils; her face was that of a young, beautiful goddess and her body curved sweetly. The wondrous figure returned his gaze with blank ivory eyes that stared with mindless disregard. Dark stood watching fixedly as her lips formed into a smile and, stepping from her pedestal, the statue entered his arms. Suddenly, the maiden's beautiful face turned, her pale skin sprouted black fur while her lips stretched and widened into a ferocious snarl as her pearly teeth lengthened into sharpened fangs. From her throat came the menacing growl of a black panther. The lashing tail wrapped around his arm, then transformed itself into a three-headed constricting snake. At last, the shape-shifter's powers of metamorphosis came to a rest as the cold, scaly body hardened to steel and became one with his armor.

Turning back, he slowly walked over to the immensely tall mirror and saw that his wounds had healed completely and the holes in his armor would be whole again by morning. A deathly silence seemed to grip the frozen assassin as he eyes locked on the dark figure who stood motionless on the other side of the mirror and was not his own reflection. The black apparition had a tall, thin body, a transparent black with a ghost-like hue that slightly shimmered. From out of the shade's mouth came the low-moaning cries of an imprisoned soul, the voice less than human and chill with death.

"Free me from my glass cell and I shall gladly serve thee, my young Master," the shadow pronounced the words with an unpleasant hiss.

The unbelieving assassin looked about in stunned nihilism, then his face turned back toward the shadow that stood trapped before him. "And why should I release you. I am content with my own shadow and have no need for another."

"Because, my Master, I possess the ultimate powers a wizard could possess and a mortal's shadow cannot," the chill voice spoke again.

Dark looked at the black shadow for a brief moment as if to object, but instead smiled wickedly and nodded in approval. "I shall release you, but upon such condition that you shall teach me and fulfill my desires in all things."

Without waiting for a response, Dark drew a circle nine feet in diameter, using the sharp claws of his steel gauntlet to entrench the ground around him. Closed within, he placed a smaller five-pointed star with ancient formulas and protective words derived from diverse ancient sources. He remembered the most important requirement in completing the binding ritual was that the circle be unbroken. In the space within the circle of protection, the conjurer's inspiration was mightily concentrated; the line that formed the circle became a defensive barrier against the soon-to-be released creature. Standing within, he began chanting, calling upon an underworld prince whose name was Asmodeus.

"*Bagabi laca bachabe*," the formula began. "*Lamac cahi achahabe*."

A wind rose suddenly inside the chamber, so strong that it sent a large desk with papers and books crashing into the far wall. A drumroll of thunder was heard, then the sound died away. The mirror seemed to open at its center, and from out of its glass confines rose the black wraith who quickly appeared at the very rim of the circle drawn in the floor.

"Will you step outside your circle, young Master?" the shadow drifted restlessly around the room.

Dark refused, there was a resigned sigh, and the shade finally asked, "Then what is your request?"

"Leaving me unharmed, you come to me freely, so I wish to make a pact with you."

"I am bound to do so," the shadow replied, then sank slowly into the assassin's own shadow and Dark found himself alone again.

XVII

Dark was instantaneously transported to his new floating home and, when he opened his black elven eyes, he was standing in the grand hall. From the corner of his eye he saw a familiar black-robed figure, an unmistakable look of smugness crossed over the mystic's bearded features.

"Hello Dark."

The mocking sound of his name interrupted the sudden silence in a broken whisper. The armored assassin turned slowly toward his grandfather and stared blankly about the massive hall at a dragon's horde scattered on the ground. Lying across a floor littered with winking jewels and gold that glittered, the new Lord of Dark Manor found his multi-headed pet. Shifting beneath his belly were piles of coins, ruby-studded necklaces, and various other valuable trinkets and bobbles in a wide assortment of precious metals.

"Is that my silver candlesticks . . . and my gold jewelry box from my private chambers?" Dark exclaimed incredulously.

"I believe it is," Mephisto teased, patting his grandson on the back.

"And why did you let him do this?" Dark muttered, quietly confused.

"Well, it's not my stuff," the old magus said, shrugging his shoulders while smiling wryly, then walked over to stand in front of the locked black chest of the Dogai, as eager as a child awaiting a present on his birthday. "Now, my young grandson, shall we proceed with the unveiling?"

For a moment there was no response at all.

"I should take your stuff . . . and sit on it . . . see how you'd like it," Dark muttered dryly under his breath.

"What was that, Dark?" Mephisto interjected quickly.

His bitter grandson shook his head in a hopeless, resigned manner, and the conversation dropped off again.

"Nothing," Dark was already standing next to him, his mask now off and safely stowed away.

"Well then, let's get on with it," the endless enchanter brushed the response aside abruptly.

Dark paused for a second, and in the distance heard the chimes of a large, ornate clock echoing loudly from the mantle above a large fireplace as it announced the hour.

"Sleek, if you would be so kind," he asked, smiling politely.

Sleek, still a part of Dark's armor, began to stir; first opening his eyes, he then squinted before raising his three snake heads and looking slowly about. Glancing down, they saw the tail of the snake, previously immobile, unravel itself from his armored arm and slowly, in a reaching motion, extend its scaly limb and place the tip into the box's keyhole. Both Dark and his grandfather did not move; they did not speak. They simply waited.

"Is this going to work?" he asked anxiously.

"I don't know," came the short reply.

"What do you mean you don't know . . . whatever!"

The once-dark surface of the Chest of the Dogai suddenly began to glow; the skilfully engraved pentagrams lit up a dully red, and each one in a different sequence. Finally, with the last of the markings lighted, a loud click resounded throughout the huge grand hall and the black gemstone box opened. Now unlocked, the container revealed not just a glass egg, but an object of art. Stylistic in technical perfection, the crystal was clear and blemish-free. The glass was ribbed with vines, and hand engraved on its clear surface a majestic crown sat. The outer shell was banded in noble metals of gold and silver with adornments of precious diamonds, rubies, and pearls. Inside was a translucent golden yolk that contained the still-beating heart of the Shadow Lord.

The black chest closed, and the contents were sealed once again as the shape-shifting Sleek removed its serpentine tail and fell back around Dark's arm. The silent pair broke into broad smiles of relief.

"So, now what do we do with it?" Dark asked flatly.

"I would not concern yourself with it now," Mephisto soothed, placing a lean hand on his grandson's shoulder.

"When the time comes for you to finally face the Shadow Lord, then and only then will you need its use."

Dark looked over at his grandfather and nodded in agreement, and the conversation dropped off again.

"Wait!" Mephisto jerked him around so sharply it sent Dark spinning to the floor. "Sorry . . . strength of a dragon—sometimes I forget." He paused a moment to help his grandson to his feet. "Now wait right here, I won't be gone long!"

The old wizard turned away abruptly and disappeared down the hallway almost at a full run, as if possessed by some spirit. Dark and the now suddenly awake Baron all watched him go without comment. Then, without missing a beat, the little Chimera laid its many heads down and went back to sleep. Noiselessly, Mephisto dashed into the library of Dark Manor and, without pausing, retrieved a book of old lore and legends and quickly rejoined Dark.

"You wanted to know what I've been up to," he spoke with heavy breath, slamming the thick book down onto the table. He then flipped through a plethora of beautiful, gold-leaf pages, until finally his hand stopped and his lean finger pointed to a specific passage. "I came across this while I was perusing Mur's . . . I mean your, extensive library."

Dark leaned over; his elven eyes scanned the title of the passage, trying hard to figure out its importance to him and how this children's story could possibly help him in his quest for vengeance.

"The One with the White Hand . . . a story told to frighten little children, so what?"

"Do you remember that night I came to you in the early hours of the morning and I told you I had to leave on business," Mephisto began again. "I went that night to meet with a man Circe said had information of the utmost importance. So I met with this man, an assassin named Fhaminn Dread, a high-level guild member from the City of Duergar. How he came about this information he did not say, but what he did say was the Grim Reaper, head of the Assassins' Guild, has obtained a most foul and heinous weapon—a scythe called

Reapers Revenge that can steal a man's soul with just a simple scratch from its ghoulish blade."

"Circe, the Sorceress . . . of the Order?" Dark asked hesitantly. "How do we know we can trust her, let alone the order, anymore?"

"We don't . . . at least not yet. But if there is any truth in her validity and the Grim Reaper has such a device for the harvesting of souls, we must act upon it," his grandfather answered quietly, his voice stern. "And in this children's story we have found our defense."

"What defense?" the grandson of the silver dragon asked anxiously.

"A wooden heart," the ancient historian replied, then he continued after a slight pause. "The story tells how individual trees and shrubs have their own inhabitants and serve as homes and shelters for a host of creatures since the earliest of times. Nymphs, also known as dryads, meaning tree, would have their bodies merge with bark and leaves so that if the tree were to be cut down, the nymph too would perish. The passage tells a tale of a willow faërie who walked in the world of mortals by day, retreating each night to her sorrowful tree. One day she met and married a mortal; a few years later she bore him a beautiful child and lived happily until one fateful morning. Now country folk rarely ventured into the shadowy woodlands, fearful of what might lurk beyond the borders of their narrow world. But on this day, the nymph's husband unwittingly entered her forest home. There he found a large willow and unknowingly chopped down her tree; the faërie died at once. Her grieving husband made two items from the willow tree—a cradle that had the power to lull the nymph's son to instant sleep, and the second was a wooden heart to hold and protect the little boy's soul. But as soon as the husband finished, the Elder Mother came and coldly murdered him and stole away the child."

"Who is the Elder Mother?" Dark queried shortly.

"She is a guardian spirit, a protector of trees," Mephisto's deep-set eyes twinkled beneath his brow as the ancient storyteller continued with his tale. “She is as pale and gaunt as a birch tree; her hands white as snow with spider legs for fingers. And if she touches your head, you go mad. And if she touches your chest, you die. After the death of the willow faërie, the One with the White Hands would now wander up and down the lanes of nearby towns, her feet falling silent on the cobblestones. Those unfortunate enough to catch a glimpse of her said that she wore green of an ancient tree spirit; in her arms she bore a sickly child.”

“She sounds fun, when do I get to meet her?” Dark spoke in jest, playfully slapping the all-too-serious narrator on the shoulder.

“Whenever you are ready,” the sage of Sommerset responded in kind. “She and the heart can be found in a forest beside the rolling hills of Dundee, in Scotland.”

“Why does that name sound so familiar?” Dark asked after a moment’s silent thought.

He paused and looked squarely over to his grandson. “Dundee is where your father was born.”

“Well, I always did want to see where he came from. I guess I’ll find out tomorrow,” replied Dark.

Only minutes later, while the two companions continued talking, the Baron was awake once again. Seeing his master was home, he suddenly rose, and before long all three of the Chimera’s heads were licking Dark with wet tongues.

“I see someone’s awake,” Dark said, pulling his hand back sharply as the dragon’s head bit him playfully. “You must be hungry. I know I’m hungry, so let’s go eat . . . you too, old man.”

Dark motioned for them both to follow him and moved away from the grand hall, drawing them down the hallway and into the dining room. He seated himself in a regal chair at the head of the table, waved to his grandfather to find a place, and easily got his young pet to sit. The master of the manor called for food and drink, and his faithful unseen servants obliged him with a great feast. All three ate like kings while Dark and Mephisto spoke at great length for several more hours as they stuffed their faces with wine and roasted lamb. There was little talk after the meal, and each one bade the other goodnight, then they rolled themselves into their comfortable beds and soon fell sound asleep.

The sleeping assassin was gently awakened by the nudging of several sniffing noses from his peaceful slumber to the unpleasant chill of the early morning. He quickly dressed himself in the armor that Lödd Strongblows had skilfully fashioned for him, then silently packed his gear and prepared to begin another journey. Within half an hour, he had gulped down a short breakfast and, with the breaking of another dawn, was soon heading northward on the back of the enchanted flying vessel.

His journey was a short one, aided by conjured winds that propelled them at three times the giant seabird's normal speed. Over calm waters and under a clear sky they flew on to Albion and ever further north into Scotland and past the stone boundary wall that divided the two territories. Their journey took them over a spur of high-peaked mountains that extended from the Highland range to the North Sea and across incised valleys and lochs carved by the action of rushing mountain streams. At the edge of a pinewood forest, he motioned for the *Albatross* to land next to a visible winding path. Dark disembarked his landed vessel and, with a thank you and a pat on her feathery shoulder, he sent Alba flying home. Then, with a word, he summoned his fiery black steed. Nightmare moved them along at a rapid pace through a winding mass of great trees and heavy foliage that became increasingly thicker as they penetrated deeper into the hills of Scotland.

The Highlands consisted of scattered villages girdled by pastures and fields of oats, millet, and barley. The people were simple farmers and sheep herders, their lives ordered by the rhythms of nature, the spring growth, the summer ripening, and the autumn bounty that brings with it sustenance for the harsh, hungry days of winter. Their existence was bound as well by the traits of the forests that encircled each hamlet.

As Dark rode, he came to a dirt track that led across golden fields of barley, down a valley, and into a wooded forest. The tract through the wood was broad and sunny, but as he followed it, the air seemed to darken and ancient trees formed a vault of shadows over his head. From time to time, he would stop and listen, but heard nothing; the silence was altogether eerie. He felt the unpleasant sensation that the trees were aware of his presence and, with eyes hidden in the denseness of the forest, watched him and waited. The track ended abruptly as Dark had come to a clearing, a small meadow bright with daisies sitting next to a still lake burdened by willows that drooped over mournfully. In the center of this clearing, standing tall and majestic, swaying rhythmically in the cool breeze, was a wide-spreading birch tree.

On the far side of the grassy meadow was a road lined with burning torches and thronged with shouting people that swept into the little clearing. The mob turned toward the single tree where Dark stood, but quickly he turned invisible before any could see him. Screaming, they drew up to him, a column of peasants carrying scythes and axes on their shoulders, but they could not see him, for the ring of invisibility protected him. He watched as the jostling throng fell to the task of cutting down the lone tree. Although the sun was shining, the birch tree felt icy as one of the brave villagers touched it with his hand before the blade of his axe sank into the white bark. The Elder Mother appeared in full-blown fury, as pale and gaunt as her tree home with her cheek cut deep and spilling red with blood. No one could mistake the unearthly light in the crone's eyes; she was one of the elder races who had long ago ruled the world and still retained formidable powers.

At first, her pale face only peered at them, drifting lightly on the wind. Then the villagers were made well aware of the faërie threat. The nymph moved toward them and gave a howl like the roaring of a winter sea. A white, rail-thin arm reached with spider-leg fingers in the air, clutching at the axe wielder's chest. When she placed her white hand over his heart, his appearance became haggard and grey in death; his lips became dry and split over a gaping black mouth as shadows now filled empty eye sockets. The rioting villagers fell silent and scared, dropping their weapons and torches as well as their bravery. They turned tail and ran wildly for their very lives through the thorny tangle of brush and hedges.

The One with the White Hand now turned back to her tree, standing tall and slender, the panels of her green dress billowing about her feet and a wooden heart held in one hand. The ancient spirit instantly saw the black-horned assassin and stopped. Her white face gazed at Dark with pale, piercing eyes. Then as if from very far away, a terrible, high-pitched scream broke the silence. As she drew closer, her screaming grew louder and more strident, her face contorting in awful agony. The Elder Mother moved toward her new prey until Dark could see the whites of her cold eyes staring into his as her merciless fingers sank hard around his neck. Upon feeling her spidery touch, his shadowy blade fell and severed the tree in two; her white hands relaxed their cruel grip on his throat. He watched as her figure became as tenuous as a ghost's, and then she faded and finally vanished amid a fine shadow of black ash that filtered gently to the ground where she had last stood.

Gently, he plucked the wooden object free from the ashen ground. As he cradled it in his palm, he could hear all around him the faint voices of children singing, slowly rising steadily toward the heavens. With the last of the singing voices fading, he turned and walked noiselessly away, and then he, too, simply vanished.

XVIII

Dark instantaneously arrived back at his cloud castle, which was still floating high above Dragon's Mouth Lake just as the sun sank beneath the rim of Mephisto's mountain home to the west. The solemn assassin casually made his way down the long, carpeted hallway to the dining room; the sound of utensils grating against golden plates along with the familiar voices of Teigue and his grandfather idly chatting could be heard in the distance. As Dark entered the room, he could see Mephisto seated at the head of a long table surrounded by platters of food. Beside him, Teigue was sitting cross-legged on the table, a thimble of red wine being consumed rapidly. And off in the corner, the Baron slept, belly up with drool sliding down all four opened mouths.

"Teigue, you're not eating," interrupted the still-masked assassin.

"You know me, Dark, I'd much rather fill up on wine than fill up on food," Teigue responded, his speech slightly slurred as his head turned to see his youthful friend. "Besides, isn't wine made from grapes, and that's a food . . . right?"

"I take it you were successful," broke in Mephisto, a half-eaten leg of lamb held tightly in his greasy hands while his mouth was covered in a thick, brown sauce.

Dark reached into the fanged mouth of his demon-faced armor and produced a small, hand-carved wooden heart that now beat as if it were somehow alive and functioning.

"Yes, I have the Heart of the Willow Nymph," Dark said with a smile. "And now there is but one item left for me to obtain."

"Ah yes, the Eye of Dagda," his grandfather answered respectively.

"The Eye of Dagda . . . not bloody likely!" Teigue hiccupped, his words slightly choked as wine dribbled down the sides of his reddened mouth. "I'm sorry Dark, but locating the tomb of the first Faërie King is quite impossible. The borders of the other world are forever shifting and transitory, making it impenetrable to most, if not all, mortals."

"What about the gem of location?" the assassin asked softly. "Why can't I just use Finders Keepers?"

A silent unseen servant pulled out a chair for his master to sit, while another invisible phantom moved over to his side and placed a steaming plate of food on the table in front of him.

"The final resting place for the High King of the Tuatha Dé Danann cannot be found by the simple magic of mortal men," Teigue's voice again choked sharply as he downed his drink with ragged gulps. "His remains lay in a world that is constantly moving, a world that might be found at the turn of a path through a forest or at the edge of the sea or even beneath the waters of a lake. Therefore, there is no way for you to get there, absolutely no way whatsoever."

Mechanically, Dark slowly sat down and began nibbling at his meal, trying hard to think of a solution to his dilemma, then absently turned his gaze toward his grandfather.

"There is one way." Mephisto, who had now finished his meal, was already puffing on his smoking pipe and blew the grisly image of a hanged man.

"I thought that was just an old wives' tale," his grandson responded in turn, his movements no longer mechanical.

"No, it is as real as you or I," responded Mephisto seriously after a few more puffs on his silver pipe. "On Samain Eve, the border between this world and the other world becomes as thin as paper, thus allowing the dead a brief moment in time to reach back through the shrouded veil that separates them from the living. At such chinks in time, placing a plait of twigs around the ankle of a dead man hanging on the gallows will awaken him once more. Then, he will be able to show you where the gateway to the secret Kingdom of Faërie lies hidden. But having touched a corpse on the night of the dead, it will hold you in its power until it sees the day's first light."

Dark stared at him incredulously.

"I know," his grandfather continued gently, shrugged, and smiled faintly. "But the summer months will pass quickly, and the magic the eye possesses is well worth the wait."

The assassin frowned, looking unconvinced. "I only hope its powers are worth the wait."

Mephisto paused, then stirred unexpectedly and quickly stood up and moved next to his brooding grandson and seated himself, his face slightly bowed. "The Eye of Dagda once belonged to a dragon named Vipera," Mephisto began again as he exhaled a great billow of smoke that turned into a crowned dragon, "a magnificent creature, as bejeweled as the fabulous treasure it was said to have guarded. Its luminous scales sparkled like diamonds; atop its horned head it wore a diadem of pearls, and in the very center of its forehead was a blood-red jewel that served as its single eye. One night each year, it was said, the creature became vulnerable. Near the ruins of an abbey in a mountain grotto, the beast would bathe in a still, clear lake. When it entered the water, it removed its precious red carbuncle and placed the stone on the ground. One day, in its blinded state, one of the four faërie princes was brave enough to approach the beast and actually steal the eye. Arawn, youngest of the king's sons, presented it to his father as a gift to help him see through the illusions of man."

"That's exactly right!" the outburst came from the tiny faërie who had succumbed to the effects of the red wine, a numbing drowsiness that seeped slowly through his body causing him to fall asleep again.

Mephisto and Dark exchanged startled looks, then both turned sharply to see Teigue, who somehow had been stripped bare of his regal vestments and now lay naked in a drunken repose on the dining table. Neither one said a word; each one's awkward gaze shifting back to focus on some imaginary point in front of them.

"Please continue," soothed the dark assassin.

"Anyway, the king took the eye and infused it with his own powerful magic and forged a new item of legacy," the ancient historian twisted his words meaningfully as he spoke, creating moving scenes with a quick puff of his long pipe. "Not only does the eye see that which cannot be seen, but it can project an illusion to surround its weaver so real, so life-like that all who would gaze upon you would see only that which you wish them to see. By no means, even magical, can its illusion be broken and, as your own abilities and talents progress, so too will those of the eye. Finally, once you have acquired the Eye of Dagda, I will teach you how to unlock the relic's potential and awaken its quiescent power with the ancient rituals of the Tuatha Dé Danann."

"So with this talisman of the High King, I could take on any form I choose," Dark replied quickly, "even Kalifen's—and no one would see that it was actually me behind this illusion . . . even with magical aid?"

"Precisely," the other acknowledged, "even inanimate objects—like being part of a stone wall, a table or chair, or even a living tree. Its powers are limitless and, in time, as you gain some degree of control over its abilities, you will begin to understand that this object has untapped potential."

"Then it is well worth the wait," Dark conceded. "But once again, you have me waiting . . . and what will I do until then?"

His voice died away in a weary murmur as he turned, looked upward, and stared transfixed at the painted picture on the ceiling. For a few brief moments no one spoke, then their silence was broken by the drunk and still naked little faërie whose faint whimpers sounded like a dog crying, his legs pumping furiously like he was running in his dream.

"For the moment do nothing, you have earned your rest," Mephisto smiled warmly, occasionally glancing over at the nude emissary of the Faërie King that left him to simply shake his head. "Besides, you should take this opportunity to hone up on your skills before you enter Duergar."

The young half-elf looked at his grandfather and nodded in agreement. Mephisto rose silently, stretching his tall frame to relieve his stiff, aching muscles and yawning loudly. His grandson rose with him and stood tacitly as he looked quickly over at his pet Chimera, who was still sleeping soundly.

"Why don't we go play a game or two of chess and you can tell me all about your latest adventure?"

Gathering his robes about his gaunt form, he reached over with one great hand and gripped Dark's armored shoulder, then turned away with him and, in the blink of an eye, both were gone.

For the months leading up to Samain Eve, the assassin remained in Sommerset during the long summer days, occupying some of his time with hunting and a new pastime, hawking, in the forests around his floating home. At night, he would feast with his grandfather in the firelit royal dining hall of Dark Manor, listening to invisible piper's music and ancient tales of the power of faërie folk. Night after night, Dark would challenge Mephisto at chess, playing the game of warfare with gold and silver men. Also during this period, he would do his daily regimen of exercise, meditation, and furthering his skill in the secret art of assassination, as well as the study of the arcane arts. And every morning till he was to leave, the son of Solus would pick wildflowers and place them on his parent's graves, his oath to them still as of yet unfulfilled.

The summer months had ended none too soon, for it was Samain Eve and the forest floor was finally ankle deep in fallen leaves. Dark awoke right away; his eyes snapped open at the sound of dawn breaking. The morning sunlight filtered down on him through stained-glass windows. He quickly came to a sitting position, squinting sharply around the brightly lit room, and saw that Baron was awake and ready to go outside. Over the last few months, it seemed the little Chimera had a growth spurt in both height and weight and now stood high enough so his shoulders reached Dark's waist. Upon his awakening, the intricately carved doors to his bedroom were politely opened after a soft knocking and, on large silk pillows, his armor, weapons, and equipment came floating into his kingly chambers, carried by several of his unseen servants. Once dressed in his black assassin's garb, Dark made his way to the landing at the top of the staircase and moved down the polished stone steps with his unholy pet in tow. When he entered the dining hall, he found Mephisto perched forward on one of the dining chairs blankly studying a map. Off to one side was a cooling plate of food that was strangely untouched.

"You know you're here so much I think I should start charging you rent," Dark exclaimed in greeting and seated himself next to the surprised old wizard.

"I can't help it," he answered truthfully, glancing at his grandson. "You have servants; it's like being on permanent vacation."

"What do you have there?" he asked with a slight smirk forming, quickly changing the subject.

"This is a map of the Emerald Isle with its five Celtic Kingdoms," the silver mage replied slowly. "The city of Ulster in the north, Connacht in the west, Leinster in the east, and the two Munsters bordering east and west at the southern tip of the island. And here, near Connacht," Mephisto now pointed to the west side on the map, "far from the city's gates on a grassy moor, this is where you will find your hanged man."

"And how is it that you came to know all of this?" he questioned suddenly, his black eyes narrowing in skeptical cynicism.

"By an old friend of your mother's, Maeve, the Warrior Queen of Connacht," the other exclaimed quickly. "Without questioning my strange request, she informed me, several days prior to the hanging, of a man found guilty of thievery."

Mephisto paused for a brief moment and looked to Dark to see if he had forgotten anything. The eager assassin grinned at his grandfather and then placed the large gem of location back into the black void of the fanged mouth of the demon face.

"Then I guess I won't need this," he acknowledged. "So when should I leave?"

"The ritual must be performed under the light of the moon, so you must leave before twilight's end," the ancient mystic explained. "And remember, it must be completed before the witching hour has begun."

He smiled quickly at Dark, who nodded soberly.

"Here, you'll need this." From beneath the sleeve of his voluminous robes, he brought forth a tough, supple twig from a weeping willow tree. "Use this to bind his ankle."

Taking hold of the long, flexible withe, Dark stowed it safely away, then summoned his staff to serve him his morning breakfast. As he ate, Mephisto related to him strange tales about the Tuatha Dé Danann—how they were an ancient and kingly warrior race that were unpredictable, that their powers were great and to be feared, especially on this night. On this night, he warned, all mortal rules were suspended and chaos reigned. For on Samain Eve, before the seasons changed, the faëries traveled abroad, their powers at their peak. He also told Dark to make his exit from the world of the Tuatha Dé Danann as quickly as possible. If he stayed past the dawn's first light, he would be trapped within the boundaries of Faërie, where one day there is equivalent to one year here.

Dark listened quietly through the series of long tales and wise reminders, all the while nodding with a perpetual half smile and the occasional nod. By the time his grandfather finished, it was growing late and he was eager to begin his long journey to the fabled Island of Ireland. Donning his mask and with his preparations complete, he closed his eyes, and when he opened them again he was seated in the cockpit of the *Albatross*. It was a dull, sunless day, a day that was damp and chilling to the bone. Dark found it even more so when they journeyed northward through the misty grey clouds in the cheerless sky, the sun still hiding its shining warmth. As the two traveled past the boundaries of Sommerset, the *Albatross* straightened her long, massive wings, moved gracefully over the roughening waters below, and soon faded off into the distance.

They sailed on for hours out over the Sea of Wonder, voyaging north all day and well into the night, trying to reach the Emerald Isle before midnight. Dark saw its outline several hours before the witching hour, just west of Albion, separated by the Irish Sea. He signaled to the *Albatross*; the sea bird then swooped down and slipped toward the shore and drifted with the wind over a ring of coastal mountains. Dark could see that the island was largely a mountainous and rocky region with dramatic green vistas filled with lush vegetation, which earned it the attributive name "The Emerald Isle."

Guided by moonlight, they soon saw in the distance the gallows tree upon the moor, where two paths met. He could see a long, black, forked shape swinging from what looked like an arm with its feet tapping gently against the thick, wooden trunk. Next to the moor was Lake Killarney, and they steered for it. Within moments, the *Albatross* slid quietly into an estuary of water so clear he could see the darting of scarlet salmon that played there. Dark made his way for a shore fringed with trees, and from their midst flowed out the carols of unknown birds. His dark figure stepped gingerly down from the giant seabird coming to stand in an apprehensive watchfulness as he stared through the grey mist that surrounded them. There was an absolute eerie silence that seemed to filter evilly through the wispy smoke, leaving an unspoken warning of death hanging in his mind.

Dark approached the hill where the living cross bore its creaking burden like ripened fruit, with only a faint wind stirring the dead leaves as he made his way to the gallows tree. The outline of the tree stood stark against the starry sky; a bundle of bones with stiffened legs was swaying gently in the breeze. From the stout branch dangled the body of a thief who had been hanged days before, its sightless eyes bulging and a blackened tongue protruding from the mouth. The assassin was relieved to see no one had cut him down, but no wise person would ever dare to touch a corpse on Samain Eve. But Dark did. He approached the hanged man without hesitation, removed the withe from the black void of the demon's mouth, and tied it around one stiffened leg. Clasping the right foot, he could feel the dents where it had been pecked and pitted with holes by black crows. Then, when he had done so, he asked the dead thief what he desired of him. The hanged man kicked out violently, sending Dark flying to the ground as the bones began to lurch about, as if it were being battered by a storm. Then, there came a low groan—not from the hanging corpse, but from the ground beneath it.

"Carry me to water," the dull voice of the corpse spoke above his head. "I was thirsty when I died."

"Take me to the tomb of the Faërie King, and you shall have your fill!" Dark exclaimed brazenly, still clutching the dead man's foot.

"Agreed," was the moaning reply.

Without further comment, he cut the body down; as quick as it fell it was up even quicker with legs wrapped around his waist and cold, dead arms around his neck. A guttural chuckle sounded with malevolence in his elven ears.

"Forward," said the hanged man.

Although he was now the dead man's tool and in its power, Dark had now acquired the corpse's vision, and so he too saw sights invisible to mortal eyes. Without a thought, Dark followed the directions given by the thief and walked forward along a track that twisted through hills and walls of large rocks. He walked for what seemed hours, his way illuminated by the full moon and by the glowing points of stars that pricked the sky. At last, the track seemed to narrow as he followed the dead man to an archway in the rock; a flight of stone steps lay just beyond.

In the archway, Dark stopped and with his light load stared out over another country, realizing at once this was no ordinary place. Spread before him as far as the eye could see were venerable and mighty oaks with apple trees that grew in abundance, heavily laden with scarlet globes. Also among them stood many hazel trees with clusters of yellow nuts, and stretching out far and wide was a smooth plain, cloaked in the green and white leaves of flowering clover. Above his head was a rosy sky where faint stars glittered silver in celestial patterns he did not recognize. In the midst of the field, a great stone staircase stood open in the grassy floor. Dark cautiously approached the crevice and peered down into the void of darkness he was soon to enter. Slowly, step by narrow step, the assassin descended down the winding stone stairs until the patterns of stonework that formed it were clearly defined. The staircase opened up at last into a twilight world with groves of trees that shone as if it were bathed under starlight. Behind the spreading groves was a great underground lake, a giant black sheet of shimmering water, and at its center arose an island spanned by a bridge of solid brass.

The corpse climbed down from Dark's back, crawled across the dirt floor to the shoreline of the black lake, and gulped heavily from its dark waters. Then, the horned assassin cautiously crossed the bridge of brass and finally made his way to where the tomb of the High King of the Tuatha Dé Danann rested.

High above the island, light glared down from no evident source and wild music soared up around him, played by no musicians. At its center was a circular pool of green; its waters were shallow around the edges but rapidly deepened to several feet toward the middle. The pool was covered by a central octagon of sculpted marble, buttressed by eight pillars, each one adorned with stylized carvings of curled leaves and flowers. The Tomb of Dagda, the Faërie King, stood under the starry vault of the octagon. His statue lay in full regalia with hands clasped around the hilt of an ornate sword and his head resting on a pillow under elaborately ornamental baldachins. The coat of arms for the House of Dagda was placed on top of this canopy of state, together with the insignia of the High King of the Tuatha Dé Danann. On the cover plate of the stone and marble tomb was inscribed, in repetition, the motto of the king, "*Ad eundum quo nemo ante iit*." Surrounding the octagon were twenty-four suits of gold plate mail, the armor shiny and well-kept. Even though they had outlived their master, the king's faithful magical guardians still stood at the ready and, although the armor was entirely empty, a faint green light seemed to flare up through the joints.

With relaxed, easy strides, Dark proceeded toward the king's tomb, his sharp elven eyes glancing uneasily at the steel sentinels and looking for any signs of movement. A moment later, he was past the edge of the pool and began walking atop its green water as if he were moving over dry land. Once again, his own eyes cast about anxiously for some sign of movement from the surrounding golden guardians as his clawed hand came to rest upon the huge, heavy marble lid of the stone coffin. With a great surge of strength from the Belt of Heroes, the lid moved. A great rush of stale air blasted Dark's senses, revealing for the first time in two thousand years the perfectly preserved body of the Faërie King.

The ruler of the Tuatha Dé Danann showed his ancestry in his unearthly beauty. The Dagda was a most handsome man; he was tall for a faërie with broad shoulders, with his hair as dark as a blackbird's tail. He wore a blue mantle with ornate clasps of red gold; his tunic was a misty mountain white, embroidered with golden animals; his long shield was chased silver and his sword gleamed with precious stones. On one royal shoulder perched a mechanical golden bird, and above the other was the famous red carbuncle of the dragon Vipera.

Woodenly, Dark moved over top of the fallen Faërie King, and his steel-clad hand closed firmly around the precious gem. He paused, his keen elven ears straining to hear any sound that dared stir. Then, slowly, he drew forth the last of his quested items, the Eye of Dagda.

"At long last my journey has finally come to an end," he silently murmured to himself, trying to close the eye on his ring, but his attempt at invisibility failed. "Well, shite."

Gazing carefully around, the black-garbed assassin assured himself that no one else was about, then darted silently over the pool's placid waters and melted instantly into the shadows of the stone pillar. For a long moment, he remained completely invisible. There, he raised his head cautiously and with keen eyes peered down the empty bridge, making certain the plate mail constructs did not move. Once again, he listened carefully for a few moments longer; he concluded the slight sound he heard was nothing more than his overactive imagination. Then, feeling a little foolish, he started to stroll confidently out from beneath the octagon canopy. As he began reaching with one foot forward, he hesitated for a split second, his elven ears fastened on the silent lake behind him.

The still surface of the black lake began to bubble upward, as billows of dark smoke poured out in gradually thickening amounts, followed by a scalding hot lick of flame that tasted his backside. As he turned, he could see high above him a fleeting shape that stood black against the cloudy vapors, its movement like a snake. A second serpentine shape shot out of the depths of the water's misty surface, then a third, fourth, and fifth swelled up like genies from a bottle until, finally, six now towered over him. Scales glittered through the smoky veil as Dark discerned a multi-headed monster that grappled with itself and flared fire from black nostrils. It was a Hydra, a creature that poisoned the Eorth and air making fields sterile; it devoured the livestock that nourished mankind as well as being known for viciously slaughtering mortals.

Six long, scaly snouts thrust forth from the vapor, and the assassin found himself regarded by eyes the size and color of yellow lemons and veiled by blinking, filmy lids. But Dark stood motionless like a man turned to stone. With cold, oily eyes the Hydra observed him; its hot, fiery breath blasted his masked cheek.

"Stop breathing on me, you ugly bastard!" Dark exploded as his steel-gauntleted fist connected with a deafening crunch to the jaw of one of the Hydra's six heads, sending it crashing into a second head in a concussed daze.

Each one of the hideous creature's six mouths gaped wide and let loose an ear-shattering roar, with howls of pain and anger, spitting black venom and white froth from its many mouths. All six horned heads lashed out and issued, in streams from cruel, sharp, fanged jaws, a flood of foul-smelling, flaming liquid. Fire sprang up, spontaneously engulfing his entire armored frame. It seemed like nothing could quench the crackle of the searing-hot flames. When the steady stream of fire finally subsided, the beast saw that the assassin was still standing; it bared its teeth and crouched for the kill. But Dark was quicker. With his eyes aglow with battle fury, he quickly took the black baton and launched himself skyward. In the air, he reacted instantly, letting loose an icy sphere of blue energy that blasted outward from the silvery mouth of the Dragon's Breath wand. A huge burst of cold frost washed out over the Hydra, flash-freezing two of the monster's black, scaly heads, instantly turning them into solid ice. As he fell back down to Eorth, his unbreakable pole impacted solidly with the two frozen heads, shattering them into thousands of sparkling shards.

The creature gave a bellowed scream as it staggered back into the shadowy waters of the lake, its remaining heads writhing back and forth in great pain. The massive, glossy, serpentine beast shot another angered hiss, its hideous fangs slicing toward the dark assassin. The Hydra's humongous body twisted and flexed as it reared out of the water. Infuriated, it took several thunderous steps toward him, but Dark darted easily out of harm's way and quickly countered and stabbed like a stinging wasp, always remaining out of reach of slashing teeth. Again and again, it struck powerfully at the lightning-quick half-elf, missing by inches as its intended victim dove to one side. The hydra struck with such force that it smashed the octagon canopy and stone tomb, causing deadly fragments of rock to shower the entire chamber.

Dark fell back against the brass bridge as the massive attacker loomed above him before snapping again at his agile form. As one of the huge serpent's heads came roaring down, tendrils of pure darkness rose silently from the ground, quickly surrounding the assassin to conceal him from his monstrous foe. Before the fanged mouth could strike, the swirling wisps of shade that obscured Dark's form dragged him down into the creature's own hulking shadow. Instantly, his lithe form leaped out of the darkness below, his shadow sword slicing in a wide arc as it severed in one powerful swing the head from the neck like a fish into two parts.

The Hydra reared upward in excruciating pain, crashing heavily into a row of gold guardians as it whipped its bulky tail from side to side. Hovering in the air, a swirling cloud of thick black smoke surrounded Dark, covering him in powerful magic that shot through with arcing bolts of lightning. His body began to quake as a giant bolt of crackling electricity exploded from his outstretched hands, striking at another head of the raging creature. The force of this new attack completely destroyed the fourth head as bloody flecks of flesh fell with a sickening splatter onto the charred floor. The Hydra spurted black blood and smoke, howling and gasping as it once again staggered back, shrieking in pain and fury. The second strike saw two more shimmering bolts streaking through the air with deadly accuracy, slashing through the unprotected flesh of the serpentine neck of the fifth head, which now slumped limp and lifeless.

This last assault threw the great, scaled body backward amid a mass of rubble, leaving the beast thrashing in agony, its great, slimy bulk a writhing mass of blood and scales. The maddened monster, still in anguish from its multiple wounds, could think only of crushing the life out of the black demonic figure that now stood before it.

With its last ounce of strength, the Hydra sprang screaming toward the armored assassin, its lone head thrown back to spit venom and fire. But Dark was upon it before it could draw another breath. As the remaining head reared one last time to strike, his shadow blade pierced its side, and the poison from its jaws trickled harmlessly to the ground. The assassin did not hesitate and moved in for the kill. Dark charged at the huge monster, bearing down on him. He thrust the sword blade upward until he felt the blade shudder as it struck and then slid into the belly of the beast. The Hydra heaved an awful sigh as ribbons of blood streaked down his dark flesh, a gaping hole in its stomach, and black bile poured from its razor-edged mouth. Almost at once, the serpent's fierce eyes glazed over as its oily mass went limp; its huge, poison-dewed body curled and crumpled like a fallen leaf. The beast's rigid black husk vanished before him, crumbling into tiny flakes that abruptly ended in a loud croak. Dark stood unblinking and stared in amazement, for the creature's form had vanished. In its place, no higher than his ankle and as wrinkled as an old woman, squatted a horny toad. As if fleeing the assassin's frightful gaze, the scared toad hopped away, fled down to the water's edge, and vanished with a splash.

Dark quickly glanced about the rubble remains of what once was the Faërie King's tomb and then dropped back among the few remaining steel sentinels left standing. The lake remained as silent as it had been before the unexpected attack, its black waters disturbingly placid. For several long moments, he stood silently still and breathed deeply before moving slowly across the bridge, and in a few seconds stood in front of the crawling thief.

"Take me back to my gallows," the corpse spoke, eyes gleaming.

So he did. When Dark had strung the body up again, he turned toward Lake Killarney. Without a thought, he wearily placed an arm around the feathered neck of the *Albatross* and used the power of the Necklace of Teleportation to transport them both home again. With the two travelers home safely, exhausted and half awake, he dragged himself to stand in front of the two stone markers to his parent's graves.

"My grief has been waiting for this day," Dark spoke as if both his parents were alive and well and standing directly in front of him. "Come tomorrow, the first of them dies!" Now the moment was finally at hand, and he would face it alone in the most savage of cities in the known world, the City of Duergar.

www.ingramcontent.com/pod-product-compliance
Ingram Content Group UK Ltd.
Pitfield, Milton Keynes, MK11 3LW, UK
UKHW021036270726
13967UKWH00013B/2810